P9-CQD-594

"A love-story, a mystery, an adventure—*Haunted* has it all, and the plot moves at a lightning-pace. Linda Winstead Jones has a magic touch with paranormal, and, yes, the pun is intended!"
—*New York Times* bestselling author
Linda Howard

A current of electricity shimmered through his arms and legs and torso.

Without hesitation, Gideon tackled Hope and threw their bodies to the floor. He and Hope landed hard just as the window shattered and a bullet slammed into the wall. They lay there for a moment, his body covering and crushing hers.

Not everywhere, but where he touched Hope there was definitely a flicker of unusual voltage. She wanted to ask about the sparks…but what if that response was one-sided? Maybe she really had imagined the lightning bolt.

But then he looked at her and damned if she couldn't feel that lightning again.

He was Gideon Raintree. Magic was in his blood.

LINDA WINSTEAD JONES

Linda Winstead Jones has written more than fifty romance books in several subgenres—historical, fairy tale, paranormal and, of course, romantic suspense. She's won the Colorado Romance Writers Award of Excellence twice, and she's a three-time RITA® Award finalist and (writing as Linda Fallon) winner of the 2004 RITA® Award for paranormal romance.

Linda lives in north Alabama with her husband of thirty-four years. She can be reached via www.eHarlequin.com or her own Web site, www.lindawinsteadjones.com.

LINDA
WINSTEAD JONES

RAINTREE:
Haunted

Silhouette® Books

nocturne™

If you purchased this book without a cover you should be aware
that this book is stolen property. It was reported as "unsold and
destroyed" to the publisher, and neither the author nor the
publisher has received any payment for this "stripped book."

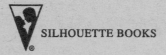

SILHOUETTE BOOKS

ISBN-13: 978-0-373-61764-7
ISBN-10:   0-373-61764-X

RAINTREE: HAUNTED

Copyright © 2007 by Linda Winstead Jones

All rights reserved. Except for use in any review, the reproduction
or utilization of this work in whole or in part in any form by any
electronic, mechanical or other means, now known or hereafter
invented, including xerography, photocopying and recording, or in
any information storage or retrieval system, is forbidden without
the written permission of the editorial office, Silhouette Books,
233 Broadway, New York, NY 10279 U.S.A.

This is a work of fiction. Names, characters, places and incidents are
either the product of the author's imagination or are used fictitiously, and
any resemblance to actual persons, living or dead, business establishments,
events or locales is entirely coincidental.

This edition published by arrangement with Harlequin Books S.A.

® and TM are trademarks of Harlequin Books S.A., used under license.
Trademarks indicated with ® are registered in the United States Patent
and Trademark Office, the Canadian Trade Marks Office and in other
countries.

www.silhouettenocturne.com

Printed in U.S.A.

Dear Reader,

Writing is almost always a solitary pastime. Yes, there are writer friends to call when characters don't cooperate or we paint ourselves into a plot corner, but for the most part we create, plot, write, revise, celebrate and occasionally scream alone.

The RAINTREE trilogy came together in a very different way. Linda, Beverly and I created, plotted, celebrated and screamed together. (And, no, we never screamed at each other. We found ourselves to be amazingly agreeable, for a trio of control freaks. <g>) We did our troubleshooting, plotting and world-building as a threesome. We put our heads together at conferences and on vacations, and before it was done, I knew their characters as well as I knew my own.

The actual writing we had to do alone, of course. Still, there were times when, as I sat at my computer, I was sure these two talented women were standing right behind me, looking over my shoulder and whispering in my ear. I always tried to listen.

This is the world we built. I thank you for coming along for the ride.

Best,

Linda Winstead Jones

With special thanks to Louis Goodrum, for the tour of Wilmington and the valuable insight.

For Linda and Beverly. What a trip this has been!

And for Leslie Wainger. Here's to butterfly years and (thankfully) missed camera moments.

Gideon

I am Raintree. It's more than a last name, more than a notation on a family tree. It's a quirk in my DNA.

It's a mark of destiny.

Long story short, magic is real. It's not only real, it exists all around us, but most people never open their eyes wide enough to see. My eyes have always been wide open. Magic is in my blood. My ancestors were called wizards, magicians and witches. They were also called demons and devils. Is it any wonder the family decided years ago to hide our gifts? *Hide,* I said, not *bury.* There's a difference. Power is a responsibility not to be denied in order to make life simple.

Each family member has a specific gift. Some are strong and some are weak; some have gifts that are more useful than others. Each Raintree has an other-worldly talent. Mine is electrical energy. I can harness the electricity that exists all around us. I can even create my own special surge of voltage. Yeah, I have a tendency to fry computers and destroy fluorescent lights, but that comes with the territory and I've learned to deal with it.

I also speak to ghosts, who are simply a form of electrical energy we don't yet fully understand. This talent comes in handy in my current profession.

I am Gideon Raintree, and I'm Wilmington, North Carolina's one and only homicide detective.

Prologue

Sunday—Midnight

The adrenaline was pumping so hard and fast that Tabby couldn't make herself stand entirely still. Even the quick climb to this third floor walkup hadn't dimmed her excitement. She wrinkled her nose in disdain as she studied the green apartment door and anxiously rose up onto her toes, then dropped down again. The paint on the door was peeling badly; the wood was warped; the number was crooked. What self-respecting Raintree would live in a dump like this one?

Tabby had been waiting for this moment for so long. Forever, it sometimes seemed. She hadn't waited *patiently*, but she had waited. Everything had to be perfect before the assault began; that had been stressed to her on more than one occasion. Finally it was time. She balanced the pizza box in her left hand as she knocked again with her right, harder and faster than she had before. A giddiness rose within her, and she savored it. She'd trained for this moment, had been practicing for almost a year, but finally the time was here.

"Who is it?" an obviously annoyed woman asked from the other side of the weathered green door.

"Pizza delivery," Tabby answered.

She listened as the security chain was undone with the slide of metal on metal and the rattle of sturdy links. A dead bolt turned, and finally—*finally*—the lock in the doorknob clicked and the door swung open.

Tabby took quick stock of the woman before her. Twenty-two years old, five foot four, green eyes, short pink hair. *Her.*

"I think there's been a mistake, unless…" the pink-haired woman began. She didn't get the chance to say another word.

Tabby forced her way into the apartment, pushing the Raintree woman back into the shabby living room and slamming the door behind her. She dropped the empty pizza box, revealing the knife she held in her left hand. "Scream and I'll kill you," she said before Echo had a chance to make a sound.

The girl's eyes got big. Funny, but Tabby had expected the Raintree eyes to be more striking. She'd heard so much about them. Echo's eyes were an average, unexciting blue-gray-green, not at all special.

One swipe and this job would be done, but Tabby didn't want it to be over too soon. Her gift was one of empathy, but rather than experiencing others' emotions, she craved their fear. Hate and horror tasted sweet when Tabby allowed her gift free rein. The dark sensations she drank in made her stronger. At this moment she fed off Echo Raintree's terror, and it felt good. It made her strong, physically and mentally. That terror fed the giddiness.

"I don't have much money," Echo said, pathetic and whining, and growing more and more afraid with every second that passed. "Whatever you want…"

"Whatever I want," Tabby repeated as she forced Echo away until her back was against the wall. Literally. What she really wanted was this girl's power. Prophesy. There was power in prophesy, properly used, though judging by this crappy apartment, Echo had not made the best of her talents. What a shame that something so extraordinary had to be wasted on this trembling doormat.

Tabby sometimes dreamed that when she killed, she absorbed the powers of her victim. It should be possible, should be an extension of her gift, but so far she hadn't been able to make it happen. One day, when her power was properly nourished as it should be, she would find the dark magic to take the next step in her own evolution.

Wishing the gift of prophesy could somehow fly from this Raintree's soul into her own, Tabby touched the girl's slender, pale throat with the tip of her knife. She made a small cut, and the girl gasped, and oh, the rush of fear that filled the air was tasty, and very, very strong.

She could play with Echo Raintree all night, but Cael wanted the job done quickly and efficiently. He'd stressed that to Tabby more than once, when she'd received her assignment. This was not the time to play but to be a soldier. A warrior. Much as she would love to stay here a while and amuse herself with the Raintree, Tabby definitely didn't want to end up on Cael's bad side.

She smiled and drew the knife very slightly away from the drop of blood on the girl's pale throat. Echo looked slightly relieved, and Tabby let the frightened woman believe, for that moment, that this was a simple robbery that would soon be over.

Nothing was over. It had just begun.

Chapter 1

When Gideon's phone rang in the middle of the night, it meant someone was dead. "Raintree," he answered, his voice rumbling with the edges of sleep.

"Sorry to wake you."

Surprised to hear his brother Dante's voice, Gideon came instantly awake. "What's wrong?"

"There's a fire at the casino. Could be worse," Dante added before Gideon could ask, "but it's bad enough. I didn't want you to see it on the morning news without some warning. Call Mercy in a couple of hours and tell her I'm all right. I'd call her myself, but I'm going to have my hands full for the next few days."

Gideon sat up, wide awake. "If you need me, I'm there."

"No, thanks. You've got no business getting on an airplane this week, and everything here is fine. I just wanted to call you before I got so tied up in red tape I couldn't get to a phone."

Gideon ran his fingers through his hair. Outside his window, the waves of the Atlantic crashed and rolled. He offered again to go to Reno and help. He could drive, if necessary. But once again Dante told him everything was fine, and they ended the call. Gideon reset his alarm for five-thirty. He would call Mercy before she started her day. The fire must have been a bad one for Dante to be so certain it would make the national news.

Alarm reset, Gideon fell back onto the bed. Maybe he'd sleep, maybe not. He listened to the ocean waves and let his mind wander. With the solstice coming in less than a week, his normal electric abnormalities were really out of whack. The surges usually spiraled out of control only when a ghost was nearby, but for the past few days, and for the week to come, it didn't take the addition of an electrically charged spirit to make appliances and electronics in his path go haywire. There was nothing he could do but be cautious. Maybe he should take a few days off, stay away from the station altogether and lie low. He closed his eyes and fell back asleep.

She appeared without warning, floating over the end of the bed and smiling down at him, as she always did. Tonight she wore a plain white dress that touched her bare ankles, and her long dark hair was unbound. Emma,

as she said she would one day be called, always came
to him in the form of a child. She was very much unlike
the ghosts who haunted him. This child came only in
dreams and was untainted by the pain of life's hardships.
She carried with her no need for justice, no heartbreak,
no gnawing deed left undone. Instead, she brought with
her light and love, and a sense of peace. And she insisted
on calling him Daddy.

"Good morning, Daddy."

Gideon sighed and sat up. He'd first seen this particular spirit three months ago, but lately her visits had
become more and more frequent. More and more real.
Who knew? Maybe he had been her father in another
life, but he wasn't going to be anyone's daddy in this
one.

"Good morning, Emma."

The spirit of the little girl drifted down to stand on
the foot of the bed. "I'm so excited." She laughed, and
the sound was oddly familiar. Gideon liked that laugh.
It made his heart do strange things. He convinced
himself that the sense of warm familiarity meant
nothing. Nothing at all.

"Why are you excited?"

"I'm coming to you soon, Daddy."

He closed his eyes and sighed. "Emma, honey, I've
told you a hundred times, I'm not going to have kids in
this lifetime, so you can stop calling me Daddy."

She just laughed again. "Don't be silly, Daddy. You
always have me."

The spirit who had told him that her name would be

Emma in this lifetime did have the Raintree eyes, his own dark brown hair and a touch of honey in her skin. But he knew better than to trust what he saw. After all, she only showed up in dreams. He was going to have to stop eating nachos before going to bed.

"I hate to tell you this, sweetheart, but in order to make a baby there has to be a mommy as well as a daddy. I'm not getting married and I'm not having kids, so you'll just have to choose someone else to be your daddy this time around."

Emma was not at all perturbed. "You're always so stubborn. I *am* coming to you, Daddy, I *am*. I'm coming to you in a moonbeam."

Gideon had tried romantic relationships before, and they never worked. He had to hide so much of himself from the women in his life; it would never do to have someone that close. And a wife and kid? Forget it. He already had to answer to the new chief, his family and a never-ending stream of ghosts. He wasn't about to put himself in a position where he would be obligated to answer to anyone else. Women came and went, but he made sure none ever got too close or stayed too long.

It was Dante's job to reproduce, not his. Gideon glanced toward the dresser, where the latest fertility charm sat ready to be packaged up and mailed. Once Dante had kids of his own, Gideon would no longer be next in line for the position of Dranir, head of the Raintree family. He couldn't think of anything worse than being Dranir, except maybe getting married and having kids of his own.

Big brother had his hands full at the moment, though, so maybe he would hold off a few days before mailing that charm. Maybe.

"Be careful," Emma said as she floated a bit closer. "She's very bad, Daddy. Very bad. You have to be careful."

"Don't call me Daddy," Gideon said. As an afterthought he added, "Who's very bad?"

"You'll know soon. Take care of my moonbeam, Daddy."

"In a moonbeam," he said softly. "What a load of…"

"It's just begun," Emma said, her voice and her body fading away.

The alarm went off, and Gideon woke with a start. He hated that freakin' dream. He glanced toward the dresser where Dante's fertility charm sat, and then he looked up, almost as if he expected to see Emma floating there. The dreams that were touched with reality were always hardest to shake.

He left the bed and the dreams behind, feeling his body and his mind come awake as he walked slowly to the French doors that opened onto a small private deck. He tossed open the drapes to reveal the ocean, drawing strength from the water as he always did. There were times when he was certain the breaking of the waves came in time with his heartbeat, and there was so much electricity in the ocean that he could smell it, taste it.

He needed to call Mercy and tell her what had happened at Dante's casino, and he would get that taken care of as soon as he had the coffee percolating. He dreaded telling her what had happened. Even though Dante was fine, she would worry.

After he made the call he would head for the office. He knew without a doubt that Frank Stiles had murdered Johnny Ray Black, but he didn't have the evidence just yet. He would, though, in time. He thought again about taking a few days off, just until the summer solstice passed. If everything was quiet at the station, he could bring the case files home and work from here.

Then Emma's final words rang in his ears, as if she were whispering to him still. "It's just begun."

Chapter 2

The small apartment had been trashed. Broken glass sparkled on anonymous beige carpet; books and carefully chosen knickknacks had been raked from the shelf to the floor; an empty pizza box lay discarded on the floor; and someone had taken a sharp blade to the old red leather sofa that sat in the middle of the room. Had the sofa been mutilated with the same knife that had killed Sherry Bishop? He didn't know. Not yet.

Gideon kept his eyes on Bishop's body while the woman behind him talked, her voice quick and high. "I thought maybe Echo was on her way home early and had ordered a pizza on her cell, you know? She does like to eat late at night, so I didn't even think…" She snorted. "Stupid. My mother will kill me when she finds out I let a wacko into the apartment."

Gideon glanced up and back. Was that an expression Sherry Bishop had used a hundred times before and automatically called upon now? Or did she not yet realize that she was dead? *My mother will kill me…*

She looked almost solid, perched on the chair behind him. As usual, she wore a faded pair of hip-hugger jeans and a T-shirt with the hem ripped to display her belly button and the piercing there. The hairdo was new.

Echo had found the body earlier this morning, after returning from a weekend trip to Charlotte. She'd immediately called him instead of dialing 911. So much for taking the week off. Gideon had made the necessary calls by cell phone, while on his way to the scene. After he'd arrived, he'd talked to Echo in the hallway. He'd calmed her down as best he could, and he'd been here to stop the first patrolmen who arrived from entering and possibly contaminating the crime scene. The uniforms stood in the hallway still, peering into the apartment like kids who weren't allowed into the candy store. Had he ever been that young?

They were all watching, but he couldn't worry about that. He already had a reputation as being odd; that was the least of his worries.

"Did you know him?" he asked softly.

"Her," Sherry said.

A woman? Gideon glanced at the body again, then at the mess the attacker had made of the apartment.

She's very bad, Daddy. Very bad. When Emma had appeared to him in the dream, Sherry Bishop had been dead for hours. Not only dead, but mutilated. The index finger of her right hand was missing, cut off after death, judging by the small amount of blood that had been shed. A neat square of her scalp, as well as a portion of blond and pink hair, had also been taken. He had a hard time comprehending that a woman had done this, but by now he should know that anything and everything was possible.

"Did you know her?"

The specter shook her head. She looked almost real, except that she wasn't entirely solid. It was as if she were manufactured entirely of a thick mist. Her pink-and-blond spiked hair, the jeans and T-shirt she wore, her pale skin. It was all slightly less than substantial. "I opened the door, she rushed in and said she wouldn't hurt me if I didn't scream, and then she hit me on my neck and…" She laid a hand over her throat and looked past Gideon to the body. Her body. "That bitch killed me, didn't she?"

"I'm afraid so. Anything you can tell me about her would be helpful."

Sherry looked at the body and gasped. "She cut off my finger? How am I supposed to play the drums with…" The ghost fell back against the couch. "Yeah, I know," she sighed. "Dead."

"Detective Raintree?" One of the patrolmen stuck his head in the room. "Are you, uh, okay?"

Gideon lifted a hand without looking at the officer. "I'm fine."

"I heard you, uh, talking."

This time Gideon did look at the kid. Hard. "I'm talking to myself. Let me know when the crime scene techs arrive."

He heard Echo start to cry again, and the officers turned to comfort her. His cousin was distracting them so he could work in peace, he knew. There wasn't a man alive who would mind comforting Echo Raintree.

The ghost of Sherry Bishop sighed again, and her form vibrated. "They can't see me, can they?"

"No," Gideon whispered.

"But you can."

He nodded.

"Why is that?"

Blood. Genetics. A curse. A gift. Electrons. "We don't have time to talk about me." He didn't know how long Sherry Bishop would remain earthbound. Maybe a few minutes more, maybe an hour, maybe a couple of days. Perhaps she would demand justice and hang around until his job was done, but he couldn't be sure. He could never be sure. Ghosts were damned unreliable. "Tell me everything you remember about the woman who attacked you."

Detective Hope Malory rushed up the stairs of the old apartment building, slowing her step as she approached the third floor. Half a dozen cops and a handful of neighbors were milling around in the hallway outside the victim's apartment, all of them trying to peer inside as if there were a show going on.

All but one petite young woman with short blond hair shot with liberal hot pink streaks. She hung back, almost as if she were afraid to see what was happening inside.

Hope took a deep breath and smoothed her navy-blue jacket as she approached. This morning she'd dressed professionally, as always, in trousers and a jacket like any other detective. Her pistol was housed in a holster at her waist, and her badge hung around her neck, so everyone could see it plainly.

The only concessions she made to her femininity were a touch of makeup and the two-inch heels. She wanted to make a good impression, since this was her first day on the job. From everything she'd heard, no matter what she said or did, her new partner was *not* going to be happy to see her.

She made her way past a couple of the officers to the doorway. One of them whispered to her, "You can't go in there." She stopped for a moment and watched Detective Gideon Raintree at work.

She'd studied his file extensively in preparation for this assignment. The man was not only a good cop, he had a solution rate that boggled the mind. Right now he was down on his haunches, studying the body and talking to himself in a low voice. Behind him, a lamp on an end table directed light on to his tightly-wound body in an odd way, as if he were caught in the spotlight. All the blinds were closed, so the room was almost dark. Everything was as he'd found it, she knew.

The photograph in Gideon Raintree's file didn't do

him justice, Hope could tell that from where she stood, even though she didn't have a clear view of his face. He was a very good-looking man with a great body—the perfectly cut suit couldn't hide that—and the fact that he needed a haircut didn't make him any less attractive. She'd always been a sucker for longish hair on a man, and very dark brown hair with just a touch of a wave hung a tad too long on Raintree's neck. No matter how conservatively he dressed, he would never completely pull off a conventional look.

The suit he wore was expensive; he hadn't bought that on a cop's salary, not unless he'd been living on macaroni and cheese for the past year. It was dark gray, perfectly fitted, and would never dare to wrinkle. The shoes were expensive, too, made of good quality leather. He had a neatly trimmed mustache and goatee, very hip, very roguish. If not for the gun and badge, Raintree wouldn't look at all like a cop.

She stepped into the room, against the whispered advice of the officer behind her. Raintree's head snapped up. "I told you..." he began, but he didn't finish his sentence. He stared at her with intense green eyes that were surprised and intelligent, and Hope got her first really good look at Gideon Raintree's face. Cheekbones and eyelashes like that on a man really should be illegal, and the way he stared at her with those narrowed eyes...

The lightbulb in the lamp behind him exploded.

"Sorry," he said, as if he had somehow made the lightbulb explode. "I'm not ready for the crime scene techs. Give me a few more minutes and I'll be out of your way." His tone was dismissive, and that rankled.

"I'm not with the Crime Scene Division," Hope said as she took a careful step forward.

His head snapped up, and he glared at her again, not so politely this time. "Then get out."

Hope shook her head. Normally she would offer her hand for a professional greeting when she got close enough, but Raintree was wearing white gloves, so she would be keeping her hands to herself. The firm businesslike handshake she usually offered the men she worked with would have to wait. "I'm Detective Hope Malory," she said. "Your new partner."

He didn't hesitate before answering with confidence, "My partner retired five months ago, and I don't need another one. Don't touch anything on your way out."

She was dismissed, and Raintree returned his attention to the body on the floor, even though he now had less light to study it by. The overhead light was dim, but she supposed it cast enough illumination over the scene. Hope had tried not to actually look at the body, but as she continued to stand her ground, she made herself take in the scene before her. It was the hair that caught her attention first. Like the woman in the hall, this victim's hair was a mixture of pale blond and bright pink. She was dressed in well-worn blue jeans and a once-white T-shirt that advertised a local music festival. She had four gold earrings in one ear and one in the other, and wore a total of five rings—a mixture of gold and silver—on her slender fingers. All nine of them.

Hope's stomach flipped. One finger had been removed, and there was a horrible bloody wound on the top of the victim's head, as if someone had tried to scalp her.

The same someone who had sliced her throat.

Hope took a deep breath to compose herself, then decided that wasn't a good idea. Death wasn't pretty, and it didn't smell nice, either. She had, of course, seen bodies before. But they hadn't been quite this *fresh,* or this mangled. It was impossible not to be affected by the sight.

Raintree sighed. "You're not going away, are you?"

Hope shook her head, and tried to casually cover her nose and mouth with one hand.

"Fine," Raintree said sharply. "Sherry Bishop, twenty-two years old. She was single and had no significant relationship at the time of her murder. Money was tight, so robbery is unlikely as a motive. Bishop was a drummer with a local band and also waitressed at a coffee shop downtown to make ends meet."

"If she was in a band, maybe a stalker fixated on her," Hope suggested.

The man who continued to squat on the floor by the body shook his head. "She was killed by a left-handed woman with long blond hair."

"How did you come up with all that information in the past, what, twenty minutes?"

"Fifteen." Gideon Raintree stood slowly.

He was over six feet tall—six-one, to be exact, according to his file—so Hope had to crane her neck to look him in the eye. His skin was warm, kissed by the sun, and this close, the green of his eyes was downright remarkable. The goatee and moustache gave him an almost devilish appearance, and somehow it suited him. When his eyes were narrowed and watchful, as they were now, he looked incredibly hard, as if he possessed no more heart than the murderers he pursued. Feeling more than a little like a coward, Hope dropped her gaze to his blue silk tie.

"From the angle of the wound, it appears that the attacker held the knife in her left hand," he explained. "The coroner will confirm that, I'm sure."

From what she'd heard, Gideon Raintree was always sure of himself. And always right. "You said *her.* How can you know the killer was a woman?"

Gideon nodded. "There's a single long blond hair on the victim's clothing. Hair that length on a man is possible, but unlikely. Again, the coroner will have to confirm."

All right, he was observant. He had done this before. He was good. "How could you possibly know the personal details of her life?" Hope asked. Drummer. No significant other. Waitress in a coffee shop. She quickly scanned the room for clues and saw none.

"Sherry Bishop was my cousin Echo's roommate."

Hope nodded. She tried to remain unaffected, but the smell was making her queasy.

Raintree stared right through her with those odd eyes of his. "This is your first homicide, isn't it?"

Again Hope nodded.

"If you're going to throw up, do it in the hallway. I won't have you contaminating my crime scene."

How thoughtful. "I'm not going to contaminate your crime scene."

"Good. If you insist on sticking around, interview the neighbors and see if they heard anything last night or early this morning."

Gladly. Hope nodded yet again, then turned to escape from the room, leaving Gideon Raintree alone with the victim. She was quite certain that he was more comfortable with the dead woman than he was with her.

His new partner was intently interviewing a nosy neighbor, and the crime scene techs were doing their thing inside the apartment. Gideon sat beside Echo on the steps that led to the fourth floor.

"Is she here?" Echo asked softly.

No one was paying them any attention at the moment. Gideon didn't expect that would last long. "She's sitting behind us."

Even though Echo knew she wouldn't see anything, she glanced over her shoulder to the deserted steps. "I'm sorry. I should've known."

Like Bishop, Echo was a young twenty-two. She was incredibly talented—as a guitar player and as a seer— but she had little or no control over her gift of prophesy. Calling her psychic wasn't quite right. She couldn't tell you where you'd left your wallet or whether or not you would marry within the next year, but she did see disasters. She dreamed of floods and earthquakes. Her nightmares came true.

Gideon had a touch of pre-cog ability, but not enough

to make a significant difference. His instincts were just a hair sharper than was normal, but he didn't dream about catastrophes and experience them as if he were there—there and unable to do anything to stop what was coming. Compared to Echo's power, he considered talking to dead people a walk in the park.

"It was painless," Gideon said as he put his arm around Echo's shoulder. "She didn't even know what happened."

"What a load of bull," Sherry muttered, her voice sour. "It hurt like hell!"

Fortunately, no one but Gideon heard her.

"Why would anyone kill Sherry?" Echo asked. The tears hadn't stopped, but they were softer now. Constant but gentle. "Everyone liked her."

"I don't know." Something Gideon didn't like niggled at his brain. Bishop hadn't recognized her killer. She'd never suspected that her life was in danger. There was no logical reason for her to be dead, much less savagely mutilated. In every case he'd had since moving to Wilmington four years ago, the victim had known the name of the killer. Drugs were the usual motive, but there had been a few crimes of misdirected passion. Murder by stranger was a rare thing. With a few notable exceptions, it took a personal connection for murder to occur.

He didn't want to scare his cousin, but there was one possibility he couldn't ignore. "Have you had any visions lately that might've put you in danger?"

Echo didn't need to be asked twice. "Do you think the person who killed Sherry was after *me?*"

"Son of a bitch!" Sherry said softly. "I never

should've dyed my hair blond and pink like Echo's. We thought it would be such a good thing for the band, you know? A trademark. A…a *thing*…" She pouted. "I thought it was so cute."

"It's just a possibility," Gideon said softly. "Look, you won't be able to stay here for a while anyway, so I want you to find yourself a quiet place to crash, and I want you to stay there until I figure this out. Where are your folks?"

"St. Moritz."

Figures. "I don't want you going that far." Besides, Echo's parents were all but useless in a crisis. "You can stay at my place for a few days."

Echo sighed and rested her head on her hands. "We have a gig next weekend, so I'm cool until then. I can call the coffee shop and tell them I won't be in this week, and then I can go to Charlotte and stay with Dewey until Friday."

Dewey. Great. The guy was a rail-thin goofy-looking saxophone player who had the hots for Echo, even though she insisted they were just friends. Still, a few days with Dewey would be better than staying around here if there was any chance the murderer had been after Echo and not Sherry. "Call me before you come back to town. You may have to cancel your gig."

Echo didn't protest, as he'd thought she might. "Maybe we should just cancel everything. We'll never find a drummer to take Sherry's place. And even if we do, it won't be the same."

Gideon didn't see Echo often. He was twelve years

older than she was, and they had no common interests. In fact, his little cousin had a wild streak that put his teeth on edge. Not that he'd always been a saint. But they were family, and he checked in on her now and then. He had even been to a smoky club to see her band play a couple of times. The music had been too loud and too angry to suit him, but the girls had all seemed to have a good time.

She was right. It would never be the same.

"You look tired."

Echo shrugged her thin shoulders. "I'm supposed to work this afternoon—you know, at the coffee shop—so I stayed up all night instead of driving home last night or trying to get up early this morning to drive back. You know how I hate to get up early."

"Yeah, I know."

"It just made more sense to stay up and drive back to grab something to eat before I had to…" Her voice hitched. "I guess I should call Mark and tell him I won't be in today, and that Sherry won't…you know."

It was difficult to say aloud. Sherry Bishop wouldn't be going back to work. Ever.

Gideon took his house key from his pocket and handed it to Echo. "Get a couple of hours sleep at my place before you head to Charlotte. You shouldn't be on the road in your condition." She nodded and slipped the key into her front pocket. "Keep your cell on," Gideon added.

None of the Raintrees advertised their gifts, but perhaps someone who had discovered Echo's ability had wanted to silence her. Because of something she'd seen or might possibly see? And why take the finger and a segment of the scalp? That alone took this case beyond anything he had ever worked, but it didn't help him. All he had were questions. Theories. More questions.

When he walked down the steps, Sherry Bishop followed. "You *are* going to find out who did this to me, aren't you?" she asked.

"I'm going to try."

"This is just so freakin' unfair. I had plans for my life, you know. Big plans. I was kinda hopin' you'd ask me out one day. I mean, you're older and all, but you're really hot anyway."

"Gee, thanks," Gideon mumbled.

Sherry gasped. "I never got a chance to wear my new boots! They were really kickin', and I got them on sale." She sighed. "Crap. Tell Echo she can have them."

"I'll tell her."

Gideon stopped at the foot of the stairs and watched his new partner as she interviewed an older woman with frizzy gray hair. He liked to work alone. It made speaking to the victims so much easier. His last partner had finally decided to believe that Gideon talked to himself and had great hunches on a regular basis. Hope Malory didn't look as if she would make things that easy for him. She didn't look at all accepting of things she did not understand.

He appreciated women. He had no plans to marry or even get involved in a serious relationship, ever, but that didn't mean he lived like a monk. Most women were attractive in some way; they all had a feature or two that could catch and hold a man's attention for a while. Hope Malory was much more than attractive. She had a classic beauty. Black hair, cut chin length, hung around her face thick and silky. Her skin was creamy pale and flawless, her eyes a serene dark blue, her lips full and rosy. She was tall, long-legged and slender, yet rounded in all the right places. She had the face of an angel, a body that wouldn't quit, and she carried a gun like she knew how to use it. Did that make her the perfect woman?

A shimmer of pure electricity ran through his body. The lights in the hallway flickered, causing everyone who was lingering in the hall to look up. At least this time nothing exploded.

"You're going to catch her, right?" Sherry Bishop pressed.

He watched Hope Malory take a few furious notes, then ask another question of the neighbor. "Catch her? Right now I'm not even planning to chase her. She's pretty, but she's not my type, and it's never a good idea to mix business with pleasure."

"Get your mind out of your pants, Raintree," Sherry said sharply. "I'm not talking about your new partner, I'm talking about the woman who killed me."

He didn't take his eyes off Malory as he answered, "I'm going to try."

"Echo says you're the best," Sherry said more kindly.

"Does she?" Hope Malory glanced his way, caught his eye, then quickly returned her attention to the neighbor.

"Yeah. And you'd better hurry, Raintree."

Gideon turned to look at Sherry Bishop. She'd faded considerably since they'd left the apartment. Soon she would move on, go home, be at peace. That was as it should be, but once that happened he would have a much harder time communicating with her. It might be possible, but it certainly wouldn't be this easy.

Malory made her way toward him with long, easy strides that spoke of confidence and grace. Her notes had been dutifully taken, and he was sure they would be complete.

"Nothing," she said softly as she came near. "Mrs. Tarleton, who lives right next door, is practically deaf, and the other neighbor was out until early this morning. No one heard anything. Everyone liked the victim and your cousin, even though they were, as Mrs. Tarleton said, young and a bit wild." She looked past Gideon to the stairway. "Maybe I should talk to your cousin."

"No."

She looked him in the eye and lifted her eyebrows slightly. "No?"

"I've already talked to Echo."

"You're her cousin, which means you're too close to her to be objective. Besides, you're a man."

"You make that sound like a bad thing."

"It can be. The point is, she might tell me things she wouldn't tell you."

"I doubt it."

The woman got her hackles up. "Should you even be working this case? After all, you have a personal connection here."

"I met Sherry Bishop one time. Maybe twice. There's no reason—"

"I'm not talking about your relationship to the victim, Raintree. Until we eliminate her, your cousin is a natural suspect."

"Echo wouldn't hurt anyone."

"You tell her, Gideon," Sherry Bishop said in an irate voice. "How dare she insinuate that Echo would do this to me?"

"You're not objective," Malory insisted.

Gideon did his best to ignore Sherry's ramblings, which had nothing at all to do with her death. "We'll establish my cousin's alibi first thing, if it'll make you feel better. Once she's eliminated from your list of suspects maybe it'll be okay with you if I do my job."

"There's no reason to get snippy."

Gideon leaned down slightly and lowered his voice. "Detective Malory, if you're determined to be my new partner I don't guess there's much I can do about it. Not at the moment, anyway. But do us both a favor and act like a detective, not a little girl."

Her nostrils flared. Ah, he'd hit a nerve. "I am not a *girl,* Raintree, you—"

"Snippy," he interrupted. "A word not used by real men anywhere."

"Fine," she said with unnecessary sharpness. "I'll just grunt a lot and scratch my ass now and then, and maybe I'll fit in."

Sherry grimaced. "I'll bet a chick like her never scratches her ass."

The truth of the matter was that Gideon knew it didn't matter what Hope Malory did or said. She was going to get under his skin big time. Like it or not, she was already there, and she was going to stay until he found a way to get rid of her. Out of sight, out of mind, right? It wasn't as if she was the only pretty woman in Wilmington.

He didn't need a partner; he didn't want one; it would never work. And in the end, it wouldn't matter.

Malory wouldn't last long.

Chapter 3

"Lunch?" Gideon glanced at his new partner briefly as he negotiated a turn in the road. The wind blew Malory's carefully styled sleek hair into her face. He could have put the top up, he supposed. Then again, why make this easy on her? She'd insisted on coming along, and he'd insisted on driving. She didn't want to know what could happen to her new, electronically handicapped car if he was too near it at the wrong moment.

"I thought you wanted to talk to that club owner," she shouted to be heard above the wind.

"He won't be in until four or later." They'd already spoken to the manager at the coffee shop where Bishop and Echo had both worked for the past seven months. Mark Nelson knew nothing of interest, but Gideon wanted to go back tonight and have a look around. Maybe the killer would be there, watching for a reaction to the news of Sherry Bishop's death.

"Okay," Malory said reluctantly. "I could eat something, I suppose."

She sounded less than enthusiastic, but Gideon figured she would never admit that the murder scene had dampened her appetite.

He made a couple of turns on narrow downtown streets and pulled into the parking lot of Mama Tanya's Café. It was late enough in the afternoon that the lunch rush was over. The gravel parking lot was practically deserted.

"Where are we, Raintree?" Malory asked suspiciously, eyeing the small concrete block building that could use a coat of paint and a bucket of spackle. And maybe a window or two.

"Mama Tanya's," he said, opening his door and stepping out. "Best soul food in town."

She followed him, her heels crunching in the gravel. "If you're trying to scare me off..." she muttered.

Gideon ignored her and stepped into the dimly lit, windowless restaurant. He hadn't been kidding when he'd said this was the best place in town for soul food. It was also a good place, filled with good people. Even the ghosts who dropped in here were happy.

"Detective Raintree." Tanya herself greeted him with a smile that deepened the wrinkles on her serene face. "The usual?"

"Yep." He grabbed his regular booth.

Tanya looked at Malory and raised her eyebrows slightly. "And for you, young lady?"

"I'll just have a salad. Vinaigrette on the side."

The order was met with silent surprise. Gideon glanced back at Tanya as Malory joined him. "Just bring her what I'm having."

Malory started to argue, then thought better of it.

"What if I don't like what you're having?" she asked when Tanya was out of hearing distance.

"You'll like it," he said.

It was the first time all day they'd been in a quiet place, alone, and he took the opportunity to study Hope Malory critically. Her hair was mussed from the ride in his convertible. She'd smoothed it with her hands but hadn't run to the ladies' room to make more extensive repairs. Her cheeks were flushed, her eyes smart. Take-no-prisoners smart. Man, she was gorgeous.

And she was pissed.

"So what are you doing here?" he asked.

"I just wanted a salad," she said softly.

"In Wilmington," he clarified. "This is a relatively small department. I know the detectives from the other divisions, and I know the uniforms. You're not one of them, so how did you end up with this ill-advised and temporary assignment as my partner?"

She didn't take the bait. "I transferred in from Raleigh. I worked vice there for the past two years."

He was surprised. She looked too young to have been a detective for two years. "How old are you?"

She didn't seem to be offended by the question, as some women might have been. "Twenty-nine."

So she was on the fast track. Ambitious, smart, maybe even a little bit greedy. "Why the move?"

"My mother lives here in Wilmington. She needs family close by, so I decided it was time to come back home."

"Is she sick?"

"No." Malory squirmed a little, obviously getting uncomfortable with the personal nature of the discussion. "She fell last year. It wasn't anything serious. She sprained her ankle and hobbled for a couple of weeks."

"But it worried you," he said. Of course it did. Malory was so earnest, so relentlessly dedicated and serious. If anything had happened to her mother, she would see it as somehow being her fault. And so here she was.

"It worried me a little," she confessed. "What about you?" she asked quickly, turning the subject of the conversation around. "Do you have family close by? Other than Echo, that is."

People who asked too many questions always made him nervous. Why did she need to know about his family? Of course, he *had* started this personal discussion. Turnabout was fair play, he supposed. "I have a sister and a niece who live in the western part of the state, a few hours away, a brother in Nevada and cousins everywhere I turn."

That last bit got a small smile out of her. Nice. Maybe she wasn't entirely earnest, after all.

"What about your parents?" she asked.

"They're dead."

Her smile faded quickly. "Sorry."

"They were murdered when I was seventeen," he said without emotion. "Anything else you want to know?"

"I didn't mean to pry."

Of course she hadn't, but his blunt answer had killed the conversation, just as he had hoped. This woman could play hell with his life on so many levels if she made even half an effort. Scary notion.

Tanya placed two very full plates on the table, along with two tall glasses of iced tea.

"Raintree," Malory said in a lowered voice, after Tanya walked away. "Everything on my plate but the turnip greens is fried."

"Yep," he answered as he dug in. "Good stuff."

They both turned their attention to eating, Hope slightly less enthusiastic than Gideon about the fare, though after a few bites she relaxed and started to enjoy the meal. Gideon was glad for the silence, but it also made him nervous, because there was a level of comfort in it.

He didn't need or want a partner. He'd tolerated Leon for three and a half years, and in the end they'd made a pretty good team. Gideon solved the cases; Leon did the paperwork and handled the bullshit. At the end of the day they both looked good and everyone was happy. Hope Malory did not look like a happy person.

"I think she's killed before," a soft voice called.

Gideon turned his head to glance into the unoccupied booth behind him. Well, it *had* been unoccupied—until Sherry Bishop arrived. She looked less solid than she had back at the apartment, but it was definitely her. "What?" he asked softly.

"Raintree," Malory began, "are you all…"

He silenced his new partner with a lifted hand but never took his eyes from Sherry.

"The woman who killed me," the ghost said. "She wasn't at all afraid or even nervous, just anxious. Wound up, the way Echo and I always were before a gig. I think she liked it. I think she enjoyed killing me."

"Raintree," Malory said again, her voice sharper than before.

Gideon lifted his hand once more, this time with a raised finger to indicate silence.

"Shake that finger at me again and I'll break it off."

Sherry Bishop disappeared, and Gideon turned around to face an angry and confused Detective Malory.

"Sorry," he said. "I was just thinking."

"You have an odd way of *thinking*."

"I've heard that before."

Something in her expression changed. Her eyes grew softer, her lips fuller, and something worse than anger appeared. Curiosity. "But apparently it works," she said. "How do you do it?"

"Think?" He knew what she was asking; he just didn't want to go there.

"I've never known a detective with a record like yours. Except for that one case last year, your record is flawless."

"I know Stiles did it, I just can't prove it. Yet."

"How?" she whispered. "How do you know?"

It was easiest to pretend that he was like everyone

else when the question came up. He had a gift for seeing small things that others missed; he had an eye for detail; he saw patterns; he was dedicated to solving each and every case. All those things were true, but they weren't the reason for his almost flawless record.

"I talk to dead people."

Malory's response was immediate and not at all unexpected. She laughed out loud. The laugh did great things to her face. Her eyes sparkled; her cheeks grew pink; her lips turned up at the corners. It struck Gideon sharply that he felt much too comfortable with Hope Malory. That laugh was nicely familiar. He could get used to this…and he couldn't allow that to happen.

Hope drove slowly past Raintree's house, and the sight of his house didn't allay her suspicions at all.

The three-story pale gray Carolina-style house right on Wrightsville Beach hadn't been bought on a cop's salary, that was for sure. This was one of the nicest areas along the strip, and he owned one of the nicest houses. She'd already done some investigating, and she knew what he'd paid for the place when he'd moved in four years ago.

There was a three-car garage at the end of a short paved driveway. She knew, even though the garage doors were down, that every bay was filled. Raintree owned a black '66 Mustang, the convertible he'd driven today; a '57 Chevy Bel Air, turquoise and cream; and a '74 Dodge Challenger in rally-red, whatever that was.

Money aside, no one was as good a cop as Gideon Raintree seemed to be. Most of the murders he'd solved were drug related, which meant he could very well be connected to someone in the community of dealers. Someone high enough up to be able to buy his own cop. Was her new partner involved with the criminal element in Wilmington?

I talk to dead people my ass.

The houses on this strip of the beach were impressive, but space was at a premium, and they had been built very close together. One colorful house after another lined this street, and Raintree's tastefully painted gray was one of the finest. Why hadn't anyone ever questioned his lifestyle?

Every detective she knew wanted to work homicide. It was high-profile; it was important. And yet five months after his partner's retirement, Raintree was still working alone—or had been, until she'd come along. The new chief had told her the other detectives weren't interested in working with Raintree. They didn't want to get lost in the shuffle, always being second man on the team, or else they knew Raintree liked to work alone and didn't want to be the one to rock the boat. In other words, if it ain't broke, don't fix it.

Hope had never minded rocking the boat.

Maybe there were completely reasonable answers to all her questions about Raintree, but then again, maybe not. She had to know, before she got herself in too deep. Before she trusted him, before she accepted him.

She knew in her gut that Raintree was a liar. Of course he lied on a regular basis: He had a penis. The question was, how deep did the lies go?

Hope parked her blue Toyota down the street, where someone was having a gathering and an extra car wouldn't stand out, and walked back to Raintree's house. It was unlikely she would see anything this late at night, but she was so curious and wound up that she couldn't possibly sleep. Since her mother never went to bed before 2:00 a.m. and the apartment over the shop was small, sleep wasn't all that easy to come by, anyway.

The house, the expensive suits, the cars…Raintree was definitely into something.

The recently-retired partner, Leon Franklin, came off as clean as a whistle when she looked into his background. Franklin had a little money in the bank, but not too much. A nice house, but not too nice. And everyone she'd talked to said Gideon Raintree was the brains of the operation. He got every homicide case in Wilmington, and he solved them all. It just wasn't natural.

Hope slipped into the darkness between Raintree's house and the less subtle yellow house next door. She'd dressed in black for this outing, so she blended into the shadows. She wasn't going to peek through a window and catch Raintree red-handed, but the more she knew about this guy, the better off she would be. There wasn't any harm in just looking around his place a bit.

Movement on the beach caught her attention, and she turned her head in that direction. Speak of the devil. Gideon Raintree was coming in from a swim, too-long hair slicked back, water dripping from his chest. He stepped from the sand onto his own private boardwalk and into more direct lighting. When the light from his deck hit him, she held her breath for a moment. He wore old, holey jeans that had been cut off just above the knees and that hung too low on his waist, thanks to the weight of the water. He wore nothing else, except a small silver charm that hung from a black cord around his neck.

"Gideon," a singsong voice called from the yellow house next to his. He stopped on the boardwalk and lifted his head, then smiled at the blonde who was leaning over her own balcony. Hope hadn't seen so much as a hint of a smile like that one all day. Yeah, the guy was definitely trouble.

"Hi, Honey." Raintree leaned against the boardwalk railing and looked up.

"We're having a party Saturday night," Honey said. "Wanna come?"

"Thanks, but probably not. I'm working a case."

"That girl I saw on the news?" Honey said, her smile fading.

"Yeah."

Another woman, a brunette this time, joined Honey at the balcony railing. "You'll have the case solved by Saturday," she said confidently.

"If I do, I'll drop by."

Both women leaned over the railing. They were wearing skimpy bathing suits, as any self-respecting beach bum would be on a warm June night. They practically preened for their neighbor's benefit.

Raintree was the kind of man a shallow woman might go for, Hope imagined. He had the looks and the bank account, and an obvious kind of charm that came with self-confidence. With those eyes and cheekbones, and the way he looked in those cutoffs, he might make a silly woman's heart race.

Hope had never been silly.

"Why don't you come on up now and have a drink with us?" Honey asked, as if the idea had just popped into her head, though she'd probably been planning to ask her studly neighbor up from the moment she'd seen him on the beach.

"Sorry. Can't do it." Raintree turned toward his own house—and Hope—and it seemed to her that he actually looked directly at her. "I have company."

Hope held her breath. He couldn't possibly see her there. Someone else was coming over, or else he was making an excuse to be polite. As if any red-blooded male would turn down "drinks" with Honey and the brunette bimbo.

"Company?" Honey whined.

"Yeah." Raintree leaned against the walkway railing again and stared into the dark space between the two houses. "My new partner stopped by."

Hope muttered a few soft curse words she almost never used, and Raintree smiled as if he could hear her. That was impossible, of course. As impossible as him seeing her standing in the shadows.

"Bring him on up," the brunette said. "The more the merrier."

"Her," Raintree responded without glancing up to his neighbors. "My new partner is a girl."

He'd said "girl" just to rile her, Hope knew, so she did her best not to react to the jibe.

"Oh." Honey sighed. "Well, you can bring her. I guess." She sounded decidedly less enthusiastic, all of a sudden.

"Thanks, but we'll pass. We have work to discuss. Isn't that right, Detective Malory?"

Busted. Hope took a few steps so that she was caught in the soft light cast from both decks. It was apparently too late to hide. Was Raintree dangerous? Maybe he was. He looked dangerous enough. Then again, she was armed and knew how to defend herself, if it came to that. Somehow, she didn't think it would.

"That's right," she said, as she walked through sand and tall sea grass to the boardwalk.

"How long have you been down there?" Honey asked.

"Just a few minutes."

"You sure were quiet."

"I was just admiring the view."

The brunette sighed. "We certainly do understand that."

Hope felt herself blush. She'd meant the *beach,* of course, but from the tone of the bimbo's voice they thought she meant... Oh, no. She did not want Raintree thinking she enjoyed looking at *him.* Even if she did. "I love the water."

"Me, too," Gideon said.

Hope bounded easily over the railing to join him.

"Come on inside," he said, turning his back on her and leading the way. "I guess you're here to talk about the Bishop case."

"Yeah," she said brightly. "I hope you don't mind me dropping by this way."

He glanced over his shoulder and smiled, wickedly amused. "Not at all, Detective Malory. Not at all."

She was up to something. Pretty Detective Hope Malory was so wound up, so filled with an electricity of her own kind, that if he laid his hands on her, they would probably both explode. Not necessarily a bad idea.

"I'm going to change." Gideon gestured toward the kitchen. "Help yourself to something to drink and I'll be right back."

Echo had slept here for a few hours and then driven to Charlotte. He'd talked to her on the phone, before heading out for a quick swim. She was still upset, but the panic had faded somewhat. Whether he liked it or not, Dewey was actually helping with the difficult situation.

It didn't take Gideon five minutes to put on dry clothes and towel dry his hair, and the entire time he kept asking himself, *Why is Malory here? What does she want?* If there were early results from the crime scene techs' study of the murder scene, they would call him, not her. If she had a theory—and that was all she could possibly have at this point—it could have been communicated by telephone. The owner of the club where Echo's band often played hadn't been any help at all. So why was Malory *here?*

He found out pretty quickly, right after stepping into the living room to find his new partner sitting in a leather chair with a glass of cold soda in one hand. "Nice place,

Raintree," she said as her eyes scanned the walls almost casually. "How do you manage this on a cop's salary?"

So that was it. She thought he was dirty, and she was here to find out *how* dirty. Did she want to join him in profitable corruption or toss his ass in jail? He would guess she was the ass-tossing sort, but he'd been wrong about women before. "My family has money." He headed for the kitchen. "I'm going to make myself something to drink."

She nodded to the opposite side of the room, where a glass of soda much like hers sat on a coaster. "I already fixed you a drink."

"How do you know what I want? Psychic?"

Again that fleeting but brilliant smile. "Your fridge was full of the stuff. I took a shot."

Gideon lowered himself into a chair. Was it coincidence that she had placed his glass as far away from her chair as possible? No. Not a coincidence at all. Malory liked to look tough, but now and then he saw a hint of the skittish beneath her skin. When she'd talked about her mother falling and how she might need her daughter, when he'd looked her in the eye…he'd seen the vulnerability in her.

She had certainly done her best to look tough tonight, in her black jeans and black T-shirt and pistol. "Family money," she said, prompting him to continue.

"Yeah."

"What kind of family money?"

"My parents and my grandparents, as well as their parents and grandparents, were all successful. And lucky."

She looked him dead in the eye in that oddly annoying way she had. "I saw Echo's apartment this morning. Is she from the poor side of the family?"

"Echo is a rebel," he explained. "Her parents very happily live off the family money. They travel, they sleep, they drink, they party. That's about it. Echo wants to earn her own way. I admire that in her, even if she does sometimes cut off her nose to spite her face."

"Are you lucky?"

He looked her over appreciatively and smiled. "Not tonight, I'm guessing."

She didn't respond to the comment, not even to bristle. "You're definitely lucky as a detective. I've seen your file."

"Goody for you. I'd like to have a look at yours."

"I'll see what I can do."

She took a drink of her soda, and he played with the condensation on his glass with one finger. If Malory got too nosy, if she asked too many damn questions, he would have to move. Dammit, he liked it here. He liked his house, and the men he worked with—most of them—and he loved being near the ocean. He had come to need it in a way he had never expected. For years he'd moved from department to department, always going to the place where he thought he was needed most. Sadly enough, his talents were called for just about everywhere, so he'd finally decided to settle down here.

If Detective Malory started investigating him and uncovered more than she should, he wouldn't be able to stay here much longer. So much for settling down. So much for home.

He was either going to have to make Hope Malory a friend or get rid of her. She didn't seem like the kind of woman who was easy to get rid of once she dug in her heels, and he wasn't sure he could make her his friend. She didn't seem to be the friendly type.

Again Malory studied the living room with critical eyes. "There's something odd about this place," she said thoughtfully. "Don't get me wrong, it's very pleasant. You have comfortable furnishings, and nice paintings on the walls. Everything matches well enough, and the lamps didn't come from a discount store or a yard sale…."

"But?" Gideon prodded.

She looked at him, then, with those curious blue eyes of hers. "The television is small and cheap, and the phone is an old land line. Most single men of a certain age who have a disposable income own a decent stereo. You have a boom box that any self-respecting fifteen-year-old would be embarrassed to carry onto the beach. Run of bad luck?"

Luck again. How could he tell her that his electronic devices had a nasty habit of exploding without warning? He owned two more small televisions, which were stored in a spare bedroom, ready for the time when this one went, and he'd never had any luck with cordless phones or digital clocks. He couldn't get too close to a vehicle that relied on computer chips, which was why he drove older models. On the rare occasions when he'd been on an airplane, he'd worn a powerful shielding charm that only Dante could fashion. He went through cell phones the way other people went through Kleenex.

"I don't watch much TV. Don't listen to much music, either. Cordless phones aren't secure."

"And you need your phone calls to be secure because…?"

Enough was enough. Gideon rose slowly to his feet. He left his drink behind and crossed the room to stand near her. "Why don't you just ask me?" he said softly.

"Ask you what?"

"Ask me if I'm dirty."

The alarm in her eyes was vivid, and he could almost see her assessing the situation. He wasn't armed, at least as far as she could tell. She was. He had a small advantage, standing over her this way, but she had the gun handy.

"Ask," he said again.

Her eyes caught and held his. "Are you?"

"No."

Her alarm faded gradually. "Something here stinks to high heaven. I just haven't figured out what, yet."

"It's the money. People can't believe that anyone would be a cop if they have any other choice."

"It's more than the money, Raintree. You're good. You're *too* good."

He leaned slightly forward, and she didn't shrink away. She smelled good. She smelled clean and sweet and tempting. She smelled comfortable and familiar. His fingers curled, as he resisted the temptation to reach out and touch her. Just a finger on her cheek or a tracing of her jaw, that was all he wanted. He kept his hands to himself.

"I made my choice a long time ago. I don't do this job because I have to. I have enough money in the bank to be a beach bum, if it suits me. I could get a job in my brother's casino—" as long as he stayed far, far away from the slot machines "—or live at the homeplace, or just do nothing at all. But when my parents were murdered, it was a couple of detectives and a handful of deputies who caught the killer and put him away. This job is important, and I do it because I can."

He did this job because he had no choice.

Her expression told him nothing. Nothing at all.

She's bad, Daddy. Very, very bad. Had Emma been warning him about Sherry Bishop's killer? Or his new partner?

Chapter 4

She'd killed the wrong woman.

Tabby was sitting in the back corner of the coffee shop, but she didn't watch the riverfront beyond the wide window, which was busy on this warm summer night; instead she kept her eyes on the patrons and the employees inside. She wouldn't have thought a place that sold coffee and cookies would be so crowded this late on a Monday night, but the small tables were filled with a mixture of both tourists and regulars, who drank decaf and munched on giant-sized cookies. Many of the regular patrons and the two young waitresses on duty sniffled as they reminisced about the deceased Sherry

Bishop. Okay, so she'd made a mistake. At least she had the pleasure of soaking in the pain and fear in the coffee shop for her trouble. Last night's exercise hadn't been a complete waste of time.

Until Tabby had seen the evening news, she'd had no idea that she'd killed the wrong woman. Satisfied and coming down off her natural high, she'd slept most of the day. When she'd awakened, she'd spent some time studying her newest souvenirs. One day she would learn of a way to use those mementos in a powerful working of magic that would give her the powers of those she'd killed. At the time she'd thought her newest victim was Raintree and therefore more powerful than the others, and so she'd touched what she'd taken with reverence and, yes, even glee. Everyone possessed some talent that could be taken, some gift that was wasted or ignored or undiscovered, but this was *Raintree*.

And then she'd turned on the television to watch the evening news, only to discover that what she'd taken had not been Raintree at all.

Who would have thought there would be two pink-haired women living in the same apartment? She sipped at her cooling coffee. Cael was going to kill her when he found out, unless she fixed her mistake, pronto. She'd been hoping Echo Raintree would be here tonight, so she could follow the girl to wherever she was staying and finish the job. But no such luck, at least not so far. The murder of both girls would raise a few eyebrows, she knew that, but what choice did she have? None.

So far Echo hadn't made an appearance. Not tonight.

Maybe she was off somewhere crying about her roommate's death, but surely she wouldn't stay away all week. If nothing else, the funeral would take place in a matter of days. Tabby didn't know the details of the arrangements, but that info would be public soon enough. There was no way Echo could stay away from her roommate's funeral. It just had to happen *this week*.

If Echo Raintree had a vision about what was to come and she warned her family, things would not go as smoothly as planned.

The door opened, and Tabby automatically turned her head to watch the couple enter the coffee shop. Her heart skipped a beat. Holy crap. Gideon Raintree. Her mouth practically watered. She wanted Gideon much more than she'd ever wanted Echo, but orders were to wait. Killing a cop would cause too much commotion, Cael said; it would raise too many questions. Later in the week, when it was almost time, then she could kill Gideon. But not tonight.

Tabby didn't think anyone had seen her near the scene of the crime last night, but she was doubly glad she'd decided to wear the short brunette wig tonight. Her head was hot, and it already itched, but at least she didn't have to worry about anyone recognizing her. She could relax, sit back and watch.

Gideon and the woman who was with him took a seat in the corner, where they could see everyone and everything in the restaurant. They were dressed casually, the woman all in black, Raintree in jeans and a faded T-shirt. Both of them were armed, though not openly. Ankle holsters for both; no badges visible. Was this an official visit? Of course it was. They were searching for Sherry Bishop's killer.

Out of the corner of her eye, Tabby studied the woman with Raintree. Cael had ordered her not to take out Gideon just yet, but what about the woman? Was she a girlfriend? Cop? Judging by the ankle holster, she would have to say cop, but maybe the woman was both colleague and bed buddy. Something was going on. No fear or sadness radiated from the couple on the opposite side of the room, but there was energy. Sexual, slightly acrimonious, uncertain energy. Whatever the relationship might be, killing the woman would definitely sidetrack Raintree if he got too close too soon. It would raise a stink, though, which Cael definitely didn't want just yet.

Tabby got antsy sitting and watching. Knowing she'd made a mistake did take some of the pleasure out of last night's outing, and she wanted more. She always wanted more. She'd already screwed up this job, so what did it matter if she killed a cop who wasn't a part of her original assignment? Getting rid of the woman would distract Gideon, and she needed him to be distracted. She needed his attention diverted to something besides Echo and the wrong damn dead woman.

Since everything had already gone wrong and Tabby didn't dare contact Cael until the job was done, his instructions didn't matter quite so much. As long as Echo and Gideon were both dead by the end of the week, she would be forgiven for any mistakes that happened along the way. She could shoot the female cop and Gideon from a distance at almost any time, but that wasn't what she wanted. Tabby didn't much care how she took out the woman, but Gideon was another matter entirely.

Gideon Raintree was a member of the royal family, next in line for Dranir, powerful in a way she could not entirely imagine. When she killed him, she wanted to be close. She wanted to be touching him when she thrust the knife that had taken Sherry Bishop's life into his heart. She wanted his blood on her hands, and a souvenir or two for her collection.

Even though she had not yet discovered a way to take the gifts she longed to steal, she did draw energy from the keepsakes she collected. Properly treated and dried, stored in a special leather bag that grew heavier with each passing year, those mementos fed her power when she was, by necessity, subdued. Cael insisted that she curb her enthusiasm, that she be cautious and not draw attention to herself and her gifts. Not yet. Not until they had taken that which was rightfully theirs. She had been very subtle and cautious in the games she played, but all that was about to change.

Yes, she could take out her target from a distance, but killing Gideon Raintree would be a powerful and delicious moment, and she wasn't yet ready to give up that moment in the name of expediency.

Tuesday—7:40 a.m.

Breakfast at the Hilton buffet, Raintree had informed her last night. It was a Tuesday morning tradition with the Wilmington PD detectives. Hope parked her Toyota in the lot and walked toward the restaurant, unconsciously smoothing a wrinkle out of her black pants and adjusting her jacket over her hips as she walked quickly toward the entrance. She was ten minutes late, but her mother had been talking her ear off as she'd left the shop, and it hadn't been easy to get away.

The group she'd been invited to join was easy to spot. A round table in the center of the restaurant was occupied by nine men, all of them in suits, all of them Wilmington detectives. Raintree stood out, even in this crowd of similarly dressed men who held jobs much like his own. He might as well have a spotlight trained on him, the way he drew the eye. The men talked to and over one another as they drank coffee, and consumed eggs and bacon and biscuits. Hope held her head high as she walked in their direction. It wasn't long before a few heads turned. Eyebrows rose. Jaws dropped.

Hope was accustomed to the initial reaction she usually aroused. She didn't look like a cop, and in the beginning there was always resentment, along with an unspoken question. Had she slept her way to the top? And if she hadn't, would she? She had to be more businesslike, more distant, more dedicated, than any man in this profession. She never would have left Raleigh and started this process all over again if not for her mother. Nothing else could have made her go through this uncomfortable initiation period for a second time.

The only vacant chair at the table was next to Raintree. She took it, and he introduced her to the other detectives. After the initial round of questions and open interest, the men returned to their discussion: Where to meet for lunch tomorrow.

Eventually the conversation turned from food to cases currently under investigation, including—but not exclusively—Sherry Bishop's murder. Through a number of outlets, state and federal, Raintree had requested the files of all unsolved murders of the same kind over the past six months, and by this afternoon he would have the majority of those files on his desk—and hers. As they talked about the case, a few important things quickly became clear. Gideon Raintree was a good cop, and the men he worked with respected and liked him.

Hope allowed herself to relax a little. Surely if Raintree was crooked, the others would know or at least suspect that something was wrong, and be mistrustful or distant or curious. She saw nothing like that at the table. Last night she'd been so certain that Raintree was somehow involved in the crimes he'd solved. Now she wasn't so sure. Did she want to believe he was a straight arrow because he was charming and good-looking as well as infuriating? She didn't want to be that shallow; she didn't want to be like those women who judged men by their looks and their well-planned words, without ever looking inside to find what was real. It was impossible to tell what a man was like from the outside, and getting to know them well enough to learn the truth was too painful. At least, it had been for her.

Eventually the detectives finished eating and peeled away from the table to start their day. Hope and Raintree left together, stepping from the restaurant into a sunny, warm morning.

"What's the plan?" Hope asked as they walked into the crowded parking lot. Her heels clicked on the asphalt. Gideon's steps were slower, steady and rhythmic.

"I want to go back to the apartment and have a look around. Maybe you can work on organizing the paperwork before the case files I requested start coming in. The neighbors' interviews need to be typed up. It'll be a day or two before we get a report from the crime lab, but you could give 'em a call and try to hurry it along."

Hope tried—very hard—not to get riled. "I'm not your secretary, Raintree."

"I didn't say you were."

"You want me to take care of the paperwork while you investigate."

"Leon didn't mind."

"I'm not Leon."

He stopped a few feet from his car and looked pointedly down at her. "I'm very well aware of that, Detective Malory."

"I'll drive today," she said.

"I'd better—"

"I'll drive," she said again, more slowly this time. She refused to allow him to dominate this partnership. Best to show him right now that she wasn't going to be pushed around.

There was a flash of something in Raintree's green eyes. Amusement, maybe. It definitely wasn't surrender. Still, all he said was, "Okay. If you insist."

Her Toyota was parked just a few spaces down from his Mustang. "Do you want to put the top up?" she asked, pointing to his convertible.

"It'll be all right," he answered casually.

She slipped her keys from the side pocket of her purse and unlocked the doors with the remote on her key chain. She opened the driver's side door while Raintree paused to look over her vehicle.

He casually placed one hand on the hood and said, "Nice car. Does it get good gas mileage?"

She almost laughed. "Significantly better than your gas guzzler."

He straightened away from the car and coolly took his place in the passenger seat, seeming perfectly at ease. Yesterday he had been insistent about driving, but today he seemed to accept his role as passenger quite well. Maybe this partnership would work out after all. Hope buckled her seat belt and turned the key in the ignition. Nothing happened.

She tried again. There was a dead-sounding click, and nothing more.

"Sounds like your starter's on the fritz," Raintree said evenly as he opened the passenger door and stepped out. "I know a guy," he said as he snagged his own car keys from his pocket and headed for his convertible. "I'll give you his number, and you can catch up with me when—"

"Oh no." Hope locked her car and followed Raintree, her own strides shorter than his but no less firm. "I'll take care of the car later. You're not leaving me here."

He glanced over his shoulder. "You're very dedicated, Detective Malory."

With the harsh sunlight on Raintree's face, she could see the faint lines around his eyes. He had probably been a pretty boy in his youth, and just enough of the pretty remained to make him interesting. He wasn't a kid anymore, though. Neither was she.

"I'm stubborn," she said. "Get used to it."

He grinned as he opened the passenger side car door for her and waited for her to step inside. She did, and then she looked up at him. "Don't do that again," she said softly.

"Don't do what?"

"Treat me like we're on a date. I'm your *partner,* Raintree. Did you ever open the door for Leon?"

"No, but he was ugly as sin and had fat, hairy legs."

She glared at him and didn't respond.

"Fine," he said as he rounded the car. "You're one of the guys. Just another cop, just another partner."

"That's right." She was still annoyed about her car, but she wasn't about to stand there waiting for a mechanic while Raintree went to the crime scene and tried to piece together any clues he might have missed yesterday.

Hope no longer believed to the pit of her soul that Gideon Raintree was crooked, but she had no proof one way or another, and she didn't know him well enough to entirely trust what her instincts told her. She'd been burned more than once by a man who hadn't been what he'd claimed to be. It wouldn't happen again.

As he pulled his car out of the parking lot, Raintree

said, "Leon called me Gideon. If you're determined to hang with me until we get this whole partner thing straightened out, you might as well do the same."

Calling him by his first name felt so personal. So friendly. How could she be *friendly* with Raintree when she still suspected, however uncertainly, that he might be corrupt?

Maybe he really was just a good cop. Maybe she would discover that he was as great a detective as he appeared to be, and his motives were nothing but noble. If that were the case, she would work with him, and learn how and why he was so good.

In truth, more than that was causing her hesitation. In spite of her down-to-earth personality and her dedication to her career, she had the very worst luck with men. She always picked the wrong guy. If there were twenty nice guys in a room and one stinker, she picked the stinker every time. She'd felt an unwanted but undeniable attraction to Gideon Raintree from the moment she'd laid eyes on him, and the last thing she needed right now was to get involved with another stinker.

"Okay, Gideon it is," she said. "I guess you might as well call me Hope."

The half smile that crossed his face made him look as if he knew something she didn't, as if he was in on a secret joke and she wasn't. "You sound so enthusiastic about the prospect, how can I refuse?"

The apartment didn't look any different than it had yesterday. It was just quieter. Deader. Sherry Bishop wasn't hanging over his shoulder, wailing about the injustice of being dead and not getting to wear her new boots. There weren't cops and neighbors hanging around in the hallway, watching. It was just him and Malory trying to piece together a very bizarre crime.

His new partner stood near the door, studying the crime scene through her own calculating eyes. She was quiet, as if she understood that he needed silence and space to do his thing. At first she had been a distraction, but he was already accustomed to her presence. It had taken him almost a year to get this comfortable with Leon.

The blinds were open to let the morning's natural light shine into the apartment. The ripped couch, the bloodstains and the wanton destruction looked obscene in the light of day, out of place and evil and *wrong*.

Standing in the quiet apartment, Gideon could almost see the progression of events. The doorbell had rung late in the evening. A woman's voice had informed Sherry Bishop that there was a pizza delivery. She opened the door, the woman rushed in and...

"There was something odd about the knife."

Gideon turned around and saw a very faint image of Sherry sitting on the couch as she had when she'd been living. Only now the couch was in shreds, and she was dead.

"The knife," he whispered as he dropped to his haunches so he was face-to-face with her. From this vantage point, she looked a little more solid.

"What?" Hope took a single step toward him.

He silenced his new partner with a raised hand. She

hated that, he knew, but he didn't want to scare Sherry off. He couldn't even afford to look away, because if he did, he might lose her. The ghost before him wouldn't last long, not in her present state. "I'm thinking out loud," Gideon said without looking at Hope.

"Oh."

"What about the knife?" he asked softly.

"It was antique looking, you know?" Bishop said. "I think maybe it was silver, and there was something fancy on the handle."

"Fancy how?"

"I couldn't see the whole grip, because that psycho bitch was holding it, but there was an engraving. Words, I think."

"What did it say?"

The ghost shrugged. "I don't know. It wasn't English, I don't think. I wasn't exactly trying to *read* at that moment." Already she was starting to fade. "She was really angry. Why was she so angry? I never did anything to—"

Sherry didn't fade away; she disappeared in an instant. Gideon remained there before the sofa, hunkered down and thinking. She'd seemed certain the killer had done this before. This afternoon, when he sat down with the files he'd requested, maybe he would be able to figure out if that was true or not. They not only had the type of weapon and wound to match, but there was the matter of the missing finger and piece of scalp. This killer took souvenirs, and that was the key that would lead him to previous victims, if there were any.

It was unusual for a serial killer to be a woman, but

it wasn't impossible. What had drawn the killer to Sherry Bishop? What had caught her eye and brought her here?

He heard and felt Hope crossing the room. She moved smoothly, silently, but he was in tune with her energy, and that was what he felt as she moved closer.

"Okay, you're spooking me a little," she said as she stopped behind him.

"Sorry." Gideon stood and turned to face her. "I want the uniforms to scour the surrounding area searching for the knife."

"They did that yesterday."

"I want them to do it again. Odds are the killer's still got it on her, but we can't take any chances. We need the murder weapon."

"It could be in the river, for all we know," she argued.

"I hope you're wrong." Sherry hadn't recognized her killer, so there was no name to go by, just a vague description, the mutilation…and that knife.

Hope's eyes softened a little. "You're taking this case kinda personally. Did you know Sherry Bishop better than you're letting on?"

"I take all my cases personally," he said.

Hope studied him carefully, as if she were trying to figure out what made him tick. Good luck.

Suddenly Emma, the wannabe daughter of his dreams, appeared, floating hazily behind Hope. Her eyes widened and she glanced toward the window and seemed to swipe at Hope with flailing hands, as if she were trying to push her. "Get down!"

Without hesitation, without even stopping to wonder at the fact that Emma had appeared while he was awake, Gideon tackled Hope and threw them both to the floor. They fell into and through Emma's image, before the girl disappeared. For a split second he was chilled by direct contact with the child who claimed to be his daughter. He and Hope landed hard, just as the window shattered and a bullet slammed into the wall. They lay there for a moment, his body covering and crushing hers.

A current of electricity shimmered through his arms and legs and torso. Not everywhere, but wherever he touched Hope there was definitely a flicker of unusual voltage that he couldn't control. She felt it, too; he knew by the way she reacted with a jolt.

After the gunshot all was silent, until they heard the shouts of an alarmed neighbor from two floors down.

Gideon rolled off Hope, drew his gun and edged toward the shattered window. She was right behind him, pistol in hand. He peered cautiously through the window, trying to see where the shot had originated. A window on the building next door was open, faded curtains ruffling slightly with the breeze. "Stay here and stay down," he ordered as he popped up and ran for the door.

"Like hell."

Hope was right behind him, and he didn't have time to stop and argue with her. Not now. She wanted to be treated like a real partner? Fine. "Third floor, fourth window from the south. I'm going up. You make the call and watch the front entrance. Nobody gets out."

For once she didn't argue with him.

* * *

Hope stood by the front door of the apartment building while Gideon ran for the stairwell. Anyone leaving would either come through this door or around the side of the building, a few feet away. Unless the shooter had already left the building, he was trapped. She made a phone call reporting shots fired at this location, and then she waited. Waiting had never been her strong suit, but sometimes it was required. Unfortunately, it gave her time to think about what had just happened, and at the moment she didn't want to think.

Had Raintree seen sunlight flashing on a muzzle? Had he heard something out of the ordinary that alarmed him? He'd tackled her a fraction of a second *before* the shot was fired, so he must have seen or heard something. Problem was, he'd been facing the wall at the time, not the window, so he couldn't have seen anything. The window had been shut, so hearing anything from across the alley would have been almost impossible. Instinct? No, instinct was too much like psychic ability, and she refused to go down that path. Two flakes in the family were quite enough.

Extraordinary intuition wasn't all she had to think about. When Gideon Raintree had landed on top of her, something odd had happened. She'd heard of chemistry, of course; she'd even experienced it a time or two. She'd certainly heard sexual attraction referred to as a spark before.

But she had never before felt an actual *spark*. A popping, charged spark. When Gideon had landed on top of her, it was as if she'd put her finger in a light socket. An electric charge had literally run through her body, from her toes to the top of her head. She'd felt it, as if lightning had danced through her blood. For a moment she'd had to fight the urge to reach out and hold on to the man above her with everything she had, not to fight the electricity off but to take it in and beg for more.

She tried to brush the memory off as imagination, but her imagination wasn't that potent. She'd felt *something;* she just didn't know what to call it.

Hope very much wanted to follow Gideon to the third floor, but until there was another officer available to guard this entrance, she wasn't going anywhere. She couldn't help but wonder what Raintree would find. Was the shooter still up there, just waiting?

A man with a solution rate like his had surely made enemies over the years. There was one open case he was continuing to investigate, many months after the fact. Had Frank Stiles, Gideon's suspect, fired that shot? Was Gideon getting too close? Or was the shooter connected to the Bishop murder? There were too many possibilities, and now was not the time for baseless theories.

A patrol car arrived, and Hope assigned the two uniformed officers to take her place on guard duty. She ran into the apartment building and to the stairwell, just as Gideon had minutes ago. She'd had partners before, and some of them had become friends. She'd lost a couple to retirement or promotion, but she'd never lost one to a bullet. Now was not the time to start.

She met Gideon on the second floor landing. "Apartment's empty," he said. "No one answering my knock at the others. Who's on the door?"

"Two uniforms, with orders not to let anyone in or out."

They took the second floor apartments, Gideon starting at one end, Hope at the other. No one had seen anything, though they had all heard the shots. Too many apartments were empty, the doors locked. Other officers arrived, the building manager was located, and in less than forty-five minutes they'd been through the entire building, floor by floor, apartment by apartment. They searched the narrow back alley. Twice. Either the shooter had escaped before they reached the building, or he was a regular tenant and they'd looked him in the eye without knowing who he was.

When the search was done, Gideon sat on the front stoop and stared out at the street, thinking. She hated to interrupt him when he was so deep in thought, but there were too many questions to leave unasked. Besides, she'd waited long enough.

She sat beside him, close but not too close. "So, who wants you dead?"

He turned his head to look at her. "What makes you think you weren't the target?"

She managed a tense smile. "I've been on the job here less than two days. I haven't had time to make any serious enemies yet. You, on the other hand…"

Gideon turned his gaze to the street again. "Yeah."

Hope leaned back slightly. "So how did you know?"

"How did I know what?"

"You tackled me before the shot was fired, Raintree," she said. "Not by much, but somehow you knew."

He was quiet for a moment. "Complaining?"

"No, but I'm definitely curious."

"Dangerous stuff, curiosity."

She wanted to ask about the sparks she'd felt, but what if that response had been one-sided? Maybe she really had imagined the lightning bolt, and it had just been surprise and maybe even her reluctant physical attraction that had made her tingle from head to toe. Then again, maybe she'd felt sparks when Gideon landed on her because it had been two years since any man had touched her.

"I live for danger," she said, half-serious.

"Let's save this conversation for later."

Even though she hated saving *anything* for later, she nodded and left him alone. She owed him that much, she supposed. "Okay. Now what?"

Gideon looked up and down the sidewalk. "Someone saw something. It's broad daylight, middle of the day, and if the shooter got out, he must've left here at a run. Somebody saw." He looked at her, and damned if she couldn't feel that lightning again, even though they were nowhere close to touching. "Let's find out who."

Chapter 5

Gideon walked down the block from the apartment building where the shots had been fired, his new partner right beside him on the sidewalk. Today was the first time he'd seen Emma outside a dream. Her appearance had told him that she was indeed more than a fantasy. The little phantom had saved his life, or Hope's, or both. He wasn't sure who would have been hit if Emma hadn't warned him to get down and flailed vainly at Hope, as if she were trying to push the woman out of the way.

She wasn't a ghost. He was convinced that she was exactly what she'd claimed to be all along: an entity that had not yet come into this world, a spirit between lives. The amount of energy it had taken to appear to him as she had was considerable, and he could no longer write

Emma off to bad dreams of a life he didn't dare to ask for. She was Raintree, all right, or one day would be.

They passed by the doorway to a corner bookstore. An older woman stood behind the counter near the window, her curious gaze turned to the street. If the shooter had come this way, she would have seen him. Gideon nodded through the glass to the nosy woman. "Why don't you ask that sales clerk if she saw anything?"

Hope, who'd been thoughtfully quiet since they'd left the building, said, "You don't want to question her yourself?"

"I need to make a phone call. Family stuff," he added, so this partner he didn't want would know he wasn't trying to leave her out of the loop. She hesitated, but finally went into the bookstore and left him standing on the sidewalk alone. He snagged his cell and hit the speed dial.

Dante answered on the second ring.

"How's everything?" Gideon asked—loudly, since there was a lot of static to talk over. Damn cell phones.

"Royally screwed," his brother answered.

"I can sympathize, trust me. I won't keep you, but I have to know. About three months ago you sent me a piece of turquoise."

"I remember."

"The blasted thing was gifted, wasn't it?" Unconsciously, he fingered the cord that hung around his neck. It was hidden by his dress shirt and tie, at the moment, but he was always aware of the power of the talisman. The silver charm that hung there carried the gift of protection, a blessing from his brother. A newly gifted charm arrived every nine days by overnight carrier. Big brother insisted, since Gideon's job came with potential dangers. The turquoise that was sitting on his bedroom dresser had obviously carried another kind of power.

Dante laughed. "I'm surprised it took you this long to figure out."

"What was the gift, exactly?"

"A glimpse of the future."

"Near future or distant?"

"It wasn't specific."

Gideon leaned against the bookstore's brick wall and cursed succinctly. Dante had made the gift nonspecific time-wise, but Emma was an entity waiting to come into this world, and she said she was coming soon.

Not necessarily. He was in control here. He made his own decisions. If he didn't want a family, then he wouldn't have one. In spite of everything he'd been taught in his life, he could not believe that he had no choice in such an important matter.

"What did you see?" Dante asked.

"None of your damn business."

Dante laughed again, then ended the conversation abruptly, as if someone had interrupted him.

Hope opened the bookstore door and stuck her head out. "Raintree, I think you're gonna want to hear this."

Tabby paced her recently rented apartment, the adrenaline still pumping amidst the faded and dusty furnishings. She'd had the woman in her sights, and it would have been an easy enough shot from the deserted apartment on the other side of the alleyway from Echo Raintree's place. Aim. Pull trigger. Watch the target fall. Run. It was a good, simple plan. Not the way she preferred to work, but still, a good enough plan to throw Raintree for a loop.

And then Gideon had knocked the target to the floor, and the bullet had been wasted. Tabby didn't know what all of Gideon's talents were, but apparently he had some kind of psychic power as well as the ability to see ghosts. He'd knocked his partner to the ground a split second *before* she'd pulled the trigger.

Tabby hated hotel rooms. There was no privacy in such places, and she needed to know that no one else had access to her things. No matter where she went, she was able to find a cheap apartment to rent, like this one. She paid a month in advance and was always long gone before the month was done. She avoided her neighbors and never *ever* brought her work home with her.

On the small kitchen table of this shabby, furnished apartment, the newly taken finger and hank of bloody hair had been treated and were drying. She sat before them and drank in the sensations they recalled so vividly. She wished for more, wished to be able to absorb the life power of her victims, but in a way she was satisfied that these things were now hers. There was such a wonderful dark mojo in her keepsakes; they soothed her even when everything else was going wrong. And at the moment it seemed that everything truly *was* going wrong.

Echo was still nowhere to be found, and that was a problem. Cael's orders had been specific. Echo was to die *first*. Tabby knew that if she called her cousin and told him what had happened, he would order her home, and then he would send someone else to finish the job she'd failed to accomplish. Her life wouldn't be worth spit if that happened. She had to finish the task she'd been given, and she had to finish it herself. Echo first, Gideon later in the week, and preferably at a time and place where she could get close enough to appreciate the experience.

Mulling over the possibilities, she reached out and barely touched a strand of spiked, pink and bloodied hair. She'd hit a couple of road bumps, but soon the Raintrees she'd been assigned to kill would be dead, and that was all that mattered. As for the woman cop, Tabby now wanted her dead on principle alone. She hated to miss.

The older lady at the bookstore had seen a woman with long blond hair walking very briskly—just short of running—away from the apartment building at exactly the right time. The long blond hair and the timing were enough to at least loosely tie the shooting to Sherry Bishop's murder. But what lay behind the crimes? It was a question Hope had no answer for.

"Sorry about your car," Gideon said. "It'll be safe in the Hilton parking lot until morning. We'll get someone out there then."

The shooting and the resulting investigation, and

then a couple of hours spent in the office they shared scanning unsolved murders outside the Wilmington area that were similar to Sherry Bishop's, had delayed them until it was too late to call a mechanic. Gideon Raintree was driving her to her mother's place. He had a thin stack of files he was taking home with him to look over later. He was hoping he would see something new if he had a fresh look.

Hope had to admit that Raintree certainly appeared to be motivated by something other than greed. Was it possible that he was truly as devoted to his job as he appeared to be? Maybe his parents' murders had inspired him and there were no secrets waiting to be uncovered. No betrayal waiting to surprise her.

Meanwhile, she was exhausted and happy to be headed home, which at the moment was her mother's apartment over The Silver Chalice, a New Age shop Rainbow Malory owned and operated in downtown Wilmington. Of course, Rainbow was not the name Hope's mother had been given at birth. Her real name was Mary. A nice, solid, normal name, Mary. But at the age of sixteen Mary had become Rainbow, and Rainbow she remained.

To Hope's horror, Gideon parked at the curb and killed the engine.

"Thanks," Hope said, exiting the Mustang quickly and doing her best to dismiss her partner. Gideon Raintree was not easily dismissed. He left the driver's seat and followed her. Luckily The Silver Chalice was two blocks from the parking space Gideon had found.

"We had this discussion, Raintree," she said sharply. "Would you have walked Leon home?"

"If someone shot at him, yes," he responded.

"Someone was shooting at *you,* not me."

"Prove it."

True enough, she couldn't prove anything. As her mother's shop grew nearer, she straightened her spine and sighed. "This is fine. Thanks."

"Is the shop still open?"

Hope glanced at her watch. In the summertime, the shop's hours were extended to suit the tourists. "Yeah, but I can't imagine there's anything in the store that would interest you."

"You don't have any idea what might interest me."

She had spent two days in this man's company, and she didn't know him at all, she realized. Hope reached the shop entrance and placed her hand on the door handle. "Don't tell my mother that someone shot at us," she said softly as she opened the door and the bell above her head chimed.

The Silver Chalice sold crystals and incense and jewelry made by local artisans. There was a display of tarot cards and runes for sale, as well as a collection of colorful silk scarves and hand-carved wooden boxes. The jewelry kept The Silver Chalice in business, but it was the New Age items that Rainbow Malory embraced. Strange, slightly off-key singing—meditation music, her mother called it— drifted from speakers overhead as Hope entered.

Rainbow looked up from her place at the counter and grinned widely. She was still very attractive at fifty-seven, though the streaks of gray in her dark hair gave away her age, as did the gentle smile lines in her face. She didn't color her hair or wear any makeup. Or a bra.

"Who's your friend?" Rainbow asked as she stepped from behind the counter. Her full, colorful skirt hung to the floor, the hem dancing around comfortable sandals.

"This is my partner, Gideon Raintree," Hope said. "He wanted to look around, but he can't stay."

Hope watched as her mother became as entranced as every other woman who discovered Gideon for the first time. Her back got a little straighter. Her smile brightened. And then she said, "You have the most beautiful aura I've ever seen."

Hope closed her eyes in utter embarrassment. She would never hear the end of this. Gideon would tell the other detectives over breakfast that Hope Malory's mother was into auras and crystals and tarot cards. She waited for the laughter to start, but instead of laughing, Gideon said, "Thank you."

Hope opened her eyes and glanced up at him. He didn't look as if he was kidding. In fact, he looked quite serious and at home here, as he began to study the merchandise on the shelves. "This is nice," he said. "Interesting products, pleasant atmosphere..."

"Atmosphere is so important. I try to fill my shop with positive energy at all times," Rainbow said.

Again Hope wanted to shrink away, but her partner didn't seem at all put off or amused. "I'll bet the tourists love this shop," he said. "It's a peaceful place."

"Why, thank you," Rainbow responded. "That's so astute of you. Of course, I knew as soon as I saw your aura…"

Not auras again. "Mom, don't talk Raintree's ear off. He has to go, anyway. He's got things to do tonight."

"Not really," he said casually. "I want to take another look at those files, but I need a little time away from them first."

She glared at him, but he ignored her as he continued to study the merchandise. If they were going to be partners, he would have to learn to take a hint.

"Join us for supper," Rainbow said, a new excitement in her voice. "I'll be closing up in twenty minutes, and there's stew in the Crock-Pot. There's more than enough for the three of us. You look hungry," she added in a motherly tone of voice.

To Hope's absolute horror, Gideon accepted her mother's invitation.

No two women could be more dissimilar. Where Hope was openly wary and more often than not tied up in knots, her mother was open and relaxed. They looked a little alike, as mothers and daughters often did, but beyond that, it was hard to believe that they'd ever lived in the same house, much less shared DNA.

Dinner was thick beef stew and homemade bread. Simple, but tasty. Gideon steered clear of the television set in the living room, and took the chair that placed him as far away from the stove and microwave as possible.

He did his best to keep any electrical surges low and controlled.

Obviously Hope wanted him to eat and get out as quickly as possible. She fidgeted; she cast decidedly uncomfortable glances his way. She was clearly embarrassed by her mother's beliefs and openness. What would his new partner say if she knew that Gideon believed in everything her mother embraced? And more. He could make her suffer and stay on after the meal was done, but Gideon did Hope a favor and declined dessert and coffee when they were offered. He said thanks and good-night, to his partner's obvious relief.

Rainbow remained in her little apartment, humming and cleaning the kitchen, and Hope walked with Gideon down the stairs.

"Sorry," she said softly when they were halfway down the stairway. "Mom's a little flaky, I know. She means well, but she never outgrew her hippie phase."

"Don't apologize. I like her. She's different, but she's also very nice." Man, did he know about being odd man out. "Different isn't always a bad thing."

"Yeah," Hope said with an audible scoff. "Try to believe that when your mother shows up for career day to talk about selling crystals and incense, and ends up heckling the CEO dad for ruining the environment and selling out to the corporate man."

Gideon couldn't help himself. He laughed.

"Trust me, you wouldn't think it was so funny if she told your first real boyfriend that he had a muddy aura and really needed to meditate in order to boost his positive energy."

"Positive energy is a good thing," Gideon said as they reached the shop, where the lights had been dimmed when Rainbow locked the door for the night.

"You don't have to patronize me," Hope said sharply. "I know my mother is odd and flaky and just plain… weird."

Gideon didn't head directly for the door. He wasn't ready to go home—not yet. He studied the crystals and jewelry in the display case, then fingered a collection of silver charms that hung suspended from a display rack. He choose one—a plain Celtic knot suspended from a black satin cord—and slipped it from the rack with one finger.

He turned his back to Hope, cupped the charm in both hands and whispered a few words. The faint gleam of green light escaped from between his fingers. The light didn't last long; neither did the words he spoke.

"What are you doing?" Hope asked, circling to face him just as the glow faded.

He slipped the charm over her head before she knew what he was planning to do. "Do me a favor and wear this for a few days."

She lifted the charm and glanced at it. "Why?"

Gideon had gifted the charm with protection. Only members of the royal family—Dante and Mercy in addition to himself—could gift charms, and they used the power sparingly. They could not bestow blessings on themselves, only others, and it was not an ability they advertised. Like everything else, it was a hidden talent that had to be carefully guarded. He didn't know if this afternoon's bullet had been meant for Hope or for him, but in either case, he would rest easier if she were protected. Nothing would shield her from everything, but the gifted charm would give her an edge. It would shield her with the positive energy she scoffed at for a few days, at least. Nine days, to be precise.

"Indulge me," he said calmly.

Hope studied the charm skeptically. "I haven't known you long enough to even consider that I should indulge your eccentricities."

"We've been shot at. That means we bond quickly as partners and you indulge me in all my eccentricities."

She was still uncertain, skeptical and wound so tight she was about to pop. The woman needed to have a little fun more than anyone he'd ever met.

While Hope was studying the Celtic knot, Gideon moved in on her. He backed her against the counter so she was trapped between his arms and the glass case. This close, he was reminded how tiny she was, how fragile. She tried so hard to be one of the guys, to be tough and independent and hard. But she was a woman, first and foremost, and she wasn't hard. She was soft, and she wasn't going anywhere, not until he was ready to let her go.

"Wear it for me," he said, his voice low. "Wear it because it'll make me feel better to know you have this lucky silver hanging around your neck."

"It's silly," she protested, obviously bothered by

the fact that she was trapped. "Besides, you don't wear such a—"

He slipped a finger beneath his collar, snagged the leather cord and drew out the talisman Dante had sent him late last week. In the light cast from the streetlamps outside her mother's shop and in the blue flashing light of the café across the street, she clearly saw the charm he wore around his neck.

"Oh," she said softly. "I did see that…once."

"Just because you can't see or feel or touch something, that doesn't mean it doesn't exist." He had never tried to explain himself to anyone, much less a woman he hadn't even known two days. Life was too short, and he didn't care what people he barely knew thought of him. But Hope was surrounded by everyday magic, through her mother, and still she rejected it. That bothered him.

"So," she said, her voice no more warm than it had been before, "do you see auras, too? Am I glowing in the dark, Raintree?"

"I don't see auras."

Was it a trick of the light, or was she relieved?

"That doesn't mean I don't believe I have one."

He wanted her transferred, for her own good as much as his own. It was safer for him to work alone, and Hope was better suited to robbery or fraud or juvenile crimes. Anything but homicide. Any partner but him. She turned her head, and her throat caught the light from the street. Her neck was pale, slender and long enough to make him wonder what it would taste like. If Hope were renting a house on the beach for a week or two, if she were a tourist or a secretary or a sales clerk, he would gladly pick her up and take her home for an evening or two.

But she was his freakin' partner, for God's sake.

Not for long.

He leaned down and pressed his mouth against her neck. She gasped as he slipped his hand between their bodies and laid his palm against her belly, lower than was proper for partners, acquaintances or friends. Her body tensed; she was about to defend herself. She was going to push him away, or knee him where it would hurt the most.

Much of the body's response was electrical, though few people seemed to realize that simple fact. Gideon understood the power of electricity very well. He'd lived with it all his life. Even now, with the solstice approaching and his abilities slightly out of whack, he had enough control to do what had to be done.

His hand fit snugly against Hope's warm belly, pressed there as if he had the right to touch her in such a way. He reached inside Hope with the electric charge he'd harnessed. Through the thick fabric of her conservative trousers, through what was probably ordinary underwear—or would she surprise him with a slip of red silk and lace?—through her skin, he touched her and made her insides quicken and pulse. He made her orgasm with a touch of his hand and a sharing of his energy.

Hope gasped, twitched and shuddered. The hand that had been about to push him away grabbed at his jacket instead and clutched the fabric tightly in a small, strong fist. She made an involuntary noise deep in her throat and stopped breathing for a moment. Just for a moment. Her thighs parted slightly; her heart beat in an irregular rhythm. He had to hold her up to keep her from falling to the floor when her knees wobbled. The response to the electricity coursing through Hope's body wasn't ordinary or conventional. She moaned; she lurched. And then she went still.

He was hard, no surprise, and they were standing so close that she was surely aware of that fact. If she kneed him now, she would do serious damage. He slowly dropped his hands and backed away.

"What did you…?" Hope didn't finish her question.

Gideon reached into his back pocket, withdrew his wallet and slipped out a ten-dollar bill. "For the charm," he said, tossing the bill onto the counter and ignoring what had just happened. "Want me to pick you up in the morning? Breakfast at the Hilton again? We'll see about getting someone out there to look at your car."

He waited for her to tell him to go to hell. She could bring him up on charges of sexual harassment, but who would believe her? *We were both fully dressed. It happened so fast. He laid a hand on me, and I came like a woman who hadn't been with a man in ten years.*

She couldn't do that. No one would ever believe her. Her only option was to tell him to go to hell and ask for another partner, to request another, more suitable, assignment.

"I think I'll skip breakfast," she said, her voice still displaying the breathless evidence of her orgasm.

Gideon smiled. Maybe it was going to be easier to scare her off than he'd thought it would be. That hope didn't last long. Still breathless, she said, "Pick me up when you're done."

After she locked the door behind Raintree, Hope rushed to the stairway and sat on the bottom step, all but crumpling there. Her knees were weak; her thighs trembled; she still couldn't breathe; her mind was spinning. What had happened, exactly?

Granted, it had been a long time since any man had touched her. And she did find Gideon attractive. He had that roguish charm that both intrigued and annoyed her. But to orgasm simply because he laid a hand on her and kissed her neck? It was impossible. Right?

Unlikely, unheard of, but apparently *not* impossible.

She leaned against the wall, hiding in the shadows, her insides still quaking a little. Her knees continued to shake, and she felt a growing dampness that told her that she wasn't finished with the man who'd aroused her and made her come in a matter of seconds. Well, mentally she was most definitely finished with him, but her body felt differently.

Gideon could hurt her so much. He could be the wrong man all over again. She couldn't do it; she simply could not take that chance. So why did she still remember the way his mustache had tickled her neck and wonder how it would feel against her mouth?

She began to fiddle with the silver doodad that hung around her neck. What she should do was rip the damn thing off and throw it away. What she should do was file charges against the SOB for daring to put his hands on her. Of course, that was probably just what he wanted and expected her to do.

What she was going to do was meet him tomorrow morning and pretend that nothing had happened. There was more to Gideon Raintree than met the eye, and she was going to find out what that *more* was.

This time of year the storms came frequently. Gideon loved storms. Most of all, he loved the lightning. Midnight had passed. He stood on the beach wearing his cutoff jeans and Dante's protection charm, and lifted his face and his palms to the clouds. Electrons filled the air. He could taste them; he could feel them.

He could still feel and taste her, too. Normally nothing distracted him when there was electricity in the air, but he still felt Hope reeling against him, clutching at his clothes, moaning and wobbling and coming more intensely than he'd expected. He could still taste her throat on his tongue. It had been an exercise meant to distract her, and instead here he was, hopelessly distracted himself, hours after he'd walked away and left her trembling and confused.

He couldn't afford to be distracted. Not now, not ever. It was the reason he always sent Emma away, the reason he mailed Dante fertility charms on a regular basis. Someone had to carry on the Raintree name, and it wouldn't be him.

What normal woman would accept who and what he was? Like it or not, there were moments when that was what he wanted more than anything. Not to be normal, not to deny who and what he was and give up his gifts. Not that, never that. But some days he craved a touch of normal in his life. Just a touch. And he couldn't have it. Nothing about his life ever had been or ever would be normal.

Hope was normal. If she knew what he was and what he could do, he would never again get close enough to touch her.

The first crack of lightning split the sky and lit the night. The bolt danced across the black sky, beautiful and bright and powerful, splintering like veins of power. He felt it under his skin, in his blood. The next bolt was closer and more powerful. It was drawn to him, as he was drawn to it. He and the lightning fed one another. He drew the energy closer; he drank it in.

The next bolt of lightning came to him. It shot through his body, danced in his blood. His eyes rolled up and back, and his feet left the sand so that he floated a few inches off the ground. He never felt more powerful than he did at moments like these, with the night cloaking him, the waves lapping close by, and the lightning running through his blood.

Gideon didn't just love the storm, he *was* the storm. Caught in the lightning show, an integral part of it, he drank in the power and the beauty. He gave back, as well, feeding the storm as it fed him. With the summer solstice coming, he didn't need the extra jolt of power the storm provided, but he wanted it. Craved it. Standing on the beach alone, fortifying his body with the power he shared with explosive nature, he could not deny who he was.

Raintree.

The next thunderbolt hit Gideon directly and blew him back several feet. He felt not as if he had been thrown but as if he were flying. Flying or not, he landed in the sand on his ass, breathless and energized and invigorated. His heartbeat raced; his breath came hard. As the storm moved on, small slivers of lightning remained with Gideon, crackling off his skin in a way that was startlingly obvious in the darkness of night. White and green and blue, the electricity danced across and inside him. He lifted a hand to the night sky and watched the fading sparks his skin generated.

Normal wasn't his thing, and it never would be. Best not to waste his time wishing for things that would never happen, impossible things like being inside Hope the next time she lurched and trembled.

If she scoffed at auras and crystals and lucky tokens, what would she think of *him?*

Chapter 6

Gideon half expected Hope to be far, far away from her mother's shop by the time he arrived at The Silver Chalice to pick her up. She'd had time to think about last night. She could be downtown, filing a report against him or requesting a transfer. Maybe she was on her way back to Raleigh, though to be honest, she didn't look like a runner. Still, it was unlikely that she would continue on as if nothing had happened.

Again she surprised him. She was waiting out front, outwardly casual, a coffee cup in one hand. As usual, she was dressed conservatively, in a gray pantsuit and white tailored blouse that would look plain on any other woman but looked incredibly hot on Hope Malory. Did she know that those tailored trousers she thought made her look professional only advertised how long and slender her legs were? And with those heels she wore— heels that were probably intended to make her look even taller than she already was—she was a knockout. If she was wearing the charm he'd given her last night, it was well hidden, just as his was.

"You shouldn't be standing out in the open," he said as he reached across and threw open the passenger side door.

"Good morning to you, too," Hope said distantly as she took her seat. "What's the plan?" If she'd had the guts to actually look him in the eye, he wouldn't have believed she was human.

"I culled out four homicides, all of them in the Southeast, that share some similarities with the Bishop murder."

"All women?"

He shook his head. "Three women, one man."

"Commonality?"

"Similar weapon and souvenirs taken. Not always fingers and hair, but souvenirs in themselves are unusual enough to make them worth looking at. There were no witnesses, and no evidence to speak of. All the victims were single. Not just unmarried, but unattached romantically and without family living close by. That could be coincidence, but…"

"I don't believe in coincidence," Hope said coolly.

"Neither do I."

He hadn't seen Sherry Bishop's ghost since yesterday, which didn't mean anything. She might show up at any moment to feed him another tidbit of useful—or not so useful—information. Or he might never see her again, in which case he was on his own.

He glanced at Hope. Not as *on his own* as he would like to be. Pretty and intriguing and smart as Hope Malory was, he didn't need or want a partner. Why was she still here? In forty-eight hours he'd tried to antagonize her and then to make her his friend. He'd disabled her car, saved her life and made her come. She should either love him or hate him, and yet here she was, cool as ever.

What would it take to rattle her?

"I called a mechanic about your car. He's going to meet us at the Hilton in ten minutes."

"Thanks," she said coolly.

"The lab analysis on Sherry Bishop should be in early this afternoon. Most of it, anyway. Once your car is taken care of, I figure we can go to the office and make some phone calls about these other murders while we wait for the report to come in."

"Fine with me. If we have the time I'd like a look at the file on Stiles, if you don't mind. He could be behind yesterday's shooting, and the blonde the bookstore clerk saw might have nothing to do with the case."

"Possible," Gideon agreed. "If we do have a serial killer on our hands, she hasn't done *this* before. She's never stuck around and targeted the investigators."

"Maybe she's scared because you're so *good*."

"Do I detect a hint of sarcasm?"

"Ah, you really are a star detective."

So…she wasn't quite as cool and distant as she pretended to be.

When they pulled into the Hilton parking lot, the mechanic was already there, waiting. Gideon parked close to Hope's Toyota and killed the engine. As he started to leave the car, she said softly, "One more thing, Raintree, before the day gets under way. Lay a hand on me again and I'll shoot you."

He hesitated with his hand on the door handle. "You mean you'll file charges against me, right?"

She looked him in the eye then, squarely and strongly. Yeah, she was entirely human, not altogether pleased with him, and more than a little rattled.

"No, I mean I'll shoot you. I handle my own problems, so if you thought you were going to send me crying to the boss asking for justice and a transfer, you were mistaken."

And how.

"I don't know how you did it, and I don't care," she continued, her voice low but strong. "Well, not much. I *am* curious, but not nearly curious enough to let this slide. From here on out, keep your hands to yourself if you want to keep them." She opened the door and stepped out, dismissing him and effectively ending the conversation.

Damn. Apparently he had himself a new partner.

Tabby took long strides along the riverfront, anxious and twitchy and unhappy. Sherry Bishop's funeral wouldn't be held until Saturday, and even then, it was being held in Indiana. Freakin' Indiana! What was she supposed to do, travel all that way on the *chance* that

Echo would be there? No, she had to be here on Sunday. Here and finished with her part of the preparations.

Time to be realistic. Time to look beyond what she wanted and concentrate on what had to be done. It was too late to get Echo first. If the Raintree prophet was going to see that something was about to happen, she'd already seen it. Maybe Echo wasn't as powerful as advertised.

Tabby had to focus on what she could do here and now, and dismiss what she couldn't. Echo was nowhere to be found, at least not at the present time, but Gideon Raintree was right here in Wilmington, so close she could almost taste him.

Raintree's neighbors were too close and too nosy. There was always someone on the beach or on a nearby deck. Taking him at home would never work. She needed privacy for what she had planned. Privacy and just a little bit of time. She wouldn't have all the time she wanted, but she definitely planned to have minutes with Raintree instead of seconds. Hours would be better, but she would take what she could get.

Raintree and his partner had been in the police station most of the day, and she wasn't stupid enough to try to take them there. Besides, she didn't want this to be quick. She wanted to be looking into Gideon's green Raintree eyes when she killed him. She wanted to be close enough to absorb any energy he emitted when he drew his last breath, and she certainly wanted a memento or two.

Fortunately, she knew exactly how to draw him out of the safety of the police station and well away from home.

The boardwalk by the river was crowded with tour-

ists and a few locals. She scanned them all, one at a time.
Someone here had to be alone. Not just by themselves
at the moment, but truly and completely *alone*. Mis-
erably isolated. Tabby scanned people quickly, dismissing one after another as inadequate for her purposes.
And then her gaze fell on the person she'd been searching for.

Alone, scared, separated from her loved ones. Uncertain, vulnerable, needy. *Perfect.*

Tabaet Ansara smiled as she focused on the redhead's
shapely back and wondered if the woman had any
inkling that she was about to die.

Wednesday—3:29 p.m.

"What do you mean, the computer chip is fried?"
Hope all but shouted into the phone. "It's practically a
new car!" Just out of warranty, in fact.

She listened to the mechanic's explanation, which
was in truth no explanation at all. He didn't know what
had happened. He only knew that a very expensive
computer chip had to be replaced. Naturally, he didn't
have the part on hand. It would take a few days to get
the new chip in and have it installed.

She banged the phone down with a vengeance, and
Raintree lifted his head slowly to look at her. "Bad news?"

"I'm without a car for a few days." She began to leaf
through the yellow pages on her desk. "Who would you
recommend I call about a rental?"

"You don't need a rental car," Raintree said.

"I'm not going to let you chauffeur me around town for days," she argued. And her mother's mode of transportation was an embarrassment. The car did get good gas mileage, but it was only slightly larger than a cigar box, and had a nasty habit of dying at stop signs and red lights.

"How are you with a stick?"

"Excuse me?"

"Standard transmission," he said, lifting his gaze to her once again. "Can you handle it?"

"Yes," she said tersely.

Raintree had taken her seriously this morning, she supposed, since he hadn't touched her all day. Not inappropriately, not casually, not at all. That was what she wanted, right? So why was she still so on edge in his presence that she wanted to scream?

"I'll loan you my Challenger," he said. "We'll run by the house tonight and I'll get you a set of keys." When she hesitated, he added, "If Leon was without a car, I'd make the same offer to him."

A part of her wanted to refuse, but she didn't. It would just be for a few days, after all. "Sure. Thanks."

Raintree sat well away from his computer, studying the thick file in his hands. They had the initial crime scene report from the Sherry Bishop case, such as it was, and were awaiting the coroner's report at any moment. Another detective, Charlie Newsom, stuck his head in the office Raintree and Hope shared—at least for the moment. He looked at Hope, openly interested with those sparkling eyes and that killer smile. Charlie was probably one of the nice guys, not a stinker at all. He didn't put her on edge in the least. "I ran that check on Stiles. He was locked up in the county jail last week for drunk and disorderly."

"He bonded out?" Gideon asked.

Charlie shook his head. "Nope. He's still there."

Which meant he couldn't possibly have been the one to take a shot at Raintree—or her—yesterday.

Gideon ran his fingers over the top photo of a woman killed in a rural part of the state four months ago. There were others just like it beneath, some with poor lighting, some from less gruesome angles, but this was the photo that spoke to him.

Marcia Cordell had very little in common with Sherry Bishop. Marcia had been a thirty-six-year-old schoolteacher in a small county school. At the time of her death she'd been wearing a loose-fitting brown dress that might have been purposely chosen to hide whatever figure she had. She wouldn't have been caught dead— or alive—with pink hair or a belly button ring. She'd lived not in an apartment but in a small house off a country road, a house she had inherited from her father when he'd passed on five years ago.

What she and Sherry did have in common was that they were both single. Instead of filling her lonely nights with music and a job at a coffee shop, Marcia Cordell had filled her emptiness with other people's children, two fat cats, and—judging by the photo on his desk— an impressive collection of snow globes from places she had never been. They'd also both been murdered with a knife that left a similar wound. Sherry had been killed by a slash to her throat, but Marcia had been stabbed half a dozen times before her throat had been cut. The angle and depth of the final wound was the same in both cases, though, and there was destruction at both scenes, as if the murderer had gone into a frenzy once the murders were done.

And one of Marcia Cordell's ears had been severed and taken.

Investigations in understaffed jurisdictions were often shoddy and incomplete, but the sheriff's office had done a fairly good job with this one. The case file was slim, but the sheriff was still actively pursuing the case and had been very cooperative over the phone. He'd invited Gideon to visit the crime scene, which had been well preserved, as Cordell had no immediate family and had left no provisions for her little house. Not that anyone was likely to want it after what had happened there.

Was it possible that Marcia Cordell's ghost was still there in that house, waiting for justice? Possible, but not necessarily likely. Still, this had been a particularly grisly murder, maybe even grisly enough to keep Marcia's spirit around for a while. If Marcia Cordell knew he was determined to find the woman who'd killed her, would she be able to rest in peace?

The stack of files on Gideon's desk was disheartening. If he had the time, he could solve them all. He could find the bad guys, put them away, send the spirits of those who had been murdered to a better place. But dammit, there was so much darkness he couldn't keep up with it all. One man couldn't possibly fix the ills of the entire world. It was a world he couldn't possibly bring a child into. He couldn't fix it all, not for a child…not for Sherry Bishop and Marcia Cordell.

"You okay, Raintree?"

He hadn't even heard Hope enter the office. "No," he said. "I'm not okay. I think we have a serial killer."

Wednesday—11:17 p.m.

Gideon hunkered down beside the body that lay atop the cheap carpet in a semirespectable hotel room. The victim's red hair covered most of her face, but he could see more than enough. Like Sherry Bishop, this woman had been killed with a knife. Unlike Sherry Bishop, this woman's death had not been quick. The scene looked more like the photos from the Marcia Cordell homicide.

Lily Clark. According to her driver's license she was thirty-one years old and had traveled here from a small town in Georgia for a week's vacation. She'd checked in with a male friend on Saturday, but according to the man at the front desk, that man hadn't been seen since Sunday afternoon. Clark had been seen in tears more than once since that time. Hope, of course, had immediately pegged the boyfriend as a suspect. Gideon already knew better.

Two murder victims in three days was unusual for Wilmington. The fact that this one was a tourist was going to cause a ruckus.

"She said my life wasn't worth a nickel," the ghost said softly. "And she was right. I didn't live the way I should've. I existed, scared of something or other more often than not. I never even thought to be afraid of something like this."

"She was trying to torment you, Lily," Gideon said gently. "Don't let her continue hurting you now. Let everything she said to you go."

Lily Clark's ghost shook her head in denial, unable to let *anything* go. "No, she was right. She said I was ugly even before she cut my face, and she said that death was best for me because no man would ever be able to love me." The spirit of the dead woman sat on the side of the bed, her hands clasped primly in her lap, her lower lip quivering. Her form was more substantial than Sherry Bishop's had ever been. She was likely to stick around for a while. "She was right," the wraith whispered.

Hope was interviewing the hotel manager, and uniformed officers were keeping everyone else out. For the moment, at least, Gideon and the ghost were alone. "No, Lily, she wasn't right. Now, I want you to forget everything she said and concentrate on what you can tell me that will help me find her. Tell me about the woman who did this to you so I can get her off the streets. Tall and blond, you said. What can you tell me about the knife she used?"

"It was old, I think. The blade was sharp, and the handle was silver. Did you see?" She pointed. "She cut off my little finger!"

And this time she hadn't waited until after death.

"Was there an engraving on the handle?"

"Yeah," Clark said, a vague touch of enthusiasm in her voice. "I couldn't tell what it said, though. It wasn't

English. When she was sitting on my chest and pointing the tip of the knife at my nose, I saw some old squiggly letters." Her red hair swayed slightly. "They didn't make any sense."

"And you never saw her before today?" Gideon said, repeating something Lily had told him when he'd first arrived on the scene.

"I was such an idiot," she wailed. "First I come here with Jerry, only to find out that he's *married,* and then I let that awful woman into my hotel room. Of course, I didn't know she was awful when I asked her in. She seemed so sweet when we met on the riverfront. We ran into each other, literally, and I spilled my lemonade all over her. I thought she'd be mad, but she just laughed. We got to talking. You know how it is. She was having boyfriend troubles, too, and we were going to go out tonight and have a few drinks and…" The ghost went still and looked at Gideon with a puzzled expression on her face. "Wait a minute. Is your name Raintree? Gideon Raintree?"

Gideon nodded, wondering with a sinking stomach how the woman knew his name.

"I almost forgot. I have a message for you."

A shiver danced down his spine. "A message?"

She nodded her head. "The woman who killed me, she said you're to meet her at midnight on the riverfront, just down from the coffee shop where the other woman she killed used to work. She said you'd know where that was. Go alone. If you don't, she'll kill someone else. I don't think she cares who, just someone like me. Some-one who won't be missed."

His sinking stomach didn't improve. Somehow the killer knew what he could do. Did she have psychic abilities herself, or had she hired a weak seer who'd just gotten lucky? The *how* didn't much matter, not now. The serial killer he was looking for had tortured and murdered this poor woman just so she would be strong enough to stick around and give him a message.

Lily Clark might never move on as she should. "Everyone is missed," he said. Lily was shaking her head, but he continued. "Everyone leaves a hole in the universe when they're taken too soon."

Her form fluttered, as if she had just become a little less substantial. "I won't," she whispered. "My first husband sure won't miss me, and my parents are just going to be angry because I never gave them grandchildren. I work with computers all day, and you know *they* won't miss me."

"I'll miss you," Gideon said, glancing down at the body and then up at the spirit on the bed. It was easier than looking at what was left of her physical form.

"Why?"

"Because if I had caught the woman who did this to you yesterday, you'd still be alive."

Lily reached out a hand as if she wanted to comfort him. Her fingers were cold, but he felt her touch very clearly. "I don't blame you."

"I blame myself."

"Do you always do that?"

Gideon's head snapped around. Hope stood in the

doorway. How long had she been there, watching and listening? "Do what?"

"Blame yourself," she said, an unexpected trace of sympathy in her voice.

"The killer wasn't the boyfriend," he said. "It's the same woman who murdered Sherry Bishop."

Hope shook her head. "I know we have the…the severed finger, but other than that, this is a completely different MO. Bishop was killed with a quick swipe. Clark was…" Her gaze flitted to the body but didn't remain there long. "She was tortured, Gideon. This was personal."

"No, this was sick." He stood. "And very much like the unsolved murder in Hale County. It's the same woman, Hope. I know it. I want an analysis on the weapon ASAP. I'd bet my job that the same knife that killed Sherry Bishop and Marcia Cordell was also used to kill Lily Clark." When he took a step toward Hope, she flinched slightly, but she didn't step back. Somehow he had to get rid of his new partner before he went to the boardwalk to meet with the killer. He couldn't tell her how he knew the psycho who had murdered two women in three days would be there, and he didn't want to put Hope in danger.

The last thing he needed was a partner he had to worry about.

"It's too late to accomplish anything tonight," he said, the weariness in his voice real enough. "We'll let the crime scene techs do their thing, and then we'll get a fresh start in the morning."

Hope cocked her head slightly, openly confused. "In the morning?"

"Yeah. In the morning. I'm tired. Let's get out of here."

For a moment all was silent but for the ghost on the bed, who continued to chatter about how stupid she had been where people were concerned. She wasn't going anywhere soon. Not tonight, in any case. As far as he knew, Sherry had already moved on, but this woman would clearly remain earthbound for a while longer.

"You go on," Hope said. "I'll stick around here for a while, just in case anything comes up."

He would feel better if he knew she was home, doors locked behind her, but that wasn't his concern. Besides, he'd spotted the cord around her neck peeking out a time or two today. She was wearing the protection charm he'd given her.

"See you in the morning," he said, turning his back on Hope and Lily Clark and the crime scene team that was waiting to go inside the bloody hotel room.

Wait until morning? No way. Two days—no, three —and she already knew that wasn't Gideon Raintree's style. Hope left the crime scene techs and trailed discreetly after Gideon. His mind was definitely elsewhere as he climbed into his Mustang and started the engine.

If she followed him in that huge and noisy red Challenger he'd loaned her, he would spot her before he got out of the parking lot. She turned to the closest person, the night manager of the hotel. "Can I borrow your car?"

"What?" he asked, confused and suspicious.

"Your vehicle," Hope said, offering her hand palm up for the keys. "I'll have it back as soon as possible, and I'll fill it up with gas."

The portly man was still less than certain.

"What am I going to do?" Hope snapped. "Steal it? I'm a cop."

He pulled his keys out of his pants pocket and reluctantly handed them over. "It's the gray pickup truck."

"Thanks." She ran to the truck, watching Raintree's taillights as he turned onto Market Street. That was *not* the way toward home.

This time of night, the streets were all but deserted. There were a few tourists still out and about, enjoying the clubs and the music in the downtown area, but trailing Raintree was easy enough to be problematic. She tried to stay back so he wouldn't know he was being followed, but she was definitely taking a chance.

There were a few possible scenarios to explain his quick exit from the hotel. He really could just be tired, but in that case he would be driving in the other direction, *toward* Wrightsville Beach. Maybe he had a date. That was probably it. He had a midnight rendezvous with some bimbo like his neighbor Honey. They were likely all *Honey* to him. Then again, maybe this was the proof she'd been waiting to find. He was meeting a drug dealer for a payoff. Maybe Lily Clark's death was connected to the other drug murders Gideon had solved in his time in the Wilmington PD, and he'd found something at the scene that alerted him to the identity of the killer.

It wasn't part of the plan to like Raintree, so why did she hope so desperately that he was going to meet some airhead for drinks and dancing and a little recreational sex? She didn't much like the idea, even though she had no claim on him and never would, but it was preferable to finding out that her initial instincts about him had been right and he was crooked. She didn't want him to be crooked. As he parked his car at the curb, she tried to come up with another scenario. One that didn't make him crooked *or* horny.

Hope drove past Raintree as he exited his Mustang, turning her head slightly so he wouldn't get a look at her face. He was so distracted, he didn't even glance at her. She turned a corner and parked in front of a closed gift shop, waiting until she saw Gideon in the rearview mirror before she left the truck.

He was headed for the riverfront. Hope stayed a good distance behind him, but close enough that she could always see the back of his head. Even though this area was well lit at night, there were plenty of shadows for her to conceal herself within. Raintree walked slowly, but with purpose and his own special brand of grace, and when he reached a particular section of the boardwalk, he stopped and leaned over the wood railing, looking down over the river.

Here was her most favorable scenario: Gideon wanted a little time alone to ponder the two murders. He was thinking in that odd way he had, winding down, putting together the pieces of the puzzle and not waiting for a Honey *or* a drug dealer. Hope stayed in the shadows and watched. One older couple passed him but didn't slow down or acknowledge him in any way other than a quick glance. Gideon continued to stare out over the river, motionless. She began to think this was a perfectly innocent evening…

And then he checked his watch. He was waiting for something. No, *someone.* Her heart sank, even though she knew she shouldn't care why he was there or who he had come to meet.

A few minutes later the tall blonde stepped out of the shadows, walking toward Raintree with a purpose of her own. He lifted his head as if he knew she was there long before he could have heard her step.

A woman. She should have known. Men like Raintree didn't live without female companionship, no matter how dedicated they might be to their jobs. She'd heard him talking to the victim back at the hotel, dragging his eyes away from the body to tell the woman who could no longer hear him that her life mattered, promising to find justice for her. And yet here he was, slipping away from a fresh investigation for a *date?* It didn't make sense, but then, what man ever did what was expected of him?

Hope was ready to slip away quietly and return the hotel manager's pickup without Raintree ever knowing that she'd once again stooped to spying on him when a niggle of warning stopped her.

The woman walking toward Raintree… Her blond hair was long and straight, matching the single strand that had been found on Sherry Bishop's body. She was taller than average, and moved in a way that advertised that she had muscles and knew how to use them.

And with her left hand she reached inside the jacket she wore and withdrew a long, wicked-looking knife.

Chapter 7

"That's her! That's her!" Lily Clark jumped up and down and pointed a shaking finger as she flailed and issued her warning. The ghost looked surprisingly solid to Gideon's eyes, but the blonde didn't seem to see her latest victim at all.

"I know," Gideon said softly.

"Shoot her," Lily instructed.

"Not yet." He wanted to discover what the blonde knew—and how. Besides, even though he knew this woman to be a murderer, shooting suspects on the river-front was definitely frowned upon.

The blonde smiled and made sure he could see the knife in her hand. Anyone sitting in the coffee shop not too far away wouldn't see anything suspicious if they glanced in this direction, because the way the woman held her jacket shielded the weapon from their view. Most of the customers weren't looking this way, anyway. Through the window he could see that they were engrossed in their own conversations, their own lives. They had no idea that a monster walked a few feet away.

"I'm here," he said, holding his hands palm up so she could see he didn't hold a weapon of his own.

"I knew you would be, Raintree," the knife-wielding blonde said as she came closer.

"You know my name. What's yours?"

Her smile widened a little. "Tabby."

Gideon suspected she was telling the truth; she didn't expect him to be around long enough to share that information with anyone else.

"What do you want, Tabby?"

"I want to talk."

"That's what she said to me," Lily said indignantly. "Don't listen to her. You're a cop. You have a gun. Shoot her!"

"Not yet," he said softly.

"What do you mean…?" Tabby began, and then she hesitated. "You're not talking to me, are you? Which one is here?" She glanced around, but her eyes never fell on Lily. "Both, maybe. No, it's got to be that whiny Clark woman. Trust me, before long you'll be more than ready to be rid of her. She just about talked my ears off before I gagged her."

In a rage, Lily threw herself at Tabby, passing right through the tall woman's body. Maybe Tabby felt something, a chill, or a bit of wind. Her step faltered a little; her smile faded.

Thanks to the torture, physical and psychological, Tabby had made Lily more substantial than most spirits. She was tied to this plane in a way most spirits weren't. With a little concentration, maybe a *lot* of concentration, Lily could affect the physical in this world she'd left behind. Maybe.

Tabby stopped less than three feet away. The place was too public for him to toss a surge of electricity her way, but when she got closer, if he could touch her and send a surge to her heart, the effect would be the same.

"You have two choices, Raintree. You can come with me without incident so we can discuss the situation privately for a while, or you can give me a hard time, and after you're dead, I'll take it out on the innocent citizens and tourists of this town you call home. You'll still be around to watch, I imagine, as a ghost who can't lift a finger to stop me." She grinned widely. "That would be very cool."

"I have a feeling it would be dangerous to go anywhere with you. Why don't we talk right here?"

"It would be very dangerous for you not to do as I say," she countered, her voice flat and her eyes hard. The grip on the knife in her left hand changed, tightening and growing more secure, more…ready. Gideon felt the tingle of electricity in his fingertips. If he had no other choice…

A young couple neared, arm in arm and oblivious to the rest of the world. Tabby moved closer. "Make a move and I'll stick 'em both before you can say boo."

Gideon remained still, sure that Tabby would do exactly as she threatened if she had the chance. The twosome passed, unaware of the danger that was so close. When they were out of earshot, Tabby smiled once again. "Are you going to come with me or not?"

"I'm going to arrest you or kill you. Your choice."

She didn't look at all afraid, not of him, not of anything. Her grin grew wide again for a split second, and then her head turned sharply and the smile disappeared altogether, with a swiftness that transformed her face. "I told you to come alone."

Gideon reached for her while she was distracted, intent on grabbing her wrist and sending a jolt to her heart. He'd never killed anyone before, but he knew it was possible, and if ever a monster deserved to die... But before he could get a grip on her, she lifted the hand that didn't hold a knife and tossed a few grains of powder into his face. The grains fell into his eyes and onto his lips and everywhere else, and he was immediately half-blinded and dizzy. He missed her, and she swung out with the knife. It wasn't a wild swing but a well-planned maneuver that slipped past his guard and took him by surprise. With a minimum of wasted motion, Tabby thrust the knife deep into his thigh.

Gideon's leg gave out from under him, and he dropped to the boardwalk with a thud. Tabby took another swipe at his hand, this one wild and unplanned. Gideon shifted his hand. The tip of the knife barely grazed his flesh, drawing a small welt of blood rather than the finger she'd no doubt wanted to collect. Her head snapped up, she cursed, and then she ran.

Half-lying, half-sitting on the boardwalk, Gideon took aim. He hesitated. His vision swam. He blinked hard. Sending a bolt of electricity into her back was possible, but had the ruckus garnered the attention of the people in the café? He wondered if he could stop her without killing her. If he killed Tabby, he would never know how she had discovered his ability to talk with the dead…how many people she'd killed…why…?

He couldn't let her get away. His hand lifted, and he called up more power than he had ever directed at another person, one who could not absorb the energy as he did.

But he didn't fire. His thinking was usually so clear, so crisp, but at this moment it was anything but. Someone familiar called his name. *Raintree!* Somewhere in those shadows ahead stood the couple that had recently walked by. He couldn't see them well, but they were there. Sure enough, the surprised and curious young man stepped into Tabby's wake and directly into Gideon's sights, and again his vision swam.

Hope, her own pistol in her hand, passed Gideon at a run. "Are you all right?"

"Yeah," he said as she cut between him and the man who'd foolishly placed himself in front of Gideon's target. "No, not really," he added, even though she was already too far away to hear his low words. "What the hell are you doing here?" He shouldn't be surprised to see Hope here; he shouldn't be surprised that she so easily gave chase. The woman was everywhere she shouldn't be.

"Call for backup!" she yelled as she kept running.

Gideon lowered his hand and leaned against the boardwalk railing, glancing down at his torn trousers. He healed quickly, but he didn't heal immediately. The scratch in his hand was already fading away, but his thigh was another matter, and whatever Tabby had tossed into his face still had him reeling. The knife had gone deep, and he tamed the flow of blood by pressing his hand to the wound. At any other time of the year he would head to the ER for stitches, but not in any week approaching an equinox or a solstice. His presence would play hell with the hospital equipment.

He pressed against the wound and did his best to concentrate, to remain lucid. A serial killer who knew what he could do. It was a nightmare. Tabby wouldn't go from town to town, not anymore. She would send him ghost after ghost after ghost, each one of them begging him for justice. She would play this game of hers until one of them was dead. Gideon's thinking grew more and more muddled. He hadn't lost that much blood, yet he felt weaker now than he had when the knife had cut into his flesh. It hadn't been sand she'd tossed into his eyes, hoping to blind him, but some kind of drug that was stealing his reason. He pressed his hand against the wound with more force. He wished for numbness, but the deep gash hurt like hell.

The lights of the coffee shop whirled, and he blinked against the oddly shifting brightness. The streetlamps above grew oblong and faded and fuzzy, and his heart wasn't pumping right. It was off beat, out of tune. In the back of his mind, Gideon knew he should be trying to get up, but more than the pain in his leg kept him immobile. His entire body was heavy, and he couldn't manage to focus on anything for more than a split second. He could think just clearly enough to know that this was bad. Very bad.

A moment later Hope was headed back toward him, moving a little more slowly than she'd been when she'd first chased after Tabby, but still moving fast. She didn't maintain her shape any better than the lights above, and he blinked against the misty vision. How on earth was she able to run in those heels?

"I lost her," she said breathlessly. "Shit, she was right *there,* and I…" She shook off her frustration and dropped down to her haunches beside him. "You look terrible. You called for backup and an ambulance, right?"

"No." His lips felt numb and heavy as he answered.

She reached for her cell phone. "You didn't call this in? Dammit, Raintree…"

He placed his hand on her wrist before she could dial. "No hospital. No backup. I just need you to drive me home."

"Home!" She moved his hand and peeled aside a portion of sliced fabric, then grimaced at his injury. "I don't think so." She pressed her surprisingly strong hand over the wound. "You need a doctor."

He shook his head. "I can't."

"You're going to have to tell her," Lily Clark said with a shake of her red head.

"I can't," he answered.

"You already said that." Hope lifted her hand slightly

and looked again at the gash in his leg, what she could see past the torn trousers. "You're not thinking straight."

"She'll understand," Lily said, almost kindly.

"No, she won't," Gideon said. He was feeling the loss of blood, as well as…something else. "No one ever understands."

"Understands what?" Hope asked. "Raintree, don't lose it on me." She tried to regain control of her cell phone so she could call 911, but Gideon still had enough strength to hold her off.

Maybe Lily was right. He hadn't trusted anyone with his secret in a long time. A very long time. Tabby knew. Did that mean the secret was out? Or soon would be? He glanced to the side to study the ghost's pale face, a face only he could see. "Maybe you're right," he said. "Maybe I can tell her the truth."

Lily nodded and smiled.

"She's going to think I'm crazy," he said.

The redhead laid a hand on his forehead, and he felt her cold touch very distinctly. He saw ghosts every day, talked to them frequently, but they rarely touched him in any way. Never like this. "Don't be like me, Gideon," Lily said. "Don't hold yourself back so much. Live well, and leave a big hole when the time comes for you to go."

He shook his head.

"Tell her."

"It's not a good idea."

"Dammit, Raintree, you're scaring the crap out of me," Hope said softly, and he could hear the concern in her voice.

Gideon turned his head to look up at Hope Malory. His head reeled. His leg didn't hurt that badly anymore, and though Hope's image was foggy, he could see that she was worried. He could see that she cared, even though she didn't want to care about him or anyone else. He hadn't told anyone what he could do in such a long time, and the last time…the last time it hadn't worked out too well.

"I didn't mean to scare you," he said. "I was just talking to Lily Clark."

Hope leaned slightly toward him. "Raintree, Lily Clark is dead."

"Yeah, I know."

Someone from the coffee shop had finally noticed the excitement on the boardwalk, and a few curious people walked toward him. He didn't have much time. "Remember when I told you I talk to dead people?"

"Yeah," Hope said.

"It was the truth."

Raintree was suffering from hallucinations. That was it.

Hope pressed against his injury harder. Hallucinations from a nasty but relatively minor knife wound to the thigh? It didn't make sense.

"That's not possible. I'm going to call 911 now…"

"There's no time to argue. I can't go to a hospital this week."

This week? "Raintree…"

"Watch this," he said tersely, then turned his gaze

toward the nearest streetlamp. In an instant the light exploded in a shower of sparks. The people who were approaching from the coffee shop stuttered and stepped back. "And the next," Raintree said softly. Another streetlamp exploded. "The next?"

"Not necessary," she said softly, turning toward the other people, who were approaching once again. She mustered a smile for them.

"Should I call an ambulance?" the burly man in the lead called. He looked like he was in charge, but this wasn't the manager they'd spoken to earlier in the week.

"No, thanks," Hope said, sounding calm. "My friend here had a little bit too much to drink and fell, and I think he got a splinter or something in his leg. If you've got a towel or some bandages or something, I'll patch him up and take him home."

It was an uninteresting explanation, and the other on-lookers turned away. "Sure," the man said, sounding disappointed. "I have a first aid kit with plenty of bandages."

"Cool," Hope said gratefully.

"Cool," Raintree echoed when the man from the coffee shop had walked away to fetch the bandages. "So you believe me?"

"Of course not," she said sternly.

"But you—"

"I believe something is up. I just haven't figured out what yet."

"I told you..." Suddenly Raintree turned his head and looked at a large expanse of air. "Yeah, she's pretty, but she's also stubborn as all get out."

"Talking to Lily Clark's ghost again?" Hope snapped.

Gideon leaned toward her. "She thinks you should be more open-minded."

"Oh, she does?"

"Yeah." Gideon looked puzzled for a moment, and then he added, "I haven't lost enough blood to feel this woozy. She tossed something in my face. A drug of some kind. Maybe even poison. This isn't good. I need to get out of here."

"You *need* a hospital."

"No. Lily says you'll take good care of me."

"That don't look like a splinter to me."

Hope's head snapped up, and she saw the man from the coffee shop staring down, suspicion in his eyes.

"Big splinter," Hope said as she took the bandages from him.

"Are you sure…?"

Hope flashed her badge at the big guy, and he held up his hands in surrender. "Never mind. None of my business."

"I'll get replacements for these bandages to you as soon as I get the chance," Hope promised.

"No problem," the man said as he backed away. "Don't worry about it." He clearly didn't quite believe her story, but he wasn't going to stir up trouble and maybe even bring some of that trouble to his own door.

Hope quickly bandaged Raintree's thigh, padding it thickly and then tying the dressing tight. He was definitely hallucinating, and he needed more care than she could give him. She quickly explained away the exploding streetlamps. He had a secret gizmo hidden somewhere, and he'd used it to short out the electrical connection somehow. Maybe it had even been a coincidence. He'd seen the lights flickering, played the long shot, and won. He certainly hadn't made the lights explode simply by looking at them. Common sense dictated that she lead Gideon out of here, put him in his Mustang and drive him to the ER.

"You still don't believe me," he said, his voice growing thicker. Was it possible that he really had been drugged? She would let a doctor figure that out. She certainly wasn't a doctor. Hell, she wasn't even a halfway decent babysitter. In years past she'd proven time and again that she couldn't even keep a goldfish alive.

"I'm sorry, Raintree," she said as she helped him up. It wasn't easy, since he was heavy and unsteady, but they managed. With her support, they should be able to get to the car and from there to the hospital. Their progress was slow, as they took one careful step and then another. To the small crowd who watched from the coffee shop, he probably did look drunk. Just as well. It was an easier explanation than the truth—whatever that might be.

Raintree muttered something low and indistinct.

"What?" Hope asked.

"I wasn't talking to you," he said gruffly.

"Of course you weren't," she answered.

A few more steps, and Raintree spoke again. "Touch her," he commanded. "You can, you know. Most ghosts can't affect the physical, but you're different, Lily. Your energy is more bound to this earth than most spirits, and if you concentrate and really, really try…"

"Cut it out, Raintree," Hope snapped. "This isn't funny anymore." Her steps faltered when it felt as if a sliver of ice brushed past her cheek, barely chilling her with its touch.

"She touched you," Raintree said as he took a small, pained step. He looked down at Hope and smiled. "Your cheek. The left one, just beneath the cheekbone."

Hope's heart stuttered much as her step had done a moment earlier. The iciness touched her stomach, as if an invisible finger had reached through her clothes.

"Stomach," Raintree said, the single word oddly heavy.

Hope licked her lips. "I don't know how you're doing that…"

The coldness wrapped itself around her ears. Both of them.

"Ears," Raintree muttered.

They walked beneath a streetlamp. The bulb didn't explode, but it did flicker a few times and then go out. Raintree turned his head back and looked up. "I can't control the energy right now. If I go into a hospital, stuff attached to sick people is going to start blowing up." He sounded a little drunk. No, he sounded a *lot* drunk. "Take me home, partner. Trust me."

Hope Malory didn't trust anyone, not anymore. She especially didn't trust cheesy parlor tricks and unbelievable explanations. But after she put Gideon into the passenger seat of the Mustang and pulled onto the road, she didn't head to the hospital. She drove toward Wrightsville Beach.

Whatever Tabby had tossed into his face was beginning to wear off. It hadn't been a lethal poison or he would be getting worse instead of better. But it *had* been a drug of some kind, meant to dull his senses. He would wonder why, but he'd seen Lily Clark's body and he knew damn well the why of it. She'd wanted to distract him, and she had.

More than that, she'd wanted time with him. She'd wanted the opportunity to torture him.

Gideon slipped the protection charm from beneath his shirt and fingered it gently. Hope would probably say the charm hadn't protected him at all, but he knew better. The knife could have hit an artery. Tabby could have decided to shoot him instead of taking a stab at his leg. He could be missing a finger right about now.

Hope might not have been behind him, literally watching his back.

"What were you doing there?" he asked.

She muttered a mild curse and kept her eyes on the road, which was deserted at this late hour. The beach was quiet. The houses that lined it were dark.

"I'm just curious," he added after a few moments of silence.

"That crap about waiting until morning before continuing with the investigation? It just didn't ring true."

"So you followed me."

"Yeah. Complaining?"

"Not at the moment."

Lily wasn't with them as they drove toward his beach house, but she was still earthbound; he knew that much. Where was she? Watching the crime scene techs study her motel room for evidence? Standing by while the coroner examined her body? Tabby had done a number on the poor woman, and convincing her spirit to move on wouldn't be easy.

"Once I get you settled, I'm calling a doctor," Hope said as she pulled into his driveway and hit the remote to open the garage door.

"No," he said.

"Dammit, Raintree!"

"I don't need a doctor."

"I saw the wound," she said stubbornly as she parked the car. "It's too deep for you to treat on your own, and I sure as hell can't take care of it. I shouldn't have humored you by bringing you home, I know, but…"

"You're already forgetting how it felt when she touched you," he said. "And you're forgetting that I saw where she touched you."

"Nice trick, Raintree," she said as she rounded the car. "One day you'll have to tell me how you do that."

"It's not a trick," he said as she opened his car door and bent down to help him stand. She kept her arm around him as they headed for the stairs that led to a door off the kitchen. The trip up those stairs would be slow, but with Hope's assistance he would make it. He hated knowing he needed anyone, but right now…right now she was his partner.

"All life is electrical," he said as they climbed, one slow step at a time. "Electricity keeps your heart beating, makes your brain work, keeps the spirit here even after the body is dead. Do you really want a technical explanation? Sorry, I don't feel up to that right now. Takes too long. Electrons, another vibrational level, does any of that make sense to you?"

"It's not plausible," she said sensibly.

"Electricity can also cause muscles and organs like the uterus to convulse, often with interesting and even pleasurable results."

"I warned you, Raintree…"

"Gideon," he said as they stepped into the kitchen and Hope switched on the lights. "If you still don't believe me, I'd be happy to provide another demonstration."

"No!" She drew away from him a little but didn't let him go. Good thing, since he wasn't sure he could stand on his own just yet. "That won't be necessary."

He smiled at her, but he knew the effort was weak. He should be glad she still didn't believe him. If he left her alone she would eventually find a way to explain it all away. Everyone did, when confronted with things they found implausible.

"I've always seen ghosts," he said as they walked toward his bedroom. "When I was little, I didn't understand that everyone didn't see them like I did. The electrical surges came later. I was twelve the first time I blew up a television. From then to fifteen, those were interesting years. But I learned how to control the power, how to harness it and use it. Still, the weeks closest to a solstice or an equinox are unpredictable. The summer solstice is almost here. Sunday." He looked down at her. "I disabled your car."

"You did not…"

"I did it, and I'll pay for the repairs. I've already made arrangements with the mechanic. I just can't take the chance of getting stranded somewhere in one of those freakin' cars with the computer chips in them. Whose idea was that, anyway? Computers have no business in a vehicle."

In his bedroom, he unbuckled his belt, and removed his weapon and badge. Hope turned on the light as he tossed off his jacket and sat on the side of the bed. "Thanks," he said as he fell back onto the mattress. "You can go home, now."

His eyes closed, and his last thought before darkness claimed him was that Hope wasn't leaving. Stubborn woman.

Tabby huddled behind the deserted storefront for a long time before she dared to leave her hiding place. She'd run and run until she couldn't run anymore, until her lungs were burning and her legs wouldn't move. If Raintree and his partner had called in help, the cops were searching way off the mark. All was silent and undisturbed. She hadn't even heard any sirens.

Maybe they hadn't called. After all, Gideon didn't want anyone to know what he could do, so how could he explain the confrontation away? He was freakish enough, but if his talents were common knowledge, he would never know any rest. Half the world would brand him a nutcase; the other half would want to use him.

She'd gotten one good stab at him, but she knew it hadn't been enough. A little to the left and she would have sliced the artery, and he would have bled to death before his pretty partner could get help. But at the last moment her hand had slipped. At least he was undoubtedly having vivid nightmares at the moment. The drug she'd blinded him with had not only given her an advantage, the effects would linger for a while. What sort of nightmares did a Raintree have? she wondered.

The partner had come out of nowhere, damn her, and she'd ruined everything. Time was running out. No more games. No more attempts at finesse. Tabby didn't do finesse well.

By Saturday night Gideon and Echo Raintree both had to be dead. If they weren't, by Sunday morning it would be Tabby who was in the ground…or in the river, or in the ocean. She didn't think Cael would bother with anything resembling a proper funeral.

A few drops of Raintree blood stained her knife and her hand. Sitting in the dark, Tabby pulled both to her face and inhaled. She closed her eyes and imagined the power she could not yet take into her own body. This was Raintree blood. It wasn't as powerful as a finger or an ear or even a tiny slice of skin, but still…*Raintree.* She'd been so close, so very close.

It was time to sit back, think on the situation and come up with a foolproof plan. She wouldn't have her time alone with Gideon, more's the pity, but he would be well dead before the end of the week.

And he wouldn't be going alone.

Chapter 8

For a long while Hope sat in a chair by Gideon Raintree's bed and watched him sleep. He tossed and turned, and then finally fell into a sleep so deep it was like death. The motionless silence scared her far more than his restlessness or the rambling or the gash in his leg.

After he'd fallen to the bed and passed out, she'd removed the bandage from his thigh, intent on calling someone if it looked half as bad as she remembered. Somehow it didn't. It was a nasty cut, no argument, but she was no longer convinced that he needed professional doctoring. It was odd, though, to see an obviously strong and healthy body laid low so completely.

She'd removed his trousers, and then she'd cleaned the wound and rebandaged it. Through the entire ordeal,

Raintree barely stirred. It had been a bit tougher to take off his shirt and tie, but she'd managed. She'd left his underwear in place. Her dedication only went so far.

With a damp washcloth, she'd wiped grains of what appeared to be sand from his face. Whatever it was, there wasn't much of it. A few specks had stuck to his goatee and his cheek, and she gently wiped away a granule that had settled near the corner of his eye. She didn't think there was enough of the substance to get any kind of analysis on, but she saved the washcloth, just in case.

She'd never actually undressed an unconscious man, and Gideon Raintree was most definitely all man. There was a dusting of hair on his chest, and his limbs were heavy and well-shaped with muscle. He had strong arms that were nicely muscled without being bulky. There was something about a man's forearms and hands, when they were built just so, that could make any woman's thoughts wander.

Besides, she couldn't look at those hands without remembering when he'd touched her. They'd both been fully dressed, and it had happened so quickly, and yet it had been intimate. Unexpected and powerful—and *intimate*.

Hope didn't want to think about that moment, not the particulars or the whys or the hows, so she attempted to concentrate on Gideon's health and well-being and put everything else in the past. This time of the night, a generous five o'clock shadow was growing in around his neatly trimmed goatee and mustache, making him look a tad grungy. It was almost a relief to realize that he could be less than perfect.

Through all her ministrations, she'd left the charm he wore beneath his suit around his neck. Since she didn't believe in lucky tokens or anything of the sort, she wasn't sure why she left the doodad alone; it just didn't seem right for her to remove it, since he believed it had some sort of power. Then again, she also couldn't explain why she was wearing the charm he had given her last night. It wasn't like her to believe in such nonsense.

When her initial round of totally inept doctoring was done, Hope sat in an uncomfortable chair she'd dragged from the corner of the room. She didn't want to leave Gideon alone or be too far away. What if he needed her? Silly thought, but still…she didn't leave.

He didn't have a modern digital clock by his bed but instead used a vintage windup alarm clock that was probably older than he was. The bedroom phone was another land line. All his talk of electricity and ghosts…she didn't believe him, but obviously *he* believed. She'd seriously considered that he was dirty; it had never so much as crossed her mind that he might be mentally unstable.

She'd used his bedside phone to call her mother, and also to call the very irate motel manager in order to tell him where she'd left his truck. He did have a spare set of keys in the motel office, thank goodness, and an officer who was still on the scene had agreed to give him a ride to his vehicle.

Hope fidgeted as she watched Gideon sleep. His story was ridiculous. It didn't make any sense at all. Ghosts. What a crock. Harnessing electrical energy?

Also too fantastic to buy. She should be able to completely dismiss everything he said as impossible or continue to go with that "mentally unstable" possibility, but there were a few other things to consider.

His record as a homicide detective.

The old cars he drove and the odd way her car had malfunctioned.

His lack of decent electrical toys and televisions and phones.

The exploding streetlamps on the riverfront.

The way he'd knocked her out of a bullet's path *before* it had been fired.

The unexpected orgasm.

Hope no longer believed in things she couldn't see with her own eyes or touch with her own hands. Her mother was partly to blame. Growing up with crystals and incense and chanting and auras had been embarrassing for Hope on more than one occasion. She'd made an effort every day of her life to remain firmly grounded in reality.

But her mother wasn't entirely to blame. Jody Landers had been the one to finally and completely blow her orderly world to pieces.

She'd loved him. Love was yet another elusive thing that could not be held or touched or smelled. Yet her love for Jody had seemed so real for a time. It had filled her world and made her happy. And it had been a lie. Turned out Jody had targeted her from day one. Their meeting had not been chance; his love had not been real. He'd been a low-level drug dealer who'd wanted a cop in his pocket as he moved up the chain of command. When she finally caught him and discovered what he'd been up to, he'd claimed that he had come to love her. But she didn't believe him, not then and not now, four years later.

She'd eventually been promoted to detective in spite of the embarrassment. Jody was in prison and would be there for some time to come, but there were still people in Raleigh who believed that she'd known all along what kind of man he was. She hated to admit it, but it wasn't only her mother's welfare that had brought her home. She'd grown tired of the suspicious looks, the whispers that would never die.

She couldn't allow herself to be tainted again by association with the wrong kind of person, the wrong kind of *man*. She was not going to be a gullible patsy ever again. So what the hell was she doing here? She didn't owe Gideon Raintree anything. Not her time or her faith or her loyalty.

Watching him sleep began to get under her skin in a way she couldn't explain away. She squirmed a little in her uncomfortable chair. This was his bed, his house, and watching him was so personal, as if she were once again spying on him, trying to discover what made him tick so she wouldn't get caught in the cross fire.

Gideon seemed to be sleeping well enough. His breathing was even and steady, his heartbeat—which she'd checked a time or two—was strong. With that in mind, Hope shook off her inexplicable need to stand guard and left the bedroom. She was thirsty, and she was hungry. She was tired, too, but she didn't think she would be getting any sleep tonight. In the kitchen she noted the old propane stove, rather than the electric stove he should have had. No microwave. Cheap toaster. She opened a few cabinets, searching for something to eat, and found one deep storage space that held two additional cheap toasters, as well as an assortment of blenders and at least three coffeepots. Her heart crawled into her throat, and she settled for toast and peanut butter and a glass of milk, all of which were consumed at the kitchen table, where she could look out over the deserted beach. In the darkness she could barely see the waves crashing onto the sand, but they did catch the moonlight as they danced to shore. It was almost mesmerizing.

She should leave now. Go home, get some sleep, drop by in the morning to pick Raintree up and either take him to the doctor or make arrangements to collect his Challenger from the motel parking lot. He probably wouldn't be able to drive for a couple of days, but they would think of some way to get his car back here where it belonged.

Movement beyond the window caught her attention. Given that someone had recently stabbed Gideon, she paid close attention and concentrated, trying to discern what had caught her eye. A glare on the windowpanes made it difficult for her to see as well as she wanted to, so she turned out the kitchen light and focused on the beach while her eyes adjusted to the darkness.

The indistinct figure of a man was walking toward the water. He moved slowly, his feet all but dragging. The night had been clear thus far, but suddenly lightning flashed in the distance. Quickly, too quickly, clouds drifted before the moon, robbing the night of the light Hope needed to see who was out there at this hour.

The thunder and lightning moved closer, a jagged bolt flashing across the sky, giving off just enough light for Hope to see what she needed to. The man on the beach was near naked, wearing only a bathing suit or a pair of shorts—or boxers. His hair was a little too long, his broad shoulders were tired, his legs were long…and his left thigh was bandaged.

Hope ran first to the bedroom. The bed she'd left Gideon sleeping in was empty. The curtains covering the large window that overlooked the ocean had been drawn back, and she realized that it wasn't just a window but French doors that opened onto an elaborate deck.

Hope ran onto the deck, certain that she could *not* have seen what she thought she'd seen. Raintree must be sleepwalking, or maybe hallucinating. If he collapsed onto the sand, she would never be able to get him back here alone. And if he walked into the ocean… Dammit, she should have insisted on taking him to the hospital! She ran down the stairs that led to the boardwalk and then to the beach, her steps uneasy once she reached the sand. She stopped to remove her pumps and tossed them aside as another bolt of lightning lit the sky and thunder rumbled.

A stroke of lightning flashed straight down and hit Gideon, and instead of a rumble the thunder was a loud, dangerous pop. Hope stumbled in the sand, her breath stolen away, fear coloring her entire world for that split second.

"Gideon!" She waited for him to fall to the ground or burst into flame, but he didn't. He stood there, arms outstretched, and yet another bolt hit him. The thunder was an earsplitting crack, and this time the lightning that found Gideon seemed to stay connected to him, until sparks generated from the blast were dancing on his skin.

Hope didn't call Gideon's name again, but she continued to run toward him. This wasn't possible, was it? A man couldn't walk onto the beach and be hit by lightning again and again and just *stand* there. As she watched the electricity dance on his skin, she remembered what her mother had said after Raintree had left the apartment Tuesday night. Hope had still been shaking from the orgasm he'd triggered with his touch, and her mother had mused with a smile, "His aura positively sparkles. I've never seen anything quite like it."

"Stop," he commanded without turning to face her. "It's not safe for you to get too close."

Hope stuttered to a halt several feet behind him. The moon had disappeared behind clouds, dimming the night, but she could see him well enough. She could see him well because he was glowing gently.

He turned to face her as the storm that had come out of nowhere rolled away, fading and suddenly not at all threatening. But Hope didn't have eyes for the storm; her gaze was riveted to the man before her. Electricity popped and swayed on his skin, a gentle glow radiating from him. He'd shaved, she noticed, doing away with his goatee and mustache. And his eyes...did they glow, or was it a trick of the light?

It couldn't be a trick of the light. There was no light except for that he himself created.

A part of her wanted to turn and run. She was not the kind of woman who would gladly and openly embrace the impossible. But her feet were rooted in the sand, and she didn't run. "I was watching from the kitchen window," she said, her voice weaker than she would have liked.

Gideon stepped toward her, and tiny sparks swirled where his bare feet sank into the sand. "I know."

Nightmares—vivid dreams of his parents and Lily Clark and all the people in between that he hadn't been able to save—had sent Gideon to the water, where he'd drawn in the lightning to feed his body and his soul, and wipe the last vestiges of the drug from his system. He hadn't walked far onto the beach before he'd realized that Hope was watching. He didn't care. Maybe it was right that she know; maybe she needed to know.

She stood a few feet away, uneasy and unsteady in the soft sand. "Are you all right?" she asked in a soft, suspicious voice.

"Yeah."

The unspoken *how?* remained between them, silent but powerful. She'd seen the streetlamps explode, been touched by a ghost's cold fingers, and still she remained skeptical. But there was no explaining this away.

Her gaze dropped to his thigh, where the electricity was working upon his damaged flesh with a ferocity she couldn't begin to understand.

"You, uh, glow in the dark, Raintree." She tried for a lighthearted tone but fell far short.

"Only when I'm turned on." He stepped toward her, and she moved out of the way. Not running, but definitely avoiding being too close.

"Very funny," she said, as they walked back toward the house.

Actually, it wasn't funny at all. The fact that he wanted this woman naked in his bed was nothing to laugh about. She was his partner, and she was one of those staunch women who questioned everything endlessly. Why? How? When? That made her a great detective, but where he was concerned, such attributes led to disaster. He'd always tried to avoid overly curious women.

He'd never been caught before. Sure, there had been times when his neighbors, awakened by the storms he drew, later asked, *Didn't I see you on the beach?* He always denied it, and they always wrote off what they'd seen to a dream or a trick of the light. After all, what he did, what he *was,* was impossible to comprehend.

"You're walking better," Hope said as they neared the wooden steps that led to his bedroom.

"I think the drug affected me more strongly than the actual wound. It's wearing off." What remained after the nightmares had passed had been washed away by the lightning.

"Good." For a moment Hope didn't say more, and then she fidgeted and said, "Okay, you have some kind of weird electrical thing going on. I'm sure there's a perfectly logical medical explanation for everything."

"Why does it have to be perfectly logical?"

"It just does."

"Nothing is perfect, and logic is subjective."

"Logic is not subjective," she argued.

He tried to usher her up the deck stairs ahead of him, but she wasn't about to let him out of her sight; she didn't want him behind her, where she couldn't see him. So he ascended first, after watching Hope collect her shoes. At least she followed him, instead of fleeing into the night. Gideon stepped into the darkened bedroom from the deck. He did glow in the dark. A little.

Hope closed the French doors behind her but left the drapes open, so they could see the waves not so far away. The sound of the surf was muted but still filled the room as it had all night. It was a comforting sound; it was the sound of home.

Gideon stood near the end of the bed, drained by the storm as well as being rejuvenated by the electrical charge that continued to dance through his body. "The logical explanation is that my family is different. More different than you can imagine."

"That's not—"

Possible, she was going to say. He didn't let her get that far. "My brother controls fire, among other things. He's Dranir, leader of the Raintree family. My sister is an empath and a talented healer, and her little girl is showing amazing promise in a number of fields. Echo is a prophet. I talk to ghosts. Should I go on?"

"That's not necessary," Hope said coolly.

"You still don't believe me."

In the near-dark room, he saw Hope shake her head. He could drop the subject, let it lie. She would request her transfer, as he'd wished for just yesterday, and he could go on about his business. She wouldn't tell anyone what she'd seen and heard here tonight, because she didn't want to appear foolish in any way. Surely she knew that no one would believe her.

But he didn't want to let her go. There was something here that he couldn't explain. He wanted Hope; of course he did. She was beautiful and smart and ran in high heels. But beneath that, there was something *more,* though he did his best to ignore it. If he slept with her, she would have to request a transfer. She wasn't fond of breaking the rules. In fact, it was probably a safe bet that she never broke the rules.

He slowly unwrapped the bandage at his thigh. At last Hope moved closer to him. "You really shouldn't do that. Not…" Her voice died away as he removed the last of the bandage and revealed the scratch there. "Yet," she finished weakly. She reached out cautiously and laid her fingers over the nearly healed wound. She licked her lips, cocked her head, and uttered a succinct word he had never expected to hear from that sweet mouth.

"How…?" She drew her fingers away, and he immediately missed them. "What did you…?"

"I'm Raintree," he said. "If you want a more detailed explanation than that, we're going to have to make a pot of coffee."

* * *

They didn't sit on opposite sides of the room this time. Gideon sat beside her on the couch, and they each held a mug steaming with hot coffee. By the light of the living room lamps she couldn't tell if he was still glowing or not. A part of her wanted to insist that what she thought she'd seen had been her usually dismal imagination running amok, but she couldn't lie to herself that way.

"You're telling me that everything my mother told me all my life is *true?*"

"I can't say, since I don't know everything she told you." Gideon leaned back and propped his bare feet on the coffee table. He'd pulled jeans on, covering the impossibly healed wound on his thigh. Those jeans were all he wore, along with the green boxers and that silver talisman that rested against his chest, hanging there from a black leather cord and as much a part of him as the color of his eyes or the way his dark hair curled by the ears.

"Auras," she threw out. That was, after all, a bone of contention between her and her mother.

"I don't see them, but they do exist," he answered plainly. "It's another energy thing. In order to see them, you have to be clairsentient."

"Yours apparently sparkles," she said grudgingly.

Gideon just gave a half-interested hum that sounded almost bored.

"Ghosts."

"Those I can attest to without question," he said, casting a glance her way.

Hope leaned her head back against the leather couch. She'd removed her jacket and her shoes but otherwise was still completely and professionally dressed. What she wouldn't give to get out of this bra and into something comfortable....

She should be running for the hills; she should be terrified of what she'd seen and heard here tonight. And here she was worrying instead about the way her bra cut into her shoulders and the flesh beneath her breasts. It was going on four forty-five in the morning, and no woman was meant to wear a bra for twenty-two hours.

"Afterlife?"

"Yes," Gideon answered almost reverently.

Hope closed her ⌐yes. There had been times when she had convinced herself that life could not possibly go beyond the physical boundaries she could see and touch. It was easier that way, most days. Believing we were here, then, one day, we were gone. No expectations, no disappointments. Listening to Gideon's simple answers...she believed him, and it felt unexpectedly good. "What's it like?"

"I don't know."

She laughed lightly. "What do you mean, you don't know? Don't the ghosts tell you anything?"

"Some things we're not meant to understand."

She nodded, oddly accepting. This conversation shouldn't seem so normal. Shouldn't she laugh? Or cry? Dance, or close herself away from the world that had just changed forever? Instead, this seemed very, very natural.

"Signs from above," she said next.

"Be more specific."

Hope lifted one hand and gestured in a casual way. "You see a rabbit cross the road, in a place where you've never seen a rabbit before. Maybe seeing a rabbit at a certain time of the day in a particular place is a sign. It's good luck or bad luck, or an indication that you're going to win the lottery or get hit by a bus."

"You really haven't studied this at all, have you?" Gideon teased.

"No. But I still want an answer." She took a long sip of coffee and waited for one.

"There are signs all around us, but we don't usually see them."

She squirmed a little, trying to get more comfortable. "Not even you?"

"Not even me. We overlook miracles every day. Then again…" Gideon shrugged slightly. "Sometimes a rabbit is just a rabbit."

The length of the day and waning adrenaline was making Hope's eyelids heavy. They drooped, but she wasn't ready to stop. Not yet. "Reincarnation."

"Definitely."

"You sound so sure."

"That's why I used the word *definitely*."

She slapped him lightly and too comfortably on the arm. "Don't tease me. I'm tired, and this is all new, and I still…" No, she couldn't say she still wasn't sure. She'd seen too much tonight not to be. Her hand remained on his arm, and it felt natural. Gideon was warm, and strong, and she liked the feel of his flesh right there, at least for now. It was soothing and spine-tingling at the same time. "If we come back again and again, and we meet the same people over and over, why don't we remember?"

"Where's the fun in that?"

"Fun?" Had he lost his mind? Life wasn't fun. Oh, there were occasional amusing moments, but for the most part, life was hard work.

"Yeah," Gideon said. "Fun. We get to make mistakes, learn how to survive, discover beauty, discover the thrill of taking a risk. We experience emotions fresh, with new eyes that haven't already been tainted or jaded by time. We face wonders with the excitement of something new and unknown, and fall in love with hearts that haven't yet been broken and battered."

"Talk about a risk," she said. Hearing Gideon talk about falling in love made her antsy. She leaned forward, placed her mug on the coffee table, reached beneath the back of her blouse, muttered a low "excuse me," unsnapped her bra and slid it off through her left sleeve.

"If you need help, all you have to do is ask," Gideon said.

"I'm fine," she said, wiggling back into place on the couch. *And ever so much more comfortable.* "Angels."

Gideon leaned back and settled in, much as she had. "Yep."

"Fairies?"

"I've never seen one, but that doesn't mean they don't exist somewhere. I'm not really sure."

She reached out a finger to touch the silver talisman on Gideon's chest. "Lucky charms?" she said softly.

He looked her in the eye, and her heart stuttered. Gideon did have amazing eyes. If she were in the market for a man, which she most certainly was not, he would do quite nicely. Not only was he beautiful in an entirely masculine way, he cared about his job. He fought for people who could no longer fight for themselves. He was justice and strength and sex…and occasionally he glowed in the dark.

"Sometimes," he finally answered.

She removed her hand from his chest and flicked her own charm out from beneath her blouse. "When I was getting ready this morning, I felt like this thing was staring at me. I'm still not entirely sure why I put it on."

"Do me a favor," Gideon said gently. "Don't take it off."

Hope nodded, then returned to her previous and very comfy position. Everything she had ever dismissed as fantasy was apparently all real. She should be screaming in denial, but instead she felt oddly calm.

"You say the Raintrees have been around for a long time."

"Yeah."

"When your ancestors married normal people, why weren't the…the… Crap, I don't know what to call it. I don't believe in magic, but for lack of a better word, it'll do. If your family has some kind of genetic magic, why hasn't it been phased out as you've bred with the common folk?"

Something about the word *bred* made them both

squirm. From the beginning there had been sexual energy between them, even when she hadn't been entirely sure he was a good guy. Still, it was too soon for energy of this sort. She never should have leaned close and touched that charm on his chest, and he never should have looked her in the eye that way.

"Raintree genes are dominant," Gideon explained.

"So, if you have kids…" She opened her eyes and turned her head to look at him, curious once again. "Do you?" she asked. "Are there little Gideon Raintrees out there somewhere drawing in lightning and talking to dead people?"

"I don't have any children," he said, his voice more solemn than before.

"But when you do…"

He was shaking his head before she had a chance to finish the sentence. "No. It's hard enough to raise a kid in this world without teaching her that a part of who she is has to be hidden away. I won't do that to a child."

"Her," Hope repeated, closing her eyes again.

"What?"

"You said her. Not it, not him. Her."

He hesitated, briefly. "I have a niece. She's the only kid I've been around for a while. That's why I said *her*."

She didn't believe him, but there wasn't any real reason for her reservations. Just instinct. But she didn't believe in instinct, did she? She believed in fact. Concrete, undisputed proof. *That* had been pretty much blown away tonight.

"You shaved," she said, turning the conversation in an absurdly normal direction.

"I woke up feeling like the drug Tabby used was still there. It wouldn't wash away."

She should've heard him moving around in the bathroom, but the house was so big…and she'd been so distracted… "I like it."

He snorted, and she smiled.

"I'm gonna sleep now," she said, her mind and her body falling toward oblivion. She was much too tired to even think about driving home, and if she did, she would only get there in time to take a quick shower, grab a bite to eat and start a new day. Here, she could sleep for an hour or two. "We'll have to get up in a couple of hours and start the Clark investigation."

"It was Tabby," Gideon said. "The blonde who killed Sherry Bishop and stabbed me."

"Yeah," Hope answered, her speech slightly slurred. "I believe you." And she did believe him. Every word he said was true. What a kick in the pants that was. "Tomorrow we have to find a way to prove it."

Chapter 9

Gideon lifted a sleeping Hope gently, and she didn't even stir. He could leave her on the couch, he supposed, but the leather wouldn't be pleasant to sleep on for very long. He laid her in his bed, instead, and she immediately rolled onto her side, grabbed a pillow and sighed.

She could sleep in her clothes, but, like the couch… not very comfortable. He unfastened her trousers, waiting with each second that passed for her to wake up and slap him. But she was a deep sleeper, or else the day's events had exhausted her. She slept on, barely moving while he removed her once-crisp gray trousers and tossed them aside.

The blouse would have to stay. He really wasn't up to getting her completely naked and then turning away.

Without the bra, which still sat on the living room couch, she would be comfortable enough.

When Hope was down to blouse and panties, he covered her with the sheet and walked on bare feet to the window. Before closing the drapes, he stood there for a few minutes and watched the waves crash onto the beach.

He'd told her more than he'd ever told anyone else. One woman had seen a glimpse—a tiny *glimpse*—of what he could do, and she hadn't been able to get away from him fast enough. That had been a long time ago. He'd run into her once, a couple of years after the split, and she had apparently forgotten all about the reason for their breakup. People did that. If they couldn't explain what they saw, they simply forgot. It was an amnesia meant to protect the mind from things that could not be accepted, he imagined, no different than forgetting the details of a car crash or any other traumatic event. Happened all the time.

Would Hope forget everything come morning? Maybe. She was a no-nonsense woman who wasn't given to believing in anything that rocked her neat little world. He could most definitely rock her world—in more ways than one.

He finally closed the drapes and returned to the bed, crawling in beside Hope. Her warmth and softness called him closer, and he answered that call. All along he'd known that if he slept with her, she would have to request a transfer, but that didn't have anything to do with the way he wanted her.

There was a double bed in the spare bedroom on the

third floor, and that was it as far as alternate sleeping arrangements were concerned. The room was used for storage, mostly, but Echo stayed here infrequently, and Mercy had visited with Eve on rare occasions, so he did keep it ready for guests. Only a glutton for punishment would fill a beach house with a selection of comfortable and welcoming guest rooms, and since Gideon preferred solitude, his lack of accommodations made perfect sense.

The single guest bed was without sheets at the moment since Echo had stripped the bed Monday before leaving for Charlotte, and it was also piled high with the files he'd brought home about the unsolved murders. He didn't feel like taking the time to clean off the bed in the name of being gentlemanly. His own bed was warm and soft, and he was drawn to Hope the way a man is drawn to his woman.

His woman. Hope was many things, but she was most definitely not his. And still he draped his arm across her waist and pulled her close before he fell asleep.

She'd slept so deeply that she didn't remember so much as a sliver of a dream. Hope burrowed into the soft mattress, trying to escape the chill. The air conditioner must be turned up high. Unusual, since her mother was usually such a stickler about conserving electricity.

The air was chilly, but she felt oddly and comfortably warm. The alarm hadn't gone off yet, which meant she could sleep a little while longer. A few more precious minutes.

Then, with a suddenness that made her twitch, she remembered where she was. Raintree's house. She'd fallen asleep on the couch, but this was no couch. It was Raintree's *bed*. She very carefully rolled over to face the man she'd been sleeping with. The reason she was so warm was that Gideon's mostly bare body was all but pressed against hers.

Still half asleep, she remained as still as possible while she studied him. They were close, closer than she'd ever thought to be with this man she had initially suspected of possible criminal misconduct. Now she knew he wasn't a dirty cop. He was just different. Very, *very* different.

He looked fine in the morning, none the worse for wear after being wounded and drugged last night. In sleep he was a little rough around the edges, unguarded, and beautiful in the special way only a handsome man could be. But if Gideon knew he was beautiful, he didn't act that way, not like some men she knew. He just *was*.

Moving cautiously so as not to wake him, she lifted the sheet that covered them both and peeked beneath. His thigh was almost healed. Last night it had been sliced deep, and now all that remained was a nasty-looking scratch. She shouldn't be surprised. Nothing connected with this man should ever surprise her again.

"Don't worry," a gruff voice rumbled. "Nothing happened."

Hope lifted her head slightly to see that Gideon's eyes were trained unerringly on her. They were sleepy still, hooded and sexy and electric.

"I was checking your *wound*," she said primly.

"I thought you were checking to see if I had my drawers on."

She slapped the sheet down, and started to roll away and leave the bed, mainly so Gideon wouldn't see how she was blushing. Her cheeks actually grew hot, and it was such a girlie reaction.

Before she could roll away, Gideon snagged her with one strong arm and pulled her back against his chest. "Don't go anywhere just yet," he said, his voice still sleepy and gruff and sexy as hell. Hope knew she could escape easily, with a gentle shove and a roll. Gideon's grasp on her wasn't binding; it was simply persuasive. Heavy and warm and comfortable. She didn't shove or roll. Instead, she laid her head on the pillow and stared away from Raintree while he held her close.

Jody hadn't often slept over at her apartment. Twice, maybe. And even then, it had been a mistake on his part. He'd fallen asleep and awakened early in the morning to make his escape. But she remembered liking this part. She very much enjoyed being held, flesh to flesh, the connection sexual and yet also much more. This was what she missed by living alone, by dedicating herself to her career and always looking at every man who so much as smiled at her as if he might turn into an ogre and bite her in the next instant.

She didn't think Gideon would bite her, but that was a potentially dangerous supposition on her part. He was a man like any other, a fact that was quickly becoming evident as he held her close.

Now was the time to leave the bed, if she was going to make her escape. If she stayed here, in his bed, if she didn't leave *right now,* she knew darn well what was going to happen. She was a fully grown woman of sound mind, twenty-nine years old and unattached. And at this moment, with her world still spinning out of control thanks to all she'd learned last night, she wanted to be held. Not just by any man, but by this one. Gideon Raintree, who talked to ghosts and inhaled lightning and occasionally glowed in the dark.

He shifted her hair aside and laid his mouth on her neck. A decided shiver worked its way through her body. Was it electricity or just *him* that made her tingle? Something paranormal or something extraordinarily *normal?* She couldn't make herself care, at the moment. This felt so good....

"I want you," he said softly.

Hope licked her lips. *I know. I want you, too.* The words danced in her head, but nothing came out.

"I'm not sure that's such a good idea, but there you have it." His hand slipped beneath her blouse to caress her bare skin, and she closed her eyes and melted. Her brain told her this was a *very bad* idea. But her body disagreed. Her body wanted the same thing Gideon wanted, though her wanting wasn't as obvious as his. Physically, at least.

Could he feel her shiver? She hadn't let a man touch her this way in a very long time, so long that this felt new and exciting and powerful.

Eyes closed and body trembling, she drank in Gideon's warmth and imagined what might be yet to come, if she allowed it. If she wanted it. She didn't have to say a word. She just had to turn in his arms, lay her mouth on his and kiss him. That was all the answer he needed, and all she was capable of giving.

His hand raked down her belly and came to rest over the soft flesh beneath her belly button, just as it had in her mother's shop when he'd pressed her against the counter and taken her by surprise. Knowing what he was about to do, she grabbed his wrist and pulled his hand slightly away.

Hope felt the disappointment in him, felt his resignation. She turned slowly so that she was facing him, his wrist still grasped in her hand. "No cheating this time," she whispered. And then she kissed him.

She should have known that he would be a great kisser. One touch, one sway of his lips over hers, and she lost the last of her doubts. She threaded her fingers in his hair and pulled him closer as her lips parted wider and she flicked her tongue against his. There were a hundred reasons why they shouldn't be here. She barely knew him; he was her partner; she'd distrusted him from day one; he was who he was.

But none of that mattered. She wanted him to kiss her, longer and more completely and with the abandon she felt unraveling inside her.

He unbuttoned her blouse while they kissed, and together they discarded it. Now she could hold him and truly be skin to skin. It was such a wonderful sensation that she couldn't help but remember what he'd said last night about discovering new and wonderful things in life. This was new. The way she wanted him, the way she spiraled out of control, the way her body was drawn to his…it was all new and beautiful.

Gideon gently rolled her onto her back, and she lay against the mattress, yearning and oddly content for someone whose heart and blood were pounding so hard they pushed away everything else. He took a nipple into his mouth and drew it deep, and she almost came off the mattress, the pleasure was so intense. Inside, she clenched, *ready* in a way she had never been before. She grabbed at Gideon, held on while he moved his attentions to the other breast. He moved as if they had all the time in the world, but she could tell that he was as close to spinning out of control as she was.

They couldn't afford to lose control completely. "Do you have a condom?" she asked hoarsely. If he said no…he couldn't say no. Surely he wouldn't say no.

"Yes," he answered, and she breathed a sigh of relief. "Good."

Gideon had such wonderful hands. They were masculine, well-shaped and strong. His fingers were long, and like everything else about this man, they were beautiful. His hands were tanned, too, thanks to hours spent on the beach. She didn't see the sun often. Her fair skin had a tendency to burn, and besides, tanning meant leisure time, and when was the last time she'd taken a real vacation? She couldn't even remember.

Gideon's sun-kissed hand skimmed over her pale flesh, and she watched him, fascinated and aroused by such a simple sight. He touched her as if she were made of porcelain, learning her curves as he went, learning the feel of her skin and inflaming her senses until she felt as if she were floating above the bed, soaring and grasping and wrapped in magic.

He snagged her panties and quickly pushed them down and off. Just like that, she was naked but for the protection charm he had made for her and insisted she wear. She slid her trembling fingers into the waistband of his boxers and pushed them down. Down and eventually off, leaving him wearing no more than she.

Before he covered himself, she wanted to touch him. She wanted to feel him in her hand, and she did. She wasn't shy, and neither was he. Not about this.

They kissed again, and this time Gideon spread her thighs and touched her while their mouths met and danced. A deep trembling had settled into her body, and nothing could stop it but the finale of this dance. There was only one possible end, only one acceptable conclusion, and that was Gideon inside her and the release they both needed. Her hands rested easily but insistently on his bare hips, her fingers gently rocking in much the way that her hips did.

He took his mouth from hers and reached for the bedside table, fumbling around and finally delving into the back of the messy drawer to snag a condom. It was a necessary but annoying delay, like stopping for gas when you were just five miles from your destination. But soon he was back, touching her again, slipping his fingers inside her and circling his thumb against her in a way that made her gasp and lurch. She had never wanted anything as much as she wanted him inside her. Now. And then he was there, pushing into her, stretching her slowly until she was accustomed to his size. She almost gasped at the sensation. Nothing had ever felt this good; no moment in her life had ever made her want to cry with the beauty of it.

Gideon made love the same way he did everything else: with complete dedication and an extraordinary level of skill. Hope closed her eyes and let him love her. He filled her body and took her to that place where she was on the edge, and he kept her there. Ribbons of pleasure danced inside her, strong and promising and demanding. Just when she was about to come, he backed away and slowed his pace, then started again.

She opened her eyes and whispered, "You're torturing me."

"Just a little."

The room was dark, thanks to the thickness of the drapes that covered the picture window and the French doors. If it hadn't been so dark, she never would have noticed the hint of a glow that rimmed the green irises of Gideon's eyes.

"You're glowing again." Oddly enough, she didn't find that fact at all disconcerting.

"Am I?"

"It's beautiful." She shifted her legs so that they were wrapped around his hips, lifted her body to his and pulled him to her, until he was buried fully inside her. He didn't draw back this time but plunged deeper and harder, faster and more completely, until she came with a cry. The release racked her body and went on even after she was sure it would end, unlike anything she had ever known before. She cried out again and grasped at Gideon's shoulders. He came with her, shuddering above and inside her.

Eventually he slowed, and so did she, and then he lay down on top of her and continued to hold her close while he remained cradled inside her. When he finally lifted his head to look down at her, she flinched a little in surprise.

"You give a whole new meaning to the word after-glow, Gideon."

He was indeed glowing a little. His eyes shone with that unnatural green light, and there was a hint of spar-kling luminescence around his body.

"Is this…normal?"

He withdrew, physically and mentally, and rolled away from her. "It's happened a time or two. I wouldn't exactly call it normal."

She reached out to touch him, to stop him, to tell him that she wasn't complaining. Quite the contrary. But he moved faster than she did and left the bed before she could touch him, heading for the bathroom.

Heart, body and soul. Gideon didn't remember exactly how he knew that all three had to be involved for the literal afterglow to happen, but he did. He took an extra minute in the bathroom to wash his face, again, and brush his teeth—again. Normally he would have done those things before, not after, but nothing about this morning had been normal.

He barely knew Hope Malory. So she was gorgeous, so she was hot, so she'd seen what he could do and hadn't fled as if a monster was on her heels. Yet. Beyond that…shit, there couldn't be anything beyond that.

She was an interesting diversion, that was all, and sleeping with her would bring an end to the unwanted partnership. She would have to ask for a transfer now, like it or not, and that was what he wanted more than anything else. So why the damn glow?

An aberration, that was the answer. Next time, if there was a next time, nothing out of the ordinary would happen, and eventually Hope would convince herself that what she'd seen had been a trick of the light or the simple aftereffect of coming so hard that she'd temporarily screwed up her own eyesight.

And she *had* come hard. What was a woman like that doing alone? She was alone in the same way he was. He knew it, the same way he knew his heart, body and soul had to be involved for what had happened to happen.

No big deal. He'd thought himself in love once before. The woman in question had seen a small hint of who he really was, and that had been the end of that. That short relationship had really screwed up his ideas of having anything normal in his life. In the end, he'd gotten over her well enough, and he would get over Hope, too.

"It's Emma who's got my head all twisted around," he muttered to the mirror, studying his too-bare chin. "Dante and his damned turquoise."

All of a sudden he saw Emma's reflection in the mirror and instinctively grabbed a towel to wrap himself in before he turned. Appearing maybe five years old today, she was floating above the tub, dressed all in white again. Her dark hair curled a bit and was fashioned into two long pigtails.

"Hi, Daddy. Did you call me?"

"No, I didn't call you."

"I heard you say my name," she protested, with all the innocence and persistence of a stubborn little girl.

A horrifying thought crossed his mind. "Were you just here?"

"No," she said, wide-eyed and growing more and more substantial as he watched. "I was waiting, and then I heard you call my name."

"Waiting for what?"

Emma smiled. "Be careful, Daddy," she said as she began to fade away. "She's very bad. Very, *very* bad."

"Who's very…?" Before he could finish the question, Emma was gone. Surely she was warning him about Tabby. A warning last night before he'd gone to the riverfront would have been nice. Not that it would have stopped him from going.

By the time he returned to the bedroom, Hope was gone. He heard her moving around in the guest bathroom down the hall. After a few minutes the bathroom door opened and she shouted, "Raintree, you wouldn't happen to have an extra toothbrush, would you?"

"Second drawer to the left," he answered.

Gideon chastised himself as he pulled his clothes for

the day from the closet. At least Hope wasn't being emotional about this. She recognized this morning for what it was: fun, in a world where there wasn't nearly enough fun. Release for two adult, apparently neglected, bodies that needed it. Just another day in a long line of days.

Yeah, Hope was hot; she was gorgeous; she was brave. But he couldn't love her, and this couldn't last.

"You must have more clothes around here that would fit me. I'd rather wear something of yours than *this!*"

"My clothes are too big for you," Gideon said sensibly. "Echo's fit just fine."

"That's a matter of opinion," Hope grumbled as she tugged on the hem of the cutoff T-shirt that revealed her belly button. She was a good three inches taller than Echo Raintree, so it was a miracle anything the other woman had left here would fit.

They'd both showered and changed clothes, but then she'd been stuck with choosing between the wrinkled blouse she'd slept in and the even more wrinkled trousers Raintree had thrown on the floor last night, or something from the drawer of clothes his cousin had left here on one of her infrequent visits.

The man didn't own an iron, or so he said. Everyone owned an iron! Hope thought as she tried to tug up the waistband of the hip-hugger jeans. Gideon claimed the dry cleaner took care of all his ironing.

Her choices were a couple of bikinis, two T-shirts with the hems ripped out to display a belly button ring

Hope did not have, and either a pair of cut-off shorts that would allow the cheeks of her butt to hang out or the tight pair of faded and ripped jeans she would normally have tossed in the garbage. For today the jeans were the lesser of two evils. They must have dragged on the ground when Echo wore them, given the frayed ends, but they were better than the cutoffs.

And not only would wearing the same clothes she'd worn yesterday be inappropriate and their hopelessly wrinkled state raise questions she didn't want to answer, this morning she'd discovered more than one spot of blood on the sleeve of her blouse and on the trousers. She didn't have a proper explanation for that, either, so she had no real choice but to make do with Echo's clothes.

At least Gideon had dressed casually, to keep her from feeling like a complete fool. His jeans actually looked good on him, and so did the T-shirt that entirely covered *his* belly button.

"We'll stop by your place later and you can change clothes," he said, turning his back on her to pour a cup of coffee.

"We'll stop by there *first*," she said.

"Maybe not," Gideon said thoughtfully. "Someone must've seen Tabby hanging around the club where Echo's band played, or at the coffee shop, or checking out the apartment building. She hasn't been invisible. The suits put some people off. People get defensive and just want to get rid of us as soon as possible, so we end up with squat. We'll go in more relaxed today, just following up with a few more questions."

Judging by the way Gideon was acting, a casual observer would have thought nothing out of the ordinary had happened this morning. He wasn't distant, but he wasn't exactly warm and cuddly, either. He was all business, and he hadn't touched her at all since he'd left the bed this morning.

Maybe having incredible casual sex with a partner he barely knew wasn't out of the ordinary for Gideon. It was certainly out of the ordinary for *her,* but she didn't necessarily want him to know that. Not if he thought what had happened was casual and unimportant.

The plan for the day was to get one of the other detectives—probably Charlie Newsom—busy collecting mug shots of anyone who matched Tabby's general description, while she and Gideon interviewed Sherry Bishop's friends, coworkers and neighbors once again. Maybe one of them had seen Tabby in the days preceding Sherry's death. Maybe one of them knew her last name. Unless they were very lucky, they wouldn't get far with nothing but "Tabby" to go on. This afternoon Gideon was meeting with a sketch artist. She wasn't sure how he would explain how he knew what the killer looked like, but somehow he would manage. She also had the washcloth she'd used to wipe away whatever Tabby had used to drug him. It was a long shot, but she planned to get that washcloth to the state lab. Unfortunately it would take weeks to get the results, and they didn't have weeks.

"My sister's coming in later today," she said. "She makes jewelry for the shop, and she has some new pieces to deliver."

Gideon lifted his head and looked at her. "You have a sister?"

Yet more evidence that they didn't know one another nearly well enough for what had happened this morning to happen. "Yeah."

"If you want to take some time and spend it with her while she's in town, I don't mind."

Of course he didn't mind. He would probably be relieved to be rid of her. "No. We see each other fairly often." *And besides, I'm the odd man out when Mom and Sunny get together.*

"Is she anything like you?" he asked, half teasing, half curious.

"No. She's two years older than me, has three little boys, and is every bit as flaky as my mother."

"So you've always been the 'normal' one?"

For a while she'd thought that to be true. She'd been so sure that she was not only normal but *right* in her skepticism. Gideon had pretty much blown that theory out of the water. "Normal is relative."

He didn't continue with the conversation. "Let's go. We're running late."

Hope grabbed her purse and followed Gideon to the stairs that led to his garage. She recognized what he was doing; she just didn't know why. He was ignoring what had happened in the hope that it would go away. He had become professional Gideon Raintree again, his mind completely on the case.

Maybe if she followed his lead and pretended that nothing had changed, they would be able to work together. They could be partners and maybe even friends. He was a good cop, and she could learn a lot working with him.

On second thought, Hope wasn't sure she could do that. The change between them was too deep to ignore. Should she take a chance and tell Gideon that she couldn't be just his partner and his friend? She was a woman who wanted all or nothing, and she had decided in the last couple of years that her only option was nothing. Maybe it would be better if she just played it safe, let Gideon back away and pretend nothing had happened.

Fortunately for both of them, she didn't have to make that decision this morning. Tabby was out there, and gut instinct told Hope that the woman was nowhere near finished.

Chapter 10

If Tabby was local, she'd never been arrested. Not as Tabby or Tabitha, at least. There was no way to be sure that was her real name, of course. Could be a nickname. Maybe her name was Catherine and it had been shortened to Cat, and then someone had started calling her Tabby and it stuck. It might be an alias, with no connection to her real name, in which case it did them no good at all. For whatever reason, the initial search on Tabby and her physical description had turned up nothing. It hadn't taken Gideon fifteen minutes to very carefully study everything Charlie had come up with. A couple of new detectives were checking out hotels in the area, in case Tabby was a visitor and not a resident. Charlie and another detective were now checking federal databases, and that would likely take a while. Hope had insisted on sending the particles of the drug Tabby had used on him to the state lab, insisting they could explain the details of how they came by the drug later, if an identification was made.

There was no way he could officially explain away what had happened last night. There was no sign of the wound in his thigh, and he couldn't reveal how he'd known to be in that place at that time without revealing that he'd spoken to Lily Clark's ghost. Somehow he didn't think the new chief or his coworkers would buy that explanation as easily as Hope had—not that he wanted them to know what he could do. To go public with his talents would not only be unwise, it was forbidden.

His current partner might be uncomfortable in Echo's clothes, but she looked great. Elegant and sleazy at the same time. The heels that barely peeked out from the frayed hem of the jeans only made the look more fetching. When they'd interviewed Sherry Bishop's friends, the men had all opened up to Hope in a way they hadn't during the first round of interviews. Unfortunately, none of them had anything startling or helpful to offer.

Right now Hope was rounding up coffee for both of them—her idea, not his—and Gideon was taking a moment's well-deserved rest in the office they shared in the police station on Red Cross Street. Now what? Tabby—for lack of a better name, that would have to do—had killed Sherry Bishop. Why? Chance? Bishop's bad luck? No. It couldn't be coincidence that all the victims were single. No one was going to come home at an inopportune time and interrupt Tabby while she was working. Tabby had tortured and killed Lily Clark just to get a message to him, and then she'd tried to add him to her list of victims.

He'd called the sheriff who'd handled the Marcia Cordell case, and they had an appointment for tomorrow afternoon. He hated the idea of leaving Wilmington even for a few hours while Tabby was on the loose, but if Marcia Cordell's ghost was hanging around that house, he not only needed to try to send her on, it was possible she might be able to add something new to what little he knew about Tabby.

Somehow he would have to find a way to leave Hope behind. She wouldn't like it if she knew what he was up to. She had accepted what he'd told her last night, but what would she think when he actually started using his gift? Would she freak out? Likely. He didn't want to leave her unguarded, but it wouldn't do for him to get too comfortable with his new partner, and that was where things were headed. Comfortable. Which meant that, deep down, he was more worried that she *would* accept what he could do.

They couldn't sleep together *and* work together; that was just asking for trouble. Truth be told, he would much rather sleep with Hope on a regular basis than accept her as a partner, but it wasn't likely that she would gently and obediently transfer to another division. Was she ever gentle or obedient? Not that he'd witnessed.

Hope entered the office with two disposable cups of

steaming coffee. Seeing her was much too much of a relief, as if she'd been gone for hours, not minutes. And that was the problem. Getting involved with her simply wasn't going to work. It was going to complicate everything. Problem was, they were already involved, things were already complicated, and he wasn't ready to let this end.

Someone had taken a shot at one of them, and if he was right, she was in danger just because she was close to him. It was too late to undo their connection. Trying to separate himself from her now would be like locking the barn door after the horses had bolted.

She set both coffee cups on his desk. "Some idiot uniform just made a pass at me. I swear, I think these clothes scream *party girl* and give off some kind of weird hormone thing. You'd think I was starring in a video of *Cops Gone Wild*. I cannot wait to get out of your cousin's clothes and into some of my own."

An unwanted anger rose up in Gideon. "Did he touch you?"

"What?" She looked at him oddly, as if she didn't understand his very simple question.

"The uniform who made a pass. Did he *touch* you?"

She sighed. "No. He just leered at my belly button and asked me what I was doing after my shift was over."

"Get his name?"

Her eyes widened, and then she shook her head. "Oh no, Raintree. We're not going there."

"Not going where?"

"You know damn well where we're not going."

"Enlighten me."

She leaned back against her own desk, which was much neater than his. Of course, she hadn't been there long enough to mess it up. "Okay, fine. If we're going to be…whatever, and I'm not sure yet that we are or we aren't; but if we *are,* there will be boundaries."

"Boundaries," Gideon repeated, half-sitting on his own desk.

"I want to be your partner, and I think I can be. I understand and accept what you can do, and I can contribute. I can be a good partner for you, Raintree, but some things are going to have to be separate. There can be no chasing after crude men who make passes at me, no staking your claim like we're cavemen and you're marking your territory, no sex on the desk or stolen kisses by the water cooler. When I'm in your bed, *if* I'm ever in your bed again, things can be different. But here in this office, I have to be your partner and nothing else. Can we do that?" she asked, as if she wasn't quite sure.

"I don't know," he said honestly. "It would be easier if you worked with someone else."

She squirmed a little, though he was sure the thought must have crossed her mind at some point that day. "I don't want to work with anyone else. I want to work homicide, and I know I can learn a lot from you. Maybe we should just write this morning off as a mistake and forget the whole thing."

Forget. Literally? A flash of anger rose up in Gideon, hot and electric. The lights overhead flickered but didn't go out. "Go ahead and forget. I don't know that I can."

Hope swallowed hard. Did she think he wouldn't see that response? he wondered.

"We're almost done here. We can go to the motel and I'll pick up the Challenger, and then I'll go home and—"

"No," he said.

"No?" Her eyebrows lifted slightly.

"I can't be sure you're safe there."

"See?" She pointed a finger at him. "This is exactly the kind of macho posturing I was trying to avoid. Would you have treated Leon this way?"

"I never fucked Leon."

Her face went red and then pale, and she pushed away from her desk and stalked out of the office. He wanted to chase her, catch her and drag her back into the office to finish this, but others were watching. And he had to admit, it was a momentarily and insanely tempting thought, to have a partner who knew what he could do and wasn't frightened by it. Someone he could count on to help with the investigation, even if they had to work it backward and upside down and inside out to get the bad guy.

So much for his determination to scare her off.

He did follow her, but at a distance. He stayed well behind Hope until they were in the parking lot, and then he easily caught up with her.

"If you're here to apologize…" she began tightly.

"I'm not," he said honestly.

She glanced at him, surprised and angry.

"I'm not apologizing for what happened, and I'm not apologizing for telling the truth just now. You're not one of the guys, Hope, and you'll never be the same kind of partner Leon was." She stopped short when he opened the passenger door for her and waited for her to get into the car.

Eventually she climbed into the passenger seat, still angry, but a little less so.

Gideon got into the driver's seat but didn't crank the engine. "You can't go home tonight because, like it or not, you're in the circle. If Tabby can't get to me, she might try to get to you. Your mother and your sister would be right there in the cross fire."

"That makes sense, I suppose," she said tightly. "I'd still like to go by the apartment and pick up a few things."

"Sure," he said, pulling out of the parking lot and heading toward The Silver Chalice. The Challenger could wait; he wasn't about to let Hope out of his sight.

As they turned off Red Cross Street, he said, "No sex on the desk, huh? Bummer."

Sunny Malory Stanton was the perfect daughter for Rainbow Malory. Her hair was a dark blond, like their father's, but other than that, she was Rainbow made over. Big smile, bigger heart. Comfy sandals, long skirt, dangling earrings. No bra.

Sunny smiled when Hope and Gideon walked through the door. She didn't even notice that her little sister's attire was totally out of character.

If Sunny showed up wearing a suit, Hope would certainly notice.

Her mother and sister were rearranging the display

of new jewelry. They were having fun, chatting away about the grandchildren, who had been left at home with their father. It would do Rainbow a world of good to spend some time with her eldest daughter.

Now to explain away spending the next few days at Gideon's beach house. Hope had been trying to come up with a good explanation since leaving the station, though she knew her mother would require no explanation at all. She would just figure that her youngest daughter had finally decided to embrace the old free love concept, and since Rainbow already liked Gideon...

No explanation was called for. Rainbow Malory looked Hope up and down, quickly took in Gideon's casual attire, and whispered, "Undercover?" as if there were a dozen people around to hear.

When Gideon opened his mouth, probably to say, "No," Hope stepped in front of him and said, "Yes," loudly enough to cover his answer. "I just need to pack a few things, and then we have to go." She didn't like to think that her family might be in danger simply because she was near, so the faster she got out of there, the better off they all would be.

She hated leaving Gideon alone with her family, but she couldn't very well ask him to come upstairs and help her pack. So she left him perusing the merchandise while she ran to the apartment above, intent on packing as quickly as she could.

Not that she could possibly be quick enough, of course. She gathered clothes, underwear, toothbrush, toothpaste, makeup. All the things she would need to make herself at home in Gideon's house.

Hope walked downstairs to find the three of them with their heads together, laughing as if someone had an old baby picture of her naked and was showing it off. Laughing as if Sunny had just told one of her embarrassing "Remember when?" stories about her little sister.

"We can go now," Hope said, her voice almost harsh.

They all three turned to look at her, and she got the feeling they knew something she didn't. She'd felt that way all her life, as if she were living on the outside looking in, as if she were missing out on some universal truth that was hidden from her and no one else.

"Yeah, okay," Gideon said, walking toward her, his eyes raking over her hungrily.

She was twenty-nine years old. She'd been involved with men before. Romantically, sexually, emotionally. And none of them had ever looked at her this way. None of them had ever looked into her with eyes that made her knees wobble.

None of them had been Gideon Raintree.

"I'm cooking Saturday night," Sunny called. "If y'all are finished with your undercover thingie, come by after the shop closes. I make a mean peach cobbler."

They said goodbye and left the shop just as three tourists—mother and daughters, judging by their similar round faces—entered, drawn there by a colorful display of wrapped stones in the window.

Hope tossed her bag into the back seat of Gideon's Mustang. She couldn't help but remember driving him home last night. He'd been so out of it that she'd been sure he would be in bed for days. She'd been certain he needed to be in the hospital. And here he was, looking as if nothing out of the ordinary had happened.

"Are they safe there?" she asked before Gideon had a chance to fire up the engine. She had seen what Tabby could do, and while she wasn't afraid for herself, the idea of a woman like that going near her family made her stomach and her heart turn.

"If I didn't think so, they wouldn't be there," Gideon answered. "They're under constant surveillance, just in case."

"How did you manage that without telling the chief everything you know?" And how did he know that was just what she needed to hear to maintain her peace of mind? Rainbow and Sunny might be flakes, but they were *her* flakes.

"I didn't tell the chief anything." He pointed to the storefront across the street, not to the busy café but to the upstairs window. "I hired a private team to keep an eye on your family, at least until Tabby is caught. Though I don't believe it's necessary," he added crisply. "Tabby wants me, and she might want you. I don't think your family's even a blip on her radar."

Twenty-four-hour surveillance didn't come cheap; she knew that. She could complain because her new partner had taken such a move without discussing it with her first, and she could offer to pay, since this was, after all, her family they were talking about. But instead she just said, "Thank you." And she meant it.

Thursday—8:37 p.m.

He wasn't surprised that Hope's bathing suit was a modest black one-piece. She looked great in it, but what he wouldn't give to see her in a skimpy bikini like the ones Echo wore when she was here. Something tiny and insubstantial, and maybe red. Beneath the conservative suits she wore to work, Hope Malory had a great body.

They'd studied the files over sandwiches and soda, but eventually they'd both started to lose what energy they had left, after last night. Words began to blur. They started making mistakes. Gideon's response to that kind of weariness was always the water.

The waves were ferocious, and night was coming, so they didn't go far from the shore. Churning salt water pummeled them both. They didn't stay close together. There was no holding hands or laughing in the surf. How could there be? He didn't yet know what they were. Partners yes, but probably not for long. Friends? No, Hope Malory was many things, but she was *not* his friend. Lovers? Maybe. It was too soon to say. One tryst did not a lover make.

As darkness crept up on them, they left the ocean and walked toward the house, a few feet of sand and an air of uncertainty separating them.

"Hi, Gideon!"

Honey, his blond next-door neighbor, leaned over her balcony and waved. He'd never once seen her in the ocean. He'd asked her about it once, and she'd said she didn't want to mess up her hair. With her hair slicked back and water dripping off her nose, Hope looked more beautiful than any other woman he'd ever seen. It was a realization he could have done without.

"Hi," he answered, his voice decidedly less enthusiastic than hers.

"Don't forget about the party Saturday night." Her eyes flitted quickly to Hope. "Are you going to be around?"

He shook his head. "Sorry, no."

"How about supper tomorrow night? We can cook out."

"I have to go out of town for the day. I'm not sure when I'll get back."

Hope glanced back at him and raised her eyebrows slightly. She was probably wondering if he was running out on her or telling Honey an out-and-out lie.

"Well, if you do get a chance on Saturday, stop by."

"Sure," he said, noncommittal and less than enthusiastic in his response.

He and Hope both reached the spigot at the foot of the stairway that led to his bedroom at the same time. They rinsed the sand off their feet.

"So where are you going tomorrow?"

"Hale County. The Cordell murder scene."

Her foot brushed against his, and she instinctively drew back. "Think it'll do any good?"

"I don't know. Maybe the ghost will still be there and can help in some way."

"After all this time?" Her question reminded her that she knew next to nothing about what he did.

"Some ghosts hang around for hundreds of years, stuck where they don't belong because they were so traumatized by life or their deaths that they can't move on. Four months is nothing."

"Do you do what you do to catch the killers, or do you try to send the ghosts of the victims to wherever it is they're supposed to be?"

"Both," he confessed.

He turned off the water, and they climbed the stairs, Hope in front, him lagging a few feet behind. What next? He wanted her, but he knew he shouldn't have her. Not couldn't, *shouldn't.*

In the end, she made the first move. At the top of the stairs she waited, and when he got there, she laid her hand on his arm, rose up on her toes and kissed him. It wasn't a sexual kiss—at least, not blatantly. It was a simple touch of her mouth to his, a hesitant, stirring kiss.

"You're a good man, Gideon. I'm sorry I suspected you of being crooked."

"That's all right," he muttered.

"No, it's not. You hide so much of yourself, and there's no way you can tell people what it is that you do. And yet you do it anyway, never taking credit, never asking for money or fame or even thanks."

"I'm a little surprised you're accepting this so easily," he said, leaning down for another kiss, because she was there and he could.

"Yeah," she whispered just before his lips touched hers again. "So am I."

The ocean had washed away Hope's worries, at least for a while, and once she'd let everything go she couldn't stop thinking about Gideon and what had happened that morning. Together they stripped off their wet bathing suits and stepped toward the master bathroom. She was sandy and salty, and she tasted Gideon on her mouth. Work was done, at least for a while, and for the moment she wasn't worried about anything but getting into the bed and staying there for a while. She felt almost wanton, which was unlike her.

Hope Malory was cautious where men were concerned, and though she'd always tried to be just like the males in her profession, she had never been aggressive in the bedroom. It was the one place where she was truly shy, where she sometimes felt reserved to the point of prim. She didn't feel at all prim now, as she gently pushed Gideon into the shower and followed him inside, stepping under the warm spray and letting it wash the last of the salt water from her skin and her hair.

"Do you ever get tired of living here?" she asked.

He ran a hand over her wet breast, almost casual and definitely familiar. There was such warmth in that hand, and she wanted more. She had a feeling she could never get enough of this man.

"Only when I get too much company," he answered. "When that happens, I just toss a few grains of sand into the bed each night, and eventually they go home."

She moved her body closer to his, unable to stop herself, not wanting to stop. "If I overstay my welcome, are you going to toss sand in my bed?" she teased.

"Not likely," he said, his voice soft and uncertain.

She wanted to ask him, *What are we, Raintree? A*

couple? Coworkers who have sex on the side? Friends?
But she didn't want to ask questions she knew he didn't
have answers for. He kissed her under the shower's
spray, and his hands wandered. So did hers. She wanted
him here and now, but there was no condom nearby, and
she wasn't about to let go of him, not yet. This felt too
good, the spray of the water, Gideon's mouth and his
hands, and the way her body responded to both. It didn't
matter what they called themselves, not yet. Maybe one
day it would matter, but for now, this was enough.

She closed her eyes while Gideon spread her legs and
touched her intimately. She could have sworn a spark
entered her body, teasing her, arousing her, fluttering
through her like a little bolt of lightning. Maybe it did.
At this point, nothing seemed impossible.

Her body began to quiver, she wanted Gideon so much.

Instead of leading her from the shower, he pressed
his palm against her belly, low, where she felt empty
and shuddery.

"I'm gonna cheat," he whispered into her ear.

"Okay," Hope whispered breathlessly, eyes closed as
everything she had was focused on touch, and touch alone.

She cried out as the orgasm washed through her with
an unexpected intensity, and if Gideon hadn't been holding
her up, she probably would have fallen to the shower floor.
But he did hold her up. He held her wet, slick body against
his, as release whipped through her like lightning.

As the orgasm faded, Gideon whispered, "Open
your eyes."

She did so, slowly. There was an odd glow in the
shower, and it didn't come from Gideon. It came from

her. Her aura, a literal afterglow, danced along her skin with little sparks of electricity. Gideon's eyes shone with a touch of green light, just a touch. The rest of the glow came from her.

He smiled. "Water is a great conductor."

He had been tempted to take Hope in the shower, condom or no condom, but Emma's frequent appearances and promises of coming soon had made him opt for another method, at least for now.

Besides, it wasn't as if they were finished.

They dried one another with a fat gray towel, then walked toward the bedroom and the bed that awaited. Hope's skin still glowed, but the luminescence was quickly fading. She didn't have the power to keep the electricity fed, as he did.

He tossed her onto the bed, and she laughed as he crawled onto the mattress to join her. She stretched beneath him, naked and damp and touched with magic.

"So," she said, reaching out to caress his face with gentle fingers. "What do girls normally say when you turn them into your own personal flashlights?"

He stroked her throat with the back of his hand. "I don't know. I've never done it before."

Her smile faded.

"I usually have to hide everything, remember?" He didn't tell her that the glow was special, that she was different, that she was so unlike other women she stunned him.

Hope shifted her body, making herself more comfortable against him. There was something most definitely different about the way his naked flesh and hers came together, something he didn't want to think about. He didn't want to *think* with her. He wanted sex. A few laughs, maybe.

"Don't hide anything from me," she said.

It was such an unexpected and startling thought, that any woman could know everything about him and stay, that Gideon almost flinched. He couldn't bare himself in every sense to anyone. Bare bodies, yes. Bare souls? Never.

He didn't want to talk about anything beyond the physical, so he spread Hope's thighs and stroked. She sighed and wrapped her fingers around him, gently, but not too gently. She caressed, and he closed his eyes and left everything behind to get lost in sensation. This was sex. It was good and right and powerful, but it was still only sex.

By the time he reached for the bedside drawer, neither of them were thinking about explanations for what this might be. It just was.

Sometimes a rabbit is just a rabbit.

Chapter 11

She should have been able to sleep like a baby, but that hadn't happened. Not yet. Her mind was spinning with a thousand questions. When Hope became so restless that she began to worry about waking Gideon, she left him sleeping in his bed while she quietly roamed the half-dark bedroom.

Moonlight from the uncovered window and a hint of illumination from a night-light in the bathroom made it easy enough to see. Gideon was a bit of a minimalist, without a lot of unnecessary stuff in his house. There were family pictures on the walls here and there, but no flower arrangements or useless knickknacks on table-tops. She ran her hands over the dresser in his bedroom. Carelessly discarded on the surface was a ceramic dish for coins, a silk tie he'd dropped in a heap, a small piece of turquoise and what she recognized as another protection charm. She ran her fingers over the small silver charm attached to the slim leather cord. A week ago, if someone had told her that something so innocent and unimportant as a piece of silver could carry the power to protect, she never would have believed it. Now she knew that many of the things she'd once believed were wrong. She lifted the charm and placed it around her neck, where it lay close to the one Gideon had given her. Tabby was out there somewhere, and besides, her heart needed all the protection it could get at the moment. Was that kind of protection even possible? Or was it too late for her?

She grabbed a T-shirt Gideon had dropped onto a chair near the dresser, pulled it over her head and very quietly walked onto the deck that overlooked the Atlantic. The sound of the surf, together with the gentle light of the moon, soothed her, and she definitely needed soothing tonight.

It wasn't like her to get deeply involved with anyone or anything so quickly. She studied all new enterprises from every angle before committing herself in any way. She always remained coldly and totally detached from any situation until she knew without doubt that a move was the right one. She'd been that way since the age of eleven, maybe even longer. She didn't make rash decisions. Not anymore.

And here she was, deeply involved with Gideon Raintree. Through the sex, his secrets and the case they were working together, she was involved to the pit of her soul.

She heard the door behind her open but didn't turn to look at Gideon. His bare feet padded toward her, and a moment later his arms encircled her. Those arms were warm and strong and wonderfully embracing. It was a nice feeling, to be held this way. She liked it. Maybe too much.

"I didn't mean to wake you," she whispered.

"Two nights together, and I wake up because you're not where you're supposed to be," he responded with a touch of displeasure in his voice.

She leaned her head back and relaxed against him. "I'm not exactly accustomed to needing anyone, either."

He slipped his hands beneath the oversized shirt she wore, raked his palms against her bare skin and cupped her breasts with familiarity. His fingers teased the sensitive nipples until she closed her eyes and swayed against him, her body responding quickly and entirely. She shouldn't want him now. She should most definitely not need him this way, with an intensity that drove away everything else. But she did.

His hands feathered over her breasts. Was that a touch of unnatural electricity that seeped through her skin and shot to her very core? Or was what she felt so intensely simply the response of a woman to a man? Gideon had such nice hands, charged or not, and he touched her as if he owned her, as if he knew exactly how to make her his in every way. He leaned down and kissed the side of her neck, familiarly and gently and amazingly arousingly. Her body quivered.

She turned in Gideon's arms, lifted her face and

kissed him. Her mouth against his, she slipped her hands around his waist. He'd walked onto the deck naked— not that anyone would be on the beach to see them at this time of night, in this near-dark—and she boldly ran her fingers against his back, his hip, his thigh. If it was true that he could make her his, then it was just as true that *she* possessed a part of *him,* at least for tonight.

He kissed her deeply, arousing her and demanding more with his lips and his tongue and his hands. Her body clenched and unclenched, quivered, and quickly spiraled out of control. So did Gideon's. She felt it in every caress of his hands; she tasted it in his kiss. Moaning low in what sounded like frustration or maybe impatience, he easily lifted her off her feet. Her legs wrapped around his waist. He was close, so close.

"Don't you need a—" she began breathlessly.

"Already thought of that," he said, his voice husky.

She shifted her body to bring him closer, to guide him into her. "You came out here wearing a condom? Pretty sure of yourself, weren't you?" she teased.

"I was overcome by optimism."

The tip of his erection teased her entrance, and she began to lower herself onto him, anxious and wanting in a way that still surprised her. She'd had more sex in the past twenty-four hours than she'd had in the past five years. And she had *never* had sex like this before, all-consuming and powerful and beautiful, without awkwardness or disappointment. She had never felt a moment's disappointment in Gideon's arms.

"I'm glad you woke up," she whispered, her mouth

resting against his ear. "I've never made love in the moonlight before."

Gideon went still. His entire body tensed, muscles tightening. "Moonlight."

He lifted her away from the railing she was partially balanced against, and carried her into the deep shadows against the house. No moonlight touched them there, and there was no railing to lean against. Gideon held her; she held him. The wall was against her back, and she felt grounded and afloat at the same time.

They were lost in complete and utter darkness when he pushed inside her, deep and hard. Hope didn't care where they were. Moonlight or daylight, darkness or sunshine. Under the covers or beneath nothing but the moon and the stars. As long as Gideon was with her, as long as he was holding her, she didn't care where they were. Instinct called her to him, but there was more than instinct here, more than intense physical need.

She hadn't thought herself in love for a very long time. Her mother, her sister, her nephews, that kind of love was all she dared to believe in. Romantic love was filled with pitfalls. She not only didn't wish for that emotion, she did her best to avoid it. Love was a trap, heartache just waiting to happen. This unexpected rush of emotion she felt for Gideon right now, while he held her and filled her and brought her closer to release, surely it was just the power of sex.

But as he made love to her, with her back to the wall and her arms and legs wrapped completely around him, she couldn't imagine any other man but Gideon making her feel this way. She could love him. She could wrap her entire world around this man and change who and what she was, who she had become. Ghosts, light shows and all, she could love him. Scary stuff.

They came together with a cry and a moan that were lost in a deep kiss. With the sounds of the surf in their ears and the moonlight inches away, with her body trembling, there was a moment of perfection when those words crossed her mind again. *I could love you.* Lost in darkness, the gentle glow of Gideon made her smile. *I love you* tugged at her lips, but she bit the words back. It was too soon for such a confession. It was also too risky.

He carried her inside the house and placed her gently on the bed. After disposing of the condom, he returned to the bed to lie beside her. She kept his T-shirt on. She liked the way it felt against her skin, this worn cotton that still smelled vaguely of Gideon.

"I'm going to get up in the morning and go to the Cordell crime scene to have a look around," he said, his voice like gravel and silk.

"You mean *we,* right?"

He hesitated. "I want you to stay here."

She rose slightly. If she hadn't just been thoroughly exhausted and satisfied, if *I love you* weren't still niggling at the edge of her brain, his words might have made her angry. Instead she smiled. "No way."

"There are other case files that need to be examined. I need you here."

"Put the top up and I'll read the files in the car."

He wrapped an arm around her waist and pulled her body against his. "Can we argue about this tomorrow?"

"Sure." Her eyes drifted closed. Maybe now she could sleep. "I like arguing with you," she said beneath her breath. "You're really cute when you get mad."

Gideon snorted, and then he laughed. "You're one of a kind, Hope Malory."

"So are you, Gideon Raintree." It was as close to *I love you* as either of them were willing to get.

Gideon woke not long after sunrise, which was normal for him. Waking with his arms around a beautiful woman was not so normal.

His sexual relationships in the past had been brief. Even in those that lasted a few weeks or even a few months, he maintained a certain distance. He didn't spend the night elsewhere or ask women to spend the night here. It was too dangerous.

Sleeping with Hope didn't feel at all dangerous. It felt right and good and natural, as if they had been sleeping together for a thousand years. And that was truly dangerous. It was so dangerous that last night he had almost forgotten Emma's words and taken Hope right there in the moonlight. He'd been wearing a condom, but no kind of protection was a hundred percent effective. Moving into the shadows before he'd buried himself inside her had simply been a precaution.

He lifted her shirt, his shirt, and laid his mouth on her flat stomach. Damn, she tasted good. She felt good, so warm and silky. He kissed her there, drawing the essence of her into his mouth, trailing the tip of his tongue up and down, sucking against her skin until he felt her hand settle in his hair.

"Good morning," she murmured, her voice sleepy and satisfied.

He answered by lifting the shirt a bit higher and pushing his hand beneath the soft cotton. The chill of her protection charm brushed against his hand as he uncovered one breast and took the nipple deep into his mouth. Hope's fingers threaded more thoroughly into his hair, and he suckled her deeper. He tasted her and savored her until one of those little moans caught in her throat.

This morning he wasn't in any hurry. He would make her come a time or two, make love to her long and hard and then leave her sleeping soundly. When she woke up and found that he was well on his way to the Cordell crime scene, she might be pissed for a while, but she would forgive him. He knew exactly how to make her forgive him.

He spread her legs and ran one finger along the tender skin of her inner thigh. Her skin was soft, the muscle of her thigh gently shaped and utterly feminine. "You have the longest legs," he said as he lifted one and laid his mouth behind the knee. She shuddered and wrapped that leg around him as his mouth moved higher. Her leg hadn't seen much sun. It was as creamy pale as any skin he had ever seen, and it fascinated him. He ran a finger up from her knee, allowing a little bit of electricity to escape. Hope laughed and twitched.

"That tickles."

"Does it?"

"Yes," she said with a sigh.

He wasn't anywhere near finished with this woman. Would he ever be? While the morning came alive, he tasted her everywhere. He made her quiver and lurch; he made her moan. After she came against his mouth, she all but threw him onto his back, determined to have her way with him, as well. Determined to make him moan. And she did. With her mouth and her hands, she studied every inch of him.

Knowing that he was as ready as a man could possibly get, Hope pulled away from him and drew the T-shirt over her head. Gideon reached for the drawer where he kept the condoms. He would have to stop by the drugstore on the way home tonight. He was almost out. And no matter how much he liked Hope, no matter how right and close and true she felt, no matter that she made him glow in the dark, he wasn't ready to go any further than this. They had great sex, but there was no guarantee that it would last. Not much in this world was truly lasting.

Hope sat on the bed, smiling and flushed and breathing hard all over again. Her black hair was mussed around her face. Perfect Hope, so carefully put together, was utterly gorgeous when she was mussed.

Mussed and naked…and wearing two charms around her neck.

Gideon dropped the wrapped condom to the bed. He forgot about pushing inside Hope and ending this torment. He forgot about everything else but those pieces of silver. "Where did you get this?" he asked as he lifted one of the charms. The one he had *not* given her.

She lifted the charm and studied it absently. "I almost forgot about this one. I found it on your dresser last night."

Gideon jumped from the bed and turned toward the dresser in question. Sure enough, Dante's fertility charm was gone. No, not *gone.* Hope was wearing it around her pretty neck. "Were you wearing that last night when we were on the deck?"

"I think so." She pushed her hair back, combing it with long, pale fingers. "Yeah, I was. I picked it up and put it on before I went outside."

He turned and stared down at her. "Why?"

"I don't know. It's pretty." She removed the charm that had not been made for her, drawing the cord over her head and ruffling her mussed hair further in the process. Not that it mattered. It was too late. Much too late. "I guess I felt the need for a little extra protection last night." She offered the talisman to him with an out-stretched hand. He didn't take it. "I'm sorry if I wasn't supposed to touch. Take it and come back to bed."

"All the protection in the world won't undo…" He stopped. One time, that was all, and he had been wearing a condom and they hadn't been in the moonlight. May-be, just maybe… He rushed into the bathroom and slammed the door.

"Gideon?" Hope called through the closed door. "Are you all right?"

Not even a little. "Fine," he answered tersely.

Fine? What a lie. He'd been this close to another

moment of absolute perfection inside Hope Malory, and then he'd seen that charm lying against her chest. Wanting someone to distraction physically was one thing. Making a baby together was another thing entirely.

Maybe everything *was* fine. He'd been thinking clearly enough to move Hope out of the moonlight last night before having sex with her. That one fact might have changed everything. Emma couldn't come to him in a moonbeam if there was no moonbeam in which to travel.

"Emma," he whispered. "Show yourself."

He waited for the spirit who claimed to be his daughter to drop in to say hello. After all, she'd shown up before when he'd called her name. But the bathroom remained silent and free of spirits of all kinds.

"You're sure you're all right?" Hope called. She was closer now, standing just on the other side of the door.

"I'm *fine!*" Gideon snapped.

She moved away, and a moment later he heard the water running in the guest bathroom. For a moment he leaned over the sink and studied his sour, bristly-cheeked reflection. He didn't look like a father; he didn't feel like a father. "Come on, Emma," he said, a bit louder than before. "This isn't funny. It isn't nice to tease. You're going to give Daddy heart failure if you don't show yourself."

The bathroom remained silent but for his own labored breathing.

Hope was special; he couldn't deny that. There was the continuing and annoying glow that told him his heart and soul were as involved as his body. Maybe, a few years down the line, if they continued to have great sex and they worked out the whole partner thing, then *maybe* he could consider the possibility that Hope was going to be a permanent fixture in his life.

But *now?*

"Come on, Emma. Sweetheart," he added. "There's no need to be hasty about this. A couple of years, maybe ten, and then I might be ready to have kids." It was a lie, and Emma likely knew it. The world wasn't fit for the innocence of a child; he saw that for himself every day.

She was pulling his leg. After all, he had moved Hope away from the early-morning moonbeams, and he'd used a condom faithfully.

And Hope had been wearing that damned fertility charm, which very well could have trumped everything.

Gideon took a quick shower, shaking off the feeling of impending doom as he toweled dry and then wrapped the towel around his waist. He found Hope in the kitchen, making coffee and scrounging around the cupboards looking for a breakfast of some sort.

She gave him a wary glance. "Are you sure you're all right?"

"Yeah." He looked at her. Most specifically, he looked at her stomach. "Come on, Emma," he whispered as Hope turned her attentions to the refrigerator. "Talk to me."

"What did you say?" Hope asked as she came out with a half gallon of milk.

"Nothing."

"Oh, I thought you said Emma." She placed the milk

on the counter, beside a box of cereal. "That's my grand-mother's name."

He almost groaned but caught himself just in time.

Hope reached for the bowls. She already knew her way around the kitchen pretty well. "My mother has her heart set on a granddaughter named Emma," she said, "but Sunny has three boys, and I'm not planning to have kids any time soon, so she's outta luck."

"Wanna bet?" Gideon asked beneath his breath.

Hope left everything she'd gathered on the counter and turned to glare at him. "Maybe I should call you Rainman instead of Raintree. You're making no sense at all this morning."

Gideon pointed to the fertility charm Hope had put around her neck once again, after he'd refused to take it from her palm. It had been meant for Dante, a broth-erly joke, a push to get the Dranir busy reproducing, but it would be just as effective on Hope.

"That talisman you lifted from the dresser last night," he said, as he continued to point a censuring finger, "is a fertility charm."

"A *what?*" Hope took a step away from him and yanked the thing from around her neck as if it might burn her. "What kind of sick person would make a fer-tility charm and leave it lying around!"

Gideon raised his empty hand. "This sick person. It was meant for my brother, not you."

Hope flung the charm at him, putting all her muscle behind it. "You really are sick," she said sharply as he caught the charm in midair. "What did your brother ever do to you to deserve that?" She looked around her immediate vicinity for something else to throw, found nothing handy and finally sat down at the kitchen table. "It didn't work," she said sensibly. "I'm sure it didn't work. That charm wasn't made for me, and we were careful. We were always careful. It's not like you have some kind of super sperm."

"Yeah," Gideon agreed, hoping she was right. If fertility charms worked without fail, Dante would have populated his own village by now. "I even moved you out of the moonlight."

"What does that have to do with anything?" she snapped.

He figured he might as well tell her everything. "For the past three months I've been dreaming about this little girl. Thanks to Dante," he added. "So don't feel too sorry for him just because I occasionally send him something he doesn't want."

"He sent you some kind of dream?"

"There have been a couple of times when I've seen Emma outside a dream. She was the one who told me to get down when Tabby took a shot at us."

"What does that have to do with moonlight, Raintree?" Hope was frustrated and irritated and maybe even a little scared. She tried to smooth her hair with agitated fingers.

"Emma told me that she's coming to me in a moonbeam."

Hope went pale. Deathly, scarily, white. As white as

the milk she'd taken from the fridge. "You should have told me that before now." She grabbed the saltshaker off the table and threw it at him, but there wasn't as much anger in the motion as before, and he caught it easily. Some of the salt escaped and fell to the floor. Out of habit, he picked up a pinch and tossed it over his left shoulder.

"Why?" Gideon asked as he set the saltshaker aside. "I didn't believe her. We make our own choices in life, and I choose not to have kids. Besides, it's just some kind of poetic nonsense. And we weren't in a moon-beam last—"

"Shut up, Raintree." Hope stood and looked long-ingly at the pepper shaker, but she walked away without throwing it at him. "You were in a moonbeam last night," she said without turning to look at him. "You were most definitely in a moonbeam."

"Where are you going?"

She lifted a hand. "I'll be right back. Don't go any-where."

A few seconds later Hope was in the kitchen again, purse in hand, face no less pale. She sat at the table, took a slim black wallet from her purse, slid her driver's license from its designated slot and tossed it to Gideon. It sailed between them like a Frisbee, hit him in the chest and landed on the floor by his feet. "Read it and weep," she said weakly.

Gideon scooped the driver's license from the floor. The picture was less than flattering, like all such photos, and still…not too bad. It was the name on the license that caught and held his attention. He gripped the license tightly and said a word not fit for little Emma's ears as he read the name again and again.

Moonbeam Hope Malory.

Chapter 12

She'd thought about having her name legally changed a thousand times, but every time she so much as mentioned it to her mother there was hell to pay. Sunshine Faith and Moonbeam Hope, those were Rainbow's daughters. They had been Sunny and Moonie for years, until Hope had grown old enough to insist that she be called by her middle name.

Gideon drove too fast, but Hope didn't say a word about him speeding. Since he'd put the top of the convertible up, she was able to leaf through the case files. That way they didn't have to talk. Or look at each other.

Several of the files were from unsolved murders that probably weren't connected to the latest killings. Most were grisly but without the connection of the missing body parts. Gathering this much information hadn't been easy. There were a number of different jurisdictions and investigators involved. Still, she saw enough similarities in a number of cases to make her uneasy.

If Tabby was a serial killer, and that was definitely possible, then why had she targeted Gideon? Why had she tried to kill him on the riverfront? It didn't fit in several ways. Unlike her other crimes, it had been attempted in a public place, and Gideon was unlike her other victims. Wasn't he? He had been alone before taking up with her. Was he still a loner, emotionally? Of course he was. What they had was just sex, which didn't exactly qualify them to be a happy couple—this morning's odd developments aside.

Hope did her best not to think about those developments. Studying the disturbing cases before her was much easier on her heart, horrifying as they were.

The file on the victim in Hale County was thin but far from shoddy. It wasn't a lack of concern that caused the file to be thin. According to Gideon, the sheriff was anxious to talk to anyone who might be able to shed light on the schoolteacher's murder, and had seemed relieved that someone had taken an interest in the case.

"Why this one?" she asked when they'd been on the road more than an hour. "There are others that fit the profile, and at least one that's closer."

"It's less than three hours away, and more importantly, the crime scene is intact," Gideon answered in a businesslike voice.

"How could it be intact after four months?"

"It's been cleaned," he explained, "but no one's moved into the house. My best shot of speaking to the victim and maybe even spotting a real clue is with this case."

He hadn't wanted her to come along today, but he hadn't argued long when she'd insisted. Was that why he was so unhappy, or was he wound tightly for more personal reasons? He sure as hell didn't want her to be pregnant. She'd never seen a man react so strongly to the very prospect. Not that she had exactly embraced the idea of parenthood with a surge of joy and giggles.

He seemed so sure that Emma was a done deal. Hope wasn't, though all his talk of moonbeams and that damned fertility charm had given her more than a moment's pause. Gideon made her look at the impossible in a whole new way. He made her want to open her eyes and her heart in a way she had refused to do in the past. But really, a *fertility* charm?

She stared out the passenger window and watched the leafy green landscape blur. It wasn't like her to meet a man on Monday and end up in his bed on Wednesday. She'd obviously hit an invisible and unexpected sexual peak of some kind, because where Gideon was concerned, she hadn't been able to control herself. That was also very much not like her. Control was her middle name. Of course, Hope Control Malory was preferable to Moonbeam Hope Malory any day.

Could've been worse. Her mother could have named her Moonbeam Chastity. Then where would she be?

They were another hour down the road, perhaps half

an hour from their destination, when Gideon said, "I'm sorry if I overreacted."

"A grown man tearing out his hair, cursing and screaming at my stomach, you call that overreacting?" she asked without emotion.

Gideon shifted his broad shoulders, fidgeting as if the car had suddenly become too small to contain him. "At least I didn't throw anything at you."

"I'm not the one who made a fertility charm and left it lying around in the bedroom for anyone to pick up."

"I said I was sorry."

She really didn't want to argue right now. In fact, she didn't want to think about the possibilities Gideon had presented to her. "Why don't we wait a while and see if there's really anything to be sorry about?"

Another awkward moment passed, and he said, "If you want to request another partner, I'll understand."

Hope almost snorted. "Is that what this is about?" she snapped. "You don't want a partner, so you go to extreme lengths to make sure—"

"No," he interrupted, then after a pause that lasted a few seconds too long, he added, "It's true. I don't want a partner."

"Then go to the chief and tell him you don't want me as a partner. Don't expect me to quit. I don't quit, Raintree. Not ever."

"He'd just assign me another one," Gideon grumbled.

She would never admit it out loud, but it hurt that Gideon didn't want to work with her. Not because they'd slept together and she felt there could be so much more, but because she'd worked so hard to get where she was, and she was damned tired of being dismissed by men who thought she couldn't do her job. She couldn't tamp her anger down. "It might be difficult to pretend to be devastated because you thought you knocked up Mike or Charlie."

Gideon didn't respond, so she glanced in his direction. He was almost smiling.

"I don't think I'm pregnant," she said sensibly, her anger fading. "We were careful. A piece of silver and a dream won't undo that." Super sperm aside.

"Maybe you're right," he said, though he didn't sound as if he believed there was a chance in hell she was.

"Even if I am…pregnant…" Damn, it was hard to say that word out loud. "That doesn't mean we have to get married or anything." The *M* word was even more difficult than *pregnant.* "You don't have to concern yourself with whatever happens to me." She said the words, but her heart did a little flip. Single and pregnant, raising a child alone, pretending she hadn't almost said *I love you* to this man who was terrified of being tied to her by a child.

"Emma's Raintree," Gideon said. "I will most definitely be concerned."

"Actually, Emma is *Malory,*" she responded. "If there *is* an Emma," she added.

"A woman who gives birth to a Raintree *becomes* Raintree, in many ways," Gideon said tersely.

"I don't think so," she responded, wondering at his statement but afraid to ask….

"You've seen what I can do," Gideon said, his voice lowered, as if someone else out here in the middle of nowhere might hear. "Emma will have her own gifts, and there's no way I can walk away and not *concern* myself with what happens to her."

They hadn't known one another long enough for Hope to be hurt because none of his concern was for her. "Maybe this time will be different. Maybe Raintree genes won't be dominant in this case." Shoot, she was talking about this kid as if it was a done deal. "If I'm pregnant. Which I'm not."

"You're pregnant," he said sourly.

"*If* I'm pregnant," she said again, "is it really such a disaster?" Her heart flipped again. Her stomach, too. Of course it was a disaster! Maybe she did think she was in love with Gideon, but they'd just met, and she had career plans, and she was pretty sure he didn't love her back.

"Yes!"

Hope turned her gaze to the blurred landscape again, so Gideon wouldn't see her face. She had no right to be devastated because he didn't want her to be pregnant. It was such a girlie reaction, to get teary-eyed over a rejection from a man she barely knew.

Maybe growing up different had been so difficult for him that he couldn't bear to watch a child go through the same struggles. But he'd turned out okay. He had a nice life, and he helped people—the living and the dead—and he had made the most of his abilities. Maybe he did have to hide a lot of himself from the world, but he hadn't hidden himself from her.

He cut the Mustang sharply onto the grassy shoulder of the road, startling Hope so that she snapped her head around to glare at him. "What are you doing?"

Gideon put the car in Park, and with the engine still running, he reached into her lap and grabbed a file. "Which one is this?" he asked, leafing through the pages and photos. "Doesn't matter, does it?" He randomly grabbed a photo and held it up. The woman in the picture was lying half-on and half-off a faded sofa, blood soaking the front of her dress and her head all but severed. "There are people in the world who do things like this," he said in a lowered voice. "If there were just a handful of the bastards, maybe I wouldn't feel sick at the very idea of exposing an innocent child to a life where this happens every day. Every day, Hope. What if Emma's like me and she's faced with the horrors of death every day of her life? What if she's like Echo and she dreams of disasters she can't do anything about? What if—" His lips snapped closed. He couldn't even finish his final thought.

How could she stay angry with him? He wasn't being petty or selfish. His panic was rooted in a fear and concern for the child he claimed he didn't want. Hope lifted her hand and touched Gideon's cheek. Her thumb brushed against his smooth chin. He didn't pull away from her, as she'd thought he might. "You've been doing this too long."

"What choice do I have? I have an ability that allows me to put the bad guys away. If I don't, some of them will get away with it. Some of the victims will be stuck here, caught between life and death." He looked her in the eye. "What do you say when a little girl asks if there are monsters in the world? *Yes* is terrifying. *No* is a lie."

She stroked his cheek. "When was the last time you had a vacation, Raintree?"

"I don't remember."

"When we catch Tabby and put her away for good, we're taking a long vacation. I like the mountains."

Gideon didn't agree that a vacation was a fine idea, but he didn't disagree, either. He placed one hand over her stomach, and that hand was gentle. "I don't like the idea of having something so important to lose," he said softly.

"Emma?" she whispered.

He lifted his head and looked her in the eye. "And you, Moonbeam Hope. Dammit, where the hell did you come from?"

She smiled at his bewilderment. "Call me Moonbeam again and I'll shoot you."

He smiled for the first time that day, and then he leaned in and kissed her quickly. "Let's get this over with. The sheriff is waiting for us."

The living room where Marcia Cordell had been murdered looked like an old lady's parlor. There were doilies on the tables, dusty silk flower arrangements that had been neglected in the four months since her death, antique furnishings that didn't match and yet somehow did. There was also a large dried bloodstain in the center of the rug in the middle of the room.

Gideon squatted down by the bloodstain, while Hope and an anxious sheriff hovered nearby. The sheriff worked the brim of his hat with meaty, nervous hands.

"I really hope you can help us out here," the man said. "Miss Cordell was a right popular teacher. Everybody loved her. Well, we thought everybody loved her. Takes a lot of hate to do what was done to her. Did you see the pictures? God-awful scene. I'll never forget it."

The man went on and on, chattering endlessly. The sheriff was nervous, and he desperately wanted help on this case. He wanted it closed. He wanted proof that someone from outside the community had done this terrible thing, so he didn't have to imagine that a man or woman he knew was capable of this kind of violence.

The ghost of Marcia Cordell was in the room, but she lurked in a corner, watchful and afraid. Still afraid.

"What kind of a man would do such a thing?" the sheriff continued. "To…to violate and murder such a sweet woman…"

Gideon's head snapped around. *Violate?* "She was sexually assaulted?"

The sheriff nodded and worked harder at the brim of his hat.

So much for the connection to Tabby. There had been no sign of sexual activity of any kind at the other scenes. "It would've been nice if that information had been included in the report you sent me."

"Miss Cordell was a decent woman. Wasn't no reason to broadcast such unpleasantness about her after she was gone. Besides, we're keeping that part of the investigation under wraps. No need to broadcast all the details to the world."

"DNA?" Hope asked crisply.

The sheriff shook his head. "No. The man who did this wore a prophylactic, the coroner said."

"Detective Malory," Gideon said in a measured and calm voice. "Would you take Sheriff Webster outside and see if he can fill in some of the blanks in the Cordell file?"

"Excellent idea," Hope said. The sheriff didn't want to leave, but when Hope took his arm and headed for the front door, he went along like a well-trained puppy.

Alone in the eerie room, Gideon turned his eyes to the far corner, where Marcia Cordell's ghost waited in a ball of unformed light. He wasn't too angry with the sheriff, even though this trip meant a day away from his current investigation, time wasted in his pursuit of Tabby. If he was here, it was for a reason. "Talk to me, Marcia," he said softly. "Tell me what happened to you."

She took form gradually, the ball of light shifting, color and shape growing more defined. Marcia Cordell had been a plump and pretty woman. She was barely five feet tall, and her long brown hair was pulled back into a bun. She suited this old-fashioned room.

"You see me," she said, her voice shaking.

"Yes, I do." Gideon remained calm and still, so he wouldn't scare her away. "Marcia, do you know you're dead?"

She nodded her head. "I saw them come and take

my body away. I screamed at them to help me, but no one heard."

"I hear you."

Marcia drifted toward him, slow and openly suspicious. One wrong move and she would disappear. She wasn't angry like Sherry and Lily. She was terrified.

"Would you tell me what happened here?" Gideon asked gently.

"I let him in, never knowing what he intended."

Him. Not Tabby, just as he'd suspected when he heard that she had been violated. Still, he could find out who'd raped and killed her, and then he could send her spirit to a better place. In that sense, his trip here had not been wasted.

Marcia Cordell's spirit sighed and drifted down to sit on a flowery sofa, her pose proper. "Dennis was always such an odd boy, but—"

"Dennis. You knew him?"

Miss Cordell gave Gideon a withering glance. It was a glance she had no doubt silenced students with over the years. "Young man, you asked me to tell you what happened, and I'm trying to do just that."

He didn't point out that he was just a couple of years younger than she had been at the time of her death, hardly a young man. She had the spirit of an older woman, as if she'd carried something into this life too strongly from another. "Sorry, ma'am," he said contritely. "Please continue."

She nodded her head. "Dennis Floyd is a neighbor. The Floyd family has been living in that house going on twenty years. Dennis was in elementary school when they moved in, and he was a pupil in my English class several years ago. He was not a good student," she said with reproach. "He stopped by that night and asked to use the phone. He said their phone was out. Of course I said yes." Her mouth thinned. "I didn't see the danger coming until he grabbed me and threw me to the floor like a…like a…" she sputtered, and her face grew red. Even in death, she could blush.

"I'm going to see that he goes away for what he did to you," Gideon said. "He'll be punished, in this life and in the next."

She nodded, obviously relieved. "Dennis needs to be punished for what he did to me. So does she."

The hairs on the back of Gideon's neck prickled. "She?"

"The woman who was with Dennis, the one who urged him on. I didn't see her, not at first. I would have had reservations about allowing a stranger into my home so late in the evening. Dennis knocked me down. He bound my arms and legs with duct tape, and left me lying on the floor while he went to the door to invite her inside." She seemed to be as incensed at having a stranger in her home as she was at being murdered.

"You didn't know this woman."

Miss Cordell shook her head. "No. Dennis called her…" She wrinkled her nose in thought. "Kitty, I think, or…"

"Tabby," Gideon said softly.

"That's it." Marcia Cordell pointed a fading and

shaking finger. "She sat in that chair over there and watched while Dennis did unspeakable things to me. She smiled, and when I screamed for help she told me that no one would hear me way out here, so far away from everyone and everything else." Her figure trembled, and she almost disappeared, as if she wanted to hide from the telling of her death. "When I cried, she asked me if I liked it. She asked me if I had always fantasized about having a young stud show up at my door to make a real woman out of me."

"She's going to pay, too," Gideon said. "I'll see to it."

Miss Cordell nodded her head. "She's the one who killed me."

"I know."

"I thought it was finally over, and then that horrible woman leaned over my body and put a knife to my belly. She…she cut me, and she enjoyed it. When she was tired of cutting, she started stabbing me and…"

Gideon listened, while Marcia Cordell told him every last detail of the way Dennis and Tabby had tortured and finally killed her. He didn't want to listen to the details, but Miss Cordell needed to tell the tale to someone who could hear her.

He listened, and then he asked, "Is there anything you can tell me about the woman? You said Dennis called her Tabby. Did he ever use a last name? Did you see what kind of vehicle she was driving? Was there anything you remember that might help me find her?"

Miss Cordell shook her head. "They left together, Dennis and that awful woman."

Which meant Dennis was likely dead, too. He couldn't imagine Tabby leaving a witness behind. "Time to go, Miss Cordell," Gideon said as he stood and looked down at her. "I promise you, I'll make sure they pay for what they did. I'll take care of them for you. Move on to the next phase of your existence and find peace. You deserve it."

"So do you," Miss Cordell whispered before she faded to nothing.

Gideon left the crime scene behind. If Dennis was still alive—unlikely, but not impossible—maybe he held the key to finding Tabby. If ever there was concrete proof that this world wasn't fit for a child, this was it.

Sheriff Webster stood by his patrol car, still working the brim of that battered hat. Gideon glanced around the overgrown yard. "Where's Detective Malory?"

"She decided to interview some of the neighbors while we were waiting for you." He nodded to a small white house down the road. It was almost a quarter of a mile away but still the closest house to Marcia Cordell's. "Detective Malory seemed to think maybe they might've seen something that night. We interviewed them all and didn't get squat, but…"

A knot of unease settled into Gideon's gut.

"Dennis Floyd drove by while we were talking and…"

The sheriff didn't get any further. Gideon turned toward the little white house and ran.

Hope glanced back toward the Cordell house. The sheriff continued to lean against his patrol car, obeying her instructions not to bother Raintree. There was no telling how long Gideon might be inside, talking to the ghost. Odd, how naturally those words came to her mind. *Talking to the ghost.*

If she could find something, any small detail, to add to what he learned, it might help. Maybe a neighbor had seen a car that night. That kind of information should have been in the report, but sometimes important facts were missed the first time around. Even if Gideon could find out who had killed the woman, they would need evidence in order to get a conviction.

"Come on in and I'll fix us some tea." Dennis Floyd was in his mid-twenties, at a guess. He was a rail-thin young man, with thinning blond hair and small, pale blue eyes. His car and his clothing had seen better years, but the house itself seemed to be well maintained. The front porch was clean, and a number of flowering plants in clay pots brightened the place considerably.

"My folks are at work," he said as he opened the screen door for her. "I used to have my own place," he added, apparently trying to impress her. "But when I was between jobs, I moved back in here. I'm workin' steady now, but the folks need a little help with the yardwork and such, so I'm doing them a favor by stayin' on."

Hope stepped into his cool, semi-dark living room. It was clean but musty, as if years of stale odors had seeped into the walls and would never wash out. There was too much clutter for her taste. The room housed too many knickknacks and ashtrays and dusty flower arrangements.

"You're investigating Miss Cordell's murder, aren't you?" Dennis asked as he walked past her.

"Yes."

He headed for the kitchen, and Hope followed. The kitchen windows were uncovered, letting in enough light to make the room cheerier than the dismal living room.

"The sheriff said the killer was some perv from out of town."

"Really? How does he know that?"

Dennis made himself busy, fetching glasses from the cupboard, filling them with ice, then taking a pitcher of tea from the fridge.

"No one around here could do such a terrible thing," he said in a lowered voice as he poured two tall glasses of iced tea. "Why, we all loved Miss Cordell."

"Did you see anything unusual that night?"

Dennis handed her a glass of tea, then leaned against the counter with his own glass in hand. "No, I don't believe I did. The sheriff asked, of course, but I didn't remember a thing that might help. Still don't, I'm afraid."

"A car that didn't belong, perhaps, or a stranger on the road?" Dennis shook his head, and Hope placed her untouched tea on the kitchen table. There was nothing of interest here, and still the hairs on her back of her neck were dancing. "Thank you for your time, Mr. Floyd. If you remember anything…"

"You know," Dennis said, straightening sharply and setting his own tea aside. "Maybe there *was* a car, now that I think about it. It passed by here, oh, about eleven o'clock or so. It was movin' real slow."

"What kind of car?"

"Fancy car, as I remember. One of them sporty cars. It was green."

Hope smiled. Dennis was lying. So she would stay a while longer? He had been leering at her, but why lie? Did he just crave the attention? Or was he curious to find out what she already knew?

Not only was this information brand-new, with no streetlamps on the narrow road, how had he been able to distinguish a color at eleven o'clock at night?

"Where were you standing," she asked, "when you saw the car on the road?"

Dennis had to take a moment to think, and to Hope's mind that proved he was lying.

"I had stepped outside to have a cigarette," he said.

Did he think she hadn't noticed the ashtrays in the living room? It wasn't necessary for him to step outside to smoke, and she knew it. But she played along. "You were in the front yard," she said.

"Yeah." He nodded. "I was in the front yard having a smoke."

"So if the green sports car had turned into Miss Cordell's driveway, you would've seen it."

He swallowed hard. "Maybe it did turn into her driveway. I can't rightly remember."

"A woman was brutally murdered, and the next morning you didn't remember that maybe you saw a car pull into her driveway?" Hope snapped.

"It was a traumatic experience," Dennis explained. "To hear that one of my favorite teachers from high school, a neighbor, had been raped and sliced up by some stranger—"

Hope very subtly moved her hand to her pistol. Sheriff Webster hadn't even told Gideon that Marcia Cordell had been sexually assaulted until they were here. He hadn't put that detail in the official report or told the newspapers, and given how protective he was of the woman's memory, odds were he hadn't started any gossip about that night, either.

With a start, Dennis realized what he'd done. He cursed, then took his glass of tea and threw it at Hope's head. She simultaneously ducked and drew her weapon. The glass flew past her head and shattered against the doorjamb behind her. Bits of broken glass, cold tea and ice cubes exploded around her.

Instead of running to the back door to escape, which was what she'd expected him to do, Dennis charged her, knocking her gun hand aside just as she fired. He grabbed her, and they both slipped on the tea and broken glass.

Hope landed on the floor hard, a struggling Dennis on top of her. She tried to bring the gun up and around, but he grabbed her wrist and pushed it away. They struggled for control of the weapon, and he was winning that struggle. For a skinny man, Dennis was strong. There were muscles in those ropey arms, and he was desperate. Only a desperate and dangerous man would do what he'd done to Marcia Cordell.

She thought of the protection charm she wore beneath her blouse, and as she fought for control, she wondered if it would do her any good at all in this particular situation.

"Did she send you after me?" Dennis asked breathlessly as he tried to take the pistol.

Was it possible that Dennis knew what Gideon could do? Did he think Marcia Cordell's ghost had given them his name?

Dennis pinned Hope to the floor with his knee and ripped the gun from her hand. One word popped into her mind, unexpected and powerful.

Emma.

Chapter 13

Gideon was halfway to the white house, running as fast as he could, when he heard the gunshot. His heart jumped into his throat.

It was hard enough to talk to the ghosts of complete strangers, people he had never seen alive, never touched, never cared about. As difficult as it was to be visited by the shells of murder victims, he'd never had to confront the battered and weary spirit of a friend—or a lover. Last night and this morning Hope had been his in a way he'd thought impossible. She knew who he was, and still she stayed. She was probably carrying his child. Probably, hell. Dante's "gift" had worked too well; it was impossible to dismiss Emma as imagination.

He didn't want to be haunted by Hope; it was too soon to lose her.

Would Emma haunt him, too?

He jumped onto the porch and burst through the front door, pistol in hand. Sounds of a struggle in the back of the house drew him there, and still at a run, he glanced into the kitchen to see a man on top of Hope. Her gun was in his hand, and he was doing his damnedest to turn it on her.

Gideon had his pistol ready, but no clear shot. Hope was holding her own, but that meant his target wasn't steady. He was rushing for Floyd in order to knock the gun away and pull him off Hope when she executed a well-planned and impressive move that simultaneously pushed the man off her and wrested the gun from his hand as her elbow slammed into his face. The entire maneuver took a few seconds, no more. With a whoosh of air and a grunt, Dennis Floyd ended up on his back, unarmed and bloody-nosed. A panting and red-faced Hope pinned him to the floor with her knee.

She lifted her head and looked at Gideon, her chest heaving with deep, quick breaths, her hair not as sleek as usual, her eyes strong and angry but also afraid. Outside, the sheriff's car pulled into the yard, and heavy footsteps sounded as the lawman made his way to the scene.

Gideon couldn't take his eyes off of Hope's face, and his heart hadn't yet slowed to a healthy pace and rhythm. He had come *this close* to losing her and Emma. He had come *this close* to being forced to bury them.

He was *this close* to asking Hope to marry him and

never again leave his sight when the clumsy sheriff blundered into the house.

Hope rose, and Gideon gladly took charge of Dennis. He hauled the little man to his feet and slammed the skinny bastard against a wall.

"Ow. Be careful of my nose," the man said, squirming. "I think she broke it."

It took all the self-control Gideon possessed to read Dennis his rights. Since he was well out of his jurisdiction, he asked the sheriff to repeat the process. At this point Dennis hadn't been charged with anything, but Gideon was taking no chance that this little man—this little monster—might get off on a technicality.

"I know what you did," Gideon said in a lowered voice.

"I...I didn't do anything," Dennis blustered.

"I don't care about you, you little pissant." Gideon pressed Dennis more forcefully against the wall. "The sheriff will take good care of you after I'm gone. I want Tabby."

Dennis swallowed hard a couple of times before answering. "I don't know anyone named Tabby." He was a very bad liar.

"Fine. Don't talk. When she finds out I've been here—and she *will* find out—I imagine she'll pay you a visit. You've seen her work, so you know what to expect when she gets her hands on you." He leaned in until his mouth was close to Dennis's ear, and he whispered, "She likes that knife of hers, doesn't she? I've run across plenty of killers who prefer a blade to a gun, but I don't think I've ever met anyone who enjoys what they do as much as Tabby does. I wonder what sort of keepsake she'll take from you, little man? What body part will she take to remember you by?"

"I just met her that day," Dennis said, his voice high and quick. "I was at the gas station, filling up and getting something cold to drink, and this woman walks up to me and says she knows what I'm thinking. I hadn't been thinking anything," Dennis said. "She put them ideas into my head."

"Bad ideas," Gideon said as he backed slightly away.

Dennis nodded. "It's true, I always did think Miss Cordell was kinda uppity, thinking she was better than everyone else...."

"You wanted to put her in her place, didn't you?" Gideon pressed Dennis harder against the wall again. "You wanted to show her who's boss."

Dennis tried to nod, but with Gideon's arm against his throat, it wasn't easy. He wanted to kill this man with his bare hands, and he could. With Hope and the sheriff watching, he could shoot the bastard or break his neck or, even better, fry his ass until there was nothing left but dust. All he had to do was allow his anger to manifest itself in a powerful jolt of electricity. He was always so careful to hide what he could do, to contain himself whenever anyone was watching. That caution had kept him from stopping Tabby when he could have, and it had kept him from using his talents on more than one murderer when they were finally in his hands. Right now, with his heart still pumping hard and the un-thinkable possibilities still too real in his mind, he didn't feel at all cautious. Gideon allowed a small shock to escape and shoot through Dennis's body.

"Ouch! What was…?"

He did it again, and Dennis began to shiver. As wound up as Gideon was, he could easily smoke this no-good waste of space and air. For Marcia Cordell. For Hope and Emma. But he didn't. Tempting as the idea was at this moment, he refused to let his anger turn him into the kind of man he'd spent his entire adult life hunting. The sheriff and the system would take good care of Dennis. And if they didn't, he could always come back.

"Tell me everything you remember about Tabby," he ordered.

The drive home had been quiet except for a few phone calls. Gideon got terrible reception on his cell, thanks to a combination of a weak signal here in the boonies and his unpredictable electrical charges, so he finally handed the phone to Hope, and she made the calls. Charlie was going to run a check on the type of car Dennis said Tabby had been driving. They still didn't have a last name for her, but maybe they could find her through the vehicle.

Hope had begun to accept that maybe, just maybe, she really was pregnant. In that moment when she'd thought she might die, when she'd expected to be shot with her own gun, the baby—or at least the possibility of the baby—had seemed very real. She'd realized she would do anything to protect Emma. What a kick in the pants that was. Hope Malory didn't have a maternal bone in her body! She liked being an aunt well enough, because she could visit her nephews and then leave when they got too rowdy or whiny. But to be a mother… She hadn't thought she was anywhere near ready, but maybe she was. Maybe.

It was after dark when they reached Gideon's house. There'd been no word from Charlie on Tabby's car, but since all they had was a make and a first name that might or might not be real, it was going to take a while. Gideon pulled into the garage and killed the engine as the garage door slowly closed behind them. He didn't immediately leave the Mustang but sat there with his gaze straight ahead and his hand resting on the steering wheel.

Hope stayed in place, too. "Do you want me to pack my stuff and leave? I know it's not a good idea for me to move back into Mom's apartment just yet, but I could—"

Gideon reached past the stick shift, grabbed the back of her head and pulled her in for a kiss. He didn't kiss her like a man who wanted her to leave. In fact, she was quite sure he had never kissed her quite this way, as if he wanted to consume her gently but entirely. When he pulled his mouth away, he did not drop his hand. "Marcia Cordell told me every vile thing that bastard did to her. At first she didn't want to talk about how she'd died, but once she got started, it seemed to do her good to get it out. She told me everything, every sick detail, and then I walk outside and the sheriff says, 'Oh, Detective Malory's down there over yonder, talking to Dennis Floyd.'"

Gideon called upon a deep and not entirely inaccurate drawl when impersonating the sheriff, and Hope laughed lightly. But she didn't laugh long.

"And I couldn't run fast enough," he said, his voice deep and soft.

"I'm not hurt." A few bruises, a lot of scary, but she wasn't really hurt.

"Not this time," he said. His thumb brushed her cheek. "But there's going to be a next time. There's going to be another Dennis, another struggle, another gunshot that makes my heart fly out of my chest. The protection charms will help, they give you an edge, and I can make sure you always have a fresh one to wear around your pretty neck. But they're not bulletproof shields, and they don't make bad guys like Dennis Floyd disappear. Dammit, Hope, I wish you'd be content to stay home and make cookies and lie on the deck under the sun and have babies and—"

"Babies?" she interrupted. "As in more than one?"

"If we're going to get married we might as well—"

"What happened to the world being too nasty to bring a child into?" she asked, only slightly panicked by the picture Gideon was painting.

"We can't go back and undo what's already done. Might as well give Emma brothers and sisters."

"Wait just a minute…"

"I didn't ask you to marry me yet, did I?" His thumb continued to caress her cheek.

"No, you didn't," she whispered.

"Marry me."

Hope licked her lips. "That's not exactly a question. It sounds more like an order."

A frustrated little moan escaped from deep in Gideon's throat. She knew this wasn't easy for him, but it wasn't easy for her, either. He was talking about marriage and children and forever. And she hadn't known him a week.

"Fine," he said. "We'll do this your way. *Will* you marry me?"

"Can I have a little time to think it over?" she asked, terrified and excited and stunned. "This is just too fast for me."

"No. You might as well learn now that I can be very impatient. I want an answer now."

It would be too easy to get caught up in this, in the way Gideon made her feel, inside and out. In the kissing and the touching and the promise of more to come. In the idea of him and Emma and babies—plural. "I never really planned to, you know, settle down and have kids and do the whole mommy thing."

"So make new plans."

If what he said about her *becoming* Raintree was true—and she had no reason to think it wasn't—she was definitely going to need a new plan.

He didn't move away but stayed close. Too close. That hand at the back of her neck was warm and strong and comforting, but she couldn't help but remember that just a few hours ago he'd been horrified at the idea of the life he was now presenting as a done deal. "If I actually said yes, you'd probably have a panic attack."

"If you say yes, I'm going to make love to you right here and now."

"In the car."

"Yep."

"With bucket seats."

He murmured in the affirmative.

Hope wrapped her arms around Gideon's neck and barely touched her lips to his. "This I gotta see."

"I think I broke something," Gideon said as he nuzzled Hope's neck. She laughed at him. He loved it when she laughed at him.

"Sex among the bucket seats was your idea, not mine."

"This is better." *This* was his bed, his woman and no clothes. It was softness and passion, boldness and demure exploration. It was a quiver and a gasp. It was the way Hope swayed and moaned when he touched her. It was the way she touched him, the way she wanted him.

He spread Hope's thighs and filled her gently. But not *too* gently.

"Nothing *seems* to be broken," she said dreamily, eyes closed and back arched.

Since he was convinced Hope was already pregnant, they hadn't bothered with a condom. Not in the car, not now. They were bare, heart and soul and body, and they were connected in a way he had never expected. Hope wanted to be his partner, and she was. In more ways than one. In all ways. In ways he had never dreamed to know.

Emma had said she was always his, in every lifetime. Maybe the same could be said of Hope. Was that why he'd felt such an undeniable and immediate pull toward her? Was that why she did not feel at all new or unknown to him?

They came together, and Hope pulled him deeper. The contractions of her body pumped him, squeezed him, and as everything slowed, she continued to sway her hips against his and hold him close.

"I love you," she said, her voice displaying exhaustion and confusion, as well as the affection she had not expected.

The words were on his lips, but he held back. He could love her this way; he could protect her as best he could and give her babies and make sure she never wanted for anything. Yes, she was undeniably his, but that didn't mean he was ready to lay it all on the line. He wasn't even sure he knew what love was anymore, but he did know that this was right. That was enough. For now.

While he was still searching for something semi-appropriate to say, he heard a trill of childish ethereal laughter. A girlish giggle, followed by a sigh and a very soft, "Told you so, Daddy." If Hope heard it, she didn't react.

He should be outraged, or at the very least surprised. But he wasn't.

"I think we've been tricked by our daughter," he said, raking a strand of black hair out of Hope's face.

Her eyes drifted open. "Tricked how?"

"You didn't get pregnant last night," he said, feeling oddly forgiving of Emma at the moment. Maybe because he was still inside Hope, satisfied and grateful and happy.

"I didn't?"

"No. You got pregnant now. Right now. Well, soon. Conception doesn't happen right away...."

Hope threaded her fingers through his hair and pulled him down for a deep, long kiss. Apparently she was feeling forgiving at the moment, too. "I know how it works, Raintree."

"Still wanna marry me?"

Without hesitation, she answered, "Yeah, I do."

Still love me? He didn't ask that question aloud. He should probably tell her that he loved her, too, or at least toss out a casual "ditto." But he didn't. The time would come when the words felt right.

Hope stroked his hair and wrapped one long leg around his, twining their limbs much as they had been earlier. She ran her foot up and down his leg.

He rose up to look down at her. "I don't want us to screw this up."

She closed her eyes and held him close. "Than let's not. Please."

There wasn't a lot to say, so they lay there, connected and touching and content. He was so rarely content.

"What you said earlier today," Hope said, her voice quick and a little shy. "I've been thinking about that."

"What did I say?" *So much...not enough...*

She raked her fingers along his neck. "Monsters."

"Oh." Not what he wanted to talk about at the moment.

"If there are monsters in the world—"

"There are, and you know it," he interrupted.

"*If* there are," she said again.

Gideon nuzzled her throat and kissed it. Now was not the time to argue.

"My mother's always talking about balance. Balance of nature, of male and female, even of good and evil. I used to dismiss that along with everything else, but she's beginning to make sense, darn it. And when you talk about monsters, I think…if the good gives up, then where will we be?"

"What's so good?"

"You," she answered without hesitation. "Us. Emma. Love. I think that's worth fighting for. I think maybe it's worth the occasional battle with a monster."

He fought monsters because it was his calling. His destiny. He didn't want his family to have to fight with him, but it was apparently the price he would have to pay in order to keep them.

Tabby sat in her apartment and carefully studied the package on the counter in the kitchenette. She disliked bombs. Not only were they unpredictable, they made it impossible for her to be close enough to drink in the fear of her victims. One minute they were alive, the next they were gone. No power, no souvenirs.

But she couldn't be picky at the moment. Time was running out.

She couldn't fail. Maybe she'd missed Echo, but Gideon was the one Cael thought of as most important to her mission. He was next in line for Dranir, a member of the royal family. He was a powerful Raintree, and his execution was necessary. Echo would be hers soon enough.

This bomb wouldn't kill Raintree, but it would draw him into the open. She would be waiting.

It was possible that Cael would still consider her mission a failure, since she hadn't killed Echo first, as planned. If her cousin were anyone else in the world, she would simply run from him when the time came. She could change her looks, change her name and take up where she'd left off. Training for this assignment had been more pleasurable than she'd imagined. It was a big country, filled with lonely people who would not be missed and sadistic little men who never dared to act on their own but were wonderfully violent when prodded.

She had become very good at prodding. If Cael didn't kill her for missing Echo, she would continue with her work after the battle was over. Maybe he would be so pleased by the act she was about to commit that he would even forgive her.

As long as she delivered Gideon Raintree's head to Cael—figuratively speaking, unfortunately—all would be well.

When she woke in Gideon's bed alone, Hope thought for a moment that it had all been a dream. Emma, Dennis, bucket seats and her foolishly uttered *I love you*. None of it was real.

But she realized soon enough that none of it had been a dream. The drapes were open, which meant Gideon was on the deck or the beach. Since it was morning, there wouldn't be a light show of any kind. Pity.

She went to the bathroom, brushed her teeth and pulled on one of Gideon's old T-shirts. It hung almost to her knees. He'd already made coffee—a quarter of the pot was gone—so she poured herself a cup and joined him on the deck. A few people were already on the beach, walking along the sand and getting their feet wet in the gentle waves.

Gideon was standing at the railing, looking out to the ocean as if he drew strength from it. Maybe he did. There was so much she didn't know about the man she had fallen in love with. Last night in bed they had laughed and made love, but this morning Gideon was serious again. His face looked as if it could be set in stone, it was so hard and unforgiving.

She knew the heart beneath that hard exterior. Hard? Sometimes. Unforgiving? Yes, when forgiveness wasn't appropriate. Nonexistent? Never.

"What's wrong?" she asked, leaning on the rail beside him.

He didn't dance around the issue. "I want you to quit work, and I don't think you will."

"You're right," she said. "At least, not any time soon. I need a little time to adjust to all this. Things have happened pretty fast."

"That's an understatement."

She leaned her head against his arm and rested there, her eyes on the ocean. "I'm a cop—just like you, Gideon. I'm not giving it up to have babies and knit and make cookies and wait at home while you do what you do. Cops have kids just like everyone else. We'll make it work."

"You'll distract me."

"So learn to deal with it."

"Why should I learn to deal with it when I have more than enough money for you to quit?"

"If money had anything to do with it, you wouldn't be doing the job, either. What we do is about more than a paycheck."

His lips thinned slightly, and then he said, "I know you think you're like every other cop, but you're not. You're mine, and I don't want to lose you."

"I'm tough," she said.

"You're fragile."

"I am not," she argued.

"Precious things are always fragile."

She didn't have an immediate response, since he'd stolen her breath away with that statement. *Precious* was not a word she'd thought he could ever speak, and yet he'd used it, however reluctantly.

He added, as if to turn her mind away from the subject, "In the beginning, I slept with you so you'd request a transfer."

"I know," she said without rancor.

"We've just upped the ante, Moonbeam. You can't be my partner anymore, and I don't trust you with anyone else."

Hope took a sip of her coffee. "Let's don't fight, not today."

His stony expression relaxed just a bit. "I thought you said I was cute when I got mad."

She laughed. "You are. I still don't want to fight with you today."

"Why not?"

The truth. Nothing but the truth. "Right now I feel too good, and I don't want to spoil it."

He wrapped an arm around her. "There are gifts that come with giving birth to a Raintree baby, gifts that are a part of being Raintree. You'll heal faster, live longer, be healthier. You and whatever children we make will have protection charms, I'll see to that. And still, if I could, I would lock you up in a place where you'd always be safe. A place where no one could ever hurt you or Emma."

"Exactly where is that place, Gideon?"

He didn't answer, because there *was* no answer; there was no such place.

"Besides," she said, "I have to help you put Frank Stiles away. Knowing is fine, but we need evidence."

He seemed perfectly willing to turn the conversation toward business. His business of stopping monsters. "There's not any. He burned the house down after he killed Johnny Ray Black. We've got no evidence."

"Then we need a confession or a witness."

"I haven't been able to obtain either."

She smiled at him. "You haven't given me a chance to try yet. I'm very good at getting confessions."

He almost smiled. "I just bet you are."

She stared out at the ocean, drinking in the beauty of it as if she, too, could literally absorb its power through her skin. How could this place already feel like home? Not the house, not the beach. Gideon. Gideon Raintree was home.

It was an oddly comforting and frightening thought, very much like the prospect of motherhood and all that would come with it.

Chapter 14

They were getting nowhere fast with the info on the vehicle Tabby had been driving four months ago. Gideon had left Charlie following up that information, trying to wring something useful from it, and then he'd headed here.

The motel room where Lily Clark had been killed had been sealed off. No one but the crime scene investigators had been in this room since she'd been murdered. Her spirit stood in the corner of the room, solid and angry.

Hope insisted that she didn't have any unnatural powers of any sort, and yet she stood back and rubbed her arms as if warding off a chill on this warm day. She sensed the anger and sadness here; she still felt the violence.

"You said you were going to get her," Lily said, so furious that her image flickered.

"I'm working on it," Gideon said softly.

Hope stood behind him, just a few feet away, listening. He had to admit that it was nice not to have to hide what he could do. It was nice to be able to talk to Lily without tricking his partner into leaving the room or pretending to be talking to himself.

"Tabby was in this room for a long time," Hope said gently. "Knowing she killed Lily Clark is one thing, but we need physical evidence. There has to be something. She must've left some kind of clue behind."

"She's careful," Gideon said as he paced at the end of the bed.

"She left a hair at the Sherry Bishop scene. She left a *witness* at the Marcia Cordell site, and that's downright sloppy. There must be something here as well." Hope walked deeper into the room. "All the crime scene techs found were a few fibers that could have been here for days. Weeks, even. This isn't exactly the cleanest motel in town. Tabby must have touched a surface she forgot to wipe down or left something behind or…"

"She took a shower after I was dead," Lily said gently, her anger fading. "She had to, because my blood was all over her. On her face and in her hair and on her clothes…I think she liked it…."

"What did she do with her bloody clothes?" Gideon asked.

"I don't know."

Gideon nodded to Hope. "My cell phone is all but useless to me today." Tomorrow was the summer solstice, and his electrical surges were coming more frequently than usual. "Call Charlie and have him get the crime scene techs in here to check the shower drain. Today," he added forcefully.

Hope pulled out her own cell phone and made the call, and Gideon walked closer to Lily Clark's much-too-solid image. "You can find those clothes for us," he said. "Your blood, a part of you, is there, and if you concentrate, you can find them. I can't guarantee that the clothes will lead us to the woman who killed you, but it's a possibility."

"I don't know how to do that," the ghost whispered.

"You can see so much more now, if you try. Think about that night. Remember what happened after. You watched Tabby walk out that door."

"Yes," Lily whispered. "I screamed at her, but she didn't hear me. I tried to stop her, but I couldn't do anything."

"Did she have the clothes with her? Were they wadded up or stuffed in a bag or—"

"She was wearing my favorite dress," Clark whined. She seemed to view that as just another indignity. "What nerve."

"What about the clothes she was wearing when she killed you? Did she have them with her when she left?"

Lily cocked her head and turned her mind back to that night, even though she undoubtedly wanted nothing more than to forget. Maybe when this was done and she moved on she *would* forget. No one should carry such painful memories with them for eternity. "No," she said thoughtfully. "All she was carrying was her purse. The knife was in it, freshly washed and wrapped in one of my nightgowns, and there wasn't room in that purse for her clothes, too. She loved that knife," the spirit added. "She touched it like it was alive."

Gideon turned to Hope, who had just ended her phone call. "The clothes are here somewhere."

"The room was searched," she said.

Gideon walked into the bathroom. "Lily, did Tabby ever carry those bloody clothes out of this bathroom? After she had that shower, did she bring the clothes back out?"

The ghost shook her head, and Gideon glanced up at the tiles in the ceiling.

It would take a few days to get solid evidence from the clothes and the towel Gideon had found hidden above the ceiling tiles, but it was a step. They didn't expect Tabby would have her name and address stitched into the clothes she'd worn, but at least they had something concrete, and there was bound to be recoverable DNA. All they needed was Tabby in custody so a match could be made.

They'd hit a dead end with the vehicle, which was all they'd gotten out of Dennis Floyd—who was locked up in a Hale County jail, still terrified that Tabby would find him, somehow. No blue Taurus in North Carolina was registered to anyone named Tabby or Tabitha, and none of the Catherines were a match. They would now begin searching all females, but damn, it was a long list.

Hope didn't think they had that kind of time before Tabby struck again.

Gideon pulled the Mustang to the curb in front of The Silver Chalice, and Hope leaned over to kiss him briefly. "Be here by seven, if you can," she said, and then she smiled. "Sunny is a better cook than I am, so you're going to have to learn to grab a good meal when you get the chance."

"Are we going to tell them the news over peach cobbler?" Gideon asked.

"Not yet." Hope wasn't sure how to tell her mother and her sister that she was going to marry this man she'd met on Monday. And as for Emma, there was no logical explanation. Not that her mother had ever required logic for anything.

Gideon nodded, visibly relieved. Maybe he wasn't ready for explanations, either. "I'll be back by seven." He was going to the station to help Charlie with the vehicle search, unable to give up just yet. Unable to rest. She supposed that was something she would have to learn to live with.

"Sure you don't want me to tag along?"

"It's Saturday, and you need some time to visit with your sister before she heads for home."

"Yeah, partners or not, it's not like we're joined at the hip or anything." So why did she hate the very idea of watching him drive away? Tabby had been quiet for a couple of days. It was possible, even probable, that she'd left town after she'd stabbed Gideon. If she had a brain in her head, she'd run that very night. Gideon had seen her, and so had Hope. Hope wasn't so sure Tabby's brain worked in any logical manner; however, anything was possible.

Even if Tabby was still around, Raintree could take care of himself. So could she. They both had protection charms, weapons and better-than-average instincts. Her eyes flitted to the building across the street.

"They're still there," Gideon said.

"For how long?"

"Until we catch Tabby or have proof that she's out of the picture."

"I'd rather catch her."

"Me, too."

He kissed her again, and she exited the Mustang. The Silver Chalice was busy, as it often was on a Saturday afternoon. Tourists and regulars perused the items for sale, and there was a class of some kind going on in a back room. Meditation, vibrational healing…things Hope had always dismissed as nonsense.

She was able to look at the people in her mother's shop with new eyes today. Maybe they knew something she didn't. Maybe they saw or heard or touched things that had always been invisible to her, the way Gideon did.

An upside-down world wasn't as unsettling as she'd imagined it might be. In fact, she was finding it more comforting than she'd thought possible.

* * *

Tabby slung the big purse off her shoulder and set it down behind a display of copper bells, partially hidden behind a book rack. This corner of the store was crowded with merchandise and was also unoccupied at the moment.

Normally she wouldn't spend a second longer than was necessary in this place. The people here sought positive energy and were, for the most part, peaceful and calm. There was no power for Tabby in being in their company. She took no joy in this place, and in fact, it made her a little antsy. Still, she could hardly run into the shop, drop off the bomb and run out again, so she pretended to be interested in the merchandise.

She glanced up when the door opened with the jingling of a bell and smiled when she saw Raintree's woman walk in. Well, this would be a nice bonus.

Even though the cop had chased her down the river-front, Tabby didn't fear being spotted here today. She was wearing a short dark wig and a baggy dress that disguised her shape. She stooped to diminish her height. There would be nothing familiar about her even if the cop noticed her. In any case, the woman wasn't even suspicious. At the moment the detective was happy to the point of distraction.

Tabby felt that happiness the same way she was able to feel fear and horror, but she took no pleasure or strength from it. She did, however, take pleasure in knowing that happiness would be short-lived.

She walked away, leaving her oversized purse behind.

* * *

It was tough to help when getting too near the computer wasn't wise, but Gideon tried. He looked at the vehicular records Charlie had printed out, and he scanned driver's license photos until the faces all started to blur. Maybe Tabby's name wasn't Tabby after all. Maybe the car had been stolen from another state and the tags switched, and had been recovered or burned by now. Whatever the reason, he was getting nowhere.

He sent Charlie home with thanks and the promise of a get-together at the beach house, and sat down with the files of the unsolved murders that might or might not be Tabby's work. Some cases came together quickly. Murderers weren't usually the brightest colors in the box, and they left massive amounts of evidence behind. Tabby, if that was indeed her name, didn't. She wiped down doorknobs; she cleaned up after herself. Dennis Floyd and the bloody clothes from the hotel and a couple of hairs were all they had. And none of those would do any good unless—until—they caught her. When they *did* catch her, all that evidence would be enough to put her away forever.

His cell phone rang, and since there was no one else around to answer for him, he did it himself. The caller ID listed a Charlotte number, which meant it was likely Echo. She probably wanted to know if it was safe for her to come home. She was going to have a fit when he told her no.

There was so much static on the line that he could barely hear her. She was frantic, that much was clear, and he heard one word clearly. *Dream.* He told her to call him again on the land line in his office. Obviously she'd had a prophetic dream that alarmed her. He'd calmed her down a hundred times, after disturbing prophesies.

He couldn't help but feel sorry for her. At least he could do something with his abilities. There were many times when it seemed as if it would never be enough, but he did make a difference. Echo couldn't, not without advertising what she could do to the public. The Raintree *never* advertised their abilities. Besides, how did you stop a disaster when the warning always came so close to the event? Minutes, sometimes. No more than an hour in most cases. Maybe, if she worked at honing her skills, the warnings would come with more lead time, but Echo was determined *not* to hone her skills.

If Emma's talents took such a sad turn, would he want her to practice so that every dream was filled with horror?

The phone on his desk rang, and he answered, "Raintree."

"I took a nap," Echo said without preamble. "I just... fell asleep on the couch, you know, and I had this dream. I don't understand this one, Gideon. It's not like the others."

"Tell me about it," he said, remaining calm.

"There was an explosion. I couldn't see where it was, but there were people," she said in a low, shaking voice. "Lots of people. They didn't know it was coming. One minute they were happy and laughing, and then... There was so much blood, and there was fire, and people were screaming...."

The odds were that it was already too late to help anyone, but he had to try. "Calm yourself and think back. There had to be a hint in the dream as to where this explosion took place. Just take a deep breath and go there, Echo. You can do it." Whether she wanted to or not, she *could* do it.

He heard her take that deep breath. "It doesn't make sense," she said, only slightly calmer. "It wasn't just people, Gideon. I mean, there were lots of people, and they were cut and burned. But the sun exploded, a big bright rainbow faded into nothing and disappeared, and the moon broke apart into a million tiny pieces...."

"I know what that means!" Gideon slammed down the phone, lifted it again and dialed The Silver Chalice. Normally he would call on the run, but his damned cell phone wouldn't do for this call. Not today. He couldn't take the chance that he would get cut off, or that Hope wouldn't be able to understand. Rainbow answered, and his heart almost returned to a normal rhythm. He wasn't too late. "This is Gideon. I need to talk to Hope."

"Hope's around here somewhere," Rainbow Malory said casually. "I just saw her looking at some new..."

"This is an emergency," Gideon interrupted. "I want you to get everyone out of the shop."

"But—"

"Now."

He hated to do this, but he had no choice. "There's a bomb in your store." Then he slammed down the phone and ran out of the office. He had other phone calls to make, but he would have to make do with the cell, interference or not.

From her seat by the window at the café across the street from The Silver Chalice, Tabby muttered a curse word as people began to stream out of the shop. Even from here, she could tell they were afraid and confused. She saw *and* felt it. Someone had found the bomb.

That didn't mean it wouldn't go off, or that she wouldn't still have Gideon Raintree right where she wanted him, but it would have been nice to have a few fireworks to enjoy before things got under way. Panic was always so lovely to enjoy, and the terror of hearing *bomb* as opposed to the terror that came from actually experiencing it were very different sensations.

She studied the people who streamed from the shop, waiting for the female cop to show. The stream of people turned into a trickle, and the woman wasn't among them. Tabby heard sirens in the near distance. Gideon Raintree was no doubt right behind the responding emergency vehicles. He might even get here before them.

Tabby took more than enough cash to pay for her coffee from the deep pocket of her oversized dress and placed it on the table. Then, with the tabletop shielding her hands from view, she removed the knife from the leather scabbard at her thigh and slipped it into her pocket, where it would be handy. Not that she was likely to need it. Much as she loved to work with her blade, she had a much more efficient weapon stashed in the back stairwell of the building across the street.

Ready for Raintree once again, determined to complete her task here and now, Tabby stood and headed outside.

The woman who owned The Silver Chalice stood on her tiptoes and searched the crowd, no doubt looking for her daughter. Tabby smiled. Maybe she would get that bonus after all.

Hope had intended just to change clothes, but her bed had looked so good that she'd fallen into it for a quick nap. After all, she hadn't exactly had lots of sleep this week. She fell asleep easily, snug in her familiar bed, warmed to her bones in a way she hadn't been warmed in a very long time.

She dreamed of Gideon and the beach, and of a dark-haired little girl who had a really great laugh. They were pleasant dreams, untouched by the stress of her job or any uncertainty about the future. There were no monsters here, not of the human variety, not of any variety.

Precious. Gideon thought she was precious. Whether he said so or not, that was love.

A door slammed, interrupting her pleasant dream of sand and laughter, and she heard Gideon calling her name. His voice was unnecessarily sharp, and it took her a moment to realize that what she heard wasn't a part of her dream.

Hope opened her eyes as he rushed into the room. "Is it seven already?" she asked as she sat up and stretched her arms over her head.

"I think there's a bomb downstairs," he said crisply. "Let's go." He didn't wait for her to respond but half lifted and half dragged her from the bed.

"I need my shoes," she protested, still muddled from sleep.

"No time," he responded, leading her toward the door that opened onto the stairway to the shop.

She was half-asleep, still fuzzy-brained and confused, and she wanted to collect her shoes and her purse and maybe an answer or two. "What do you mean, you *think* there's a bomb?" That didn't make any sense at all. There either was a bomb or there wasn't.

"Echo had a dream." Gideon's jaw clenched, and a muscle twitched there.

"I wondered how you found out about the bomb so fast."

They both spun to face the woman who stood by the kitchen door. She held a semiautomatic pistol in one hand, and with the other she removed a dark wig and shook out the long blond strands of her hair. Tabby was armed differently today, and she didn't look at all inclined to run.

Gideon had one hand on the doorknob to the stairwell, the other gripping Hope's arm. He smoothly placed his body in front of hers.

"Gideon Raintree," Tabby said with a crooked smile. "This isn't exactly what I'd planned, but I can't say I'm disappointed. When I saw the bomb squad arrive I was disappointed, because I'd hoped to have a little time with your girlfriend before you showed up. Still, I suppose this will do."

Gideon dropped Hope's arm and pushed her aside as he smoothly drew his weapon. Her own weapon was in the other room, resting on the bedside table. She'd never thought she might need it here, and in an instant she understood the violation Sherry Bishop and Marcia Cordell and all the other victims had felt when Tabby had entered their homes.

Tabby's aim never wavered. Her smile barely faded as she glanced at Gideon's weapon. "Shoot me and you'll never find out where the second bomb is, or when it's scheduled to go boom."

Chapter 15

"What do you want?" Gideon tried to ease Hope toward the door, doing his best to place himself between the two women.

"First thing, I want you and your girlfriend away from that door."

"She's my partner, not my girlfriend," Gideon said, knowing a close connection to him was a very bad idea at this particular moment.

"Liar," Tabby said. "I can feel the connection rolling off both of you like the tide outside your window."

Apparently the blonde had seen him and Hope together. She knew where he lived, too, which was more than a little disturbing. "You don't need her," Gideon said as he took a step toward Tabby.

"You don't know what I need, Raintree," Tabby snapped. "If your girl tries to leave before I say she can go, not only will I shoot her, I'll make sure you don't know where the second bomb is until it's too late."

He took another step toward the woman with the gun. "I'll ask you one more time. What do you want?"

"I want both of you dead by the end of the day, and I want Echo. Where the hell is she?"

"You want Echo?" Gideon said calmly. "Is that all? Give me the location of the second bomb and we'll talk."

Tabby held the gun as if she were comfortable with it, as if she'd been in this very position many times before. "You'd give up your cousin so easily?"

He needed her to believe that he would trade his cousin's life in order to save many others, so he remained calm as he answered, "Yes. For the bomb and Hope, you can have her."

"You're cold," Tabby said. "Sensible and predictably noble, but cold. Stop right there, and very carefully put that gun on the floor."

Lily Clark took shape beside Tabby and swiped vainly at the woman who had killed her. "There's not another bomb. Don't listen to her, Gideon! She's trying to trick you. She tricked me, and she tricked other people, too. I know that now. Don't let her trick you."

Did Lily know something he didn't, or was it a guess? Maybe there wasn't another bomb, but he couldn't be sure.

"None of this will make any difference if we don't

hurry up," Gideon said as he dipped down to place his pistol on the floor. "How long before the bomb downstairs goes off?" He wanted to know how much time he had to get Hope out of here, if the bomb squad didn't get the device neutralized. They were in the building working on the bomb at this very moment; he heard male voices and the hum of motorized equipment downstairs.

"We have a few minutes," Tabby said, flipping her hair in a caricature of girlishness. "Long enough for us to finish our business. Much as I would love to spend a little time with you and your girl, I need to hurry. I have a party to go to tonight, and I want to make myself extra special pretty."

Gideon knew there was a rarely used back stairway that was kept locked, except when Rainbow took the trash to the Dumpster in the alleyway. Obviously Tabby had entered the building that way. She could have shot them both in the back when she'd come out of the kitchen. They wouldn't have known she was there until it was too late. Why hadn't she? Why was she so intent on dragging out the confrontation?

And where the hell was the team he'd hired to keep an eye on this place? Dammit, someone should know Tabby was here. They should have been watching all the entrances to the building, locked or not.

The fact remained: if Tabby simply wanted him dead, he would already be dead.

"Let's finish our business, then." He could take Tabby down with one motion; he just needed her to move the weapon aside so Hope wouldn't take a bullet if the automatic weapon the blonde was holding went off when she went down.

The psycho reached into the roomy pocket of her dress and drew out the knife she'd used to kill Sherry Bishop and Lily Clark and so many others. So that was the way of it. She wanted him dead, but not quickly and not from a distance. He could use that to get himself closer, to make sure Hope wasn't harmed in any way.

"Tell me why," Gideon said as he took a step forward. Since he was unarmed and she had two weapons, Tabby didn't feel threatened, and she didn't tell him to step back or stop moving forward.

"Who cares why?" Lily Clark said frantically, jumping up and down. "Just kill her! Don't let her get away with this."

Gideon turned his gaze to the ghost. Lily was strong. She had the power to affect this reality if she tried hard enough. If she wanted it badly enough. "I need you to move that weapon aside."

"I'm not moving anything," Tabby said, not yet realizing that Gideon wasn't speaking to her. Lily didn't realize it yet, either.

"I need you to shift the barrel of that gun away from me and Hope."

Clark's eyes went wide, and her figure shimmered. "Me?"

"Yes, you."

Tabby finally put two and two together. "You're not talking to me, are you? Well, good luck. I've killed a lot of people. I've even felt like maybe their ghosts were watching me. But none of them ever laid a hand on me. You know why? They can't. They're *dead*. All that's left when I'm done is a pitiful spit of energy that can't do anything but moan and cry to you. They're pathetic."

Lily's misty hand reached for Tabby's gun and wafted through it without creating so much as a wobble.

"I don't feel anyone trying to move my gun," Tabby said, brandishing the weapon almost wildly. "See? I'm in control here. No ghost is going to touch me *or* my weapon." She quit jiggling the pistol and took aim at Hope. "I want to feel you die in my hands, Raintree. I don't care about her. She can die right here and now."

Gideon threw himself between Hope and the gun just as Lily finally made contact. The ghost's misty hand grabbed the barrel and shoved upward. A surprised Tabby lost control of the weapon. It swung wildly up and then to the side, and a bullet slammed harmlessly and loudly into the ceiling before Lily managed to knock the weapon from Tabby's hand.

The pistol hit the floor and skittered away, coming to rest half beneath the sofa. Hope ran toward the weapon to retrieve it, while Gideon lifted his hand and directed a bolt of electricity at Tabby before she could reach for the pistol she'd lost. He could fry her heart from this distance, but he didn't want her dead. Not yet.

Was there a second bomb or not? He had to know. The bolt he let loose knocked Tabby backward and to the floor, where she landed hard. But she didn't lose her grip on the knife.

"What the hell was that?" she asked breathlessly as

she looked up at Gideon. "They didn't tell me you could do that."

"Who's *they*, Tabby?" If she wasn't working alone, then this wasn't over by a long shot.

"Wouldn't you like to know?"

Gideon dragged the blonde to her feet and wrested the knife out of her hand, tossing it away. She tried to fight but was weakened by the electricity he'd called upon to stop her. Hope held on to Tabby's weapon and fetched her own pistol. She stood more beside than behind him, her own pistol pointed unwaveringly at Tabby.

"Where's the other bomb?" he asked.

Tabby just smiled, and he gave her a small jolt to remind her of what he could do. "I can stop your heart with one jolt," he said quietly. "I can pop you with more electricity than your brain can handle. Don't think I won't."

"Go ahead. I have worse waiting for me if I walk out of here and leave you alive. Besides, we're going up in a big boom any minute now. Tick-tock. Tick-tock." She grinned at him. "Afraid?" She closed her eyes and took a long, deep breath, inhaling deeply and holding it.

"Hope, check on the bomb squad," Gideon said without turning to look at her. "If they don't have the device neutralized, get out of the building."

She edged to the door. "I'll get a status report, but I'm not walking out of here without you."

"Don't be stupid."

Hope left the room without responding, leaving Gideon alone with Tabby. "How touching," she whispered, opening her eyes once again. "What are you planning to do, Raintree? Get married and make little freaks? Settle down and pretend you're just any old cop? Good luck. Even if…well, let's just say it's never gonna happen, and we both know it."

He ignored her attempt to distract him. "Where's the other bomb?"

"Wouldn't you like to know?"

"It's in your best interest to cooperate, Tabby. Is that your real name?" he asked almost casually. "Tabby?"

The woman didn't answer. She worked her mouth oddly, and before Gideon realized what she was up to, she bit into something she'd had hidden in her mouth. Instantly her body bucked and her eyes rolled back in her head. A few seconds later, she went slack.

Gideon muttered every foul word he knew as he dragged Tabby from the room. Hope met him on the stairs. "The bomb was a simple mechanism, and it's already been disabled. What happened?"

"Tabby had some kind of poison hidden in her mouth, and when she realized she wasn't going to get away, she bit into it. Dammit!" Considering the almost paralyzing dust she'd thrown into his face, he should have seen this coming. He needed to know about the other bomb. He also wanted to know what she'd meant when she talked about "them." Were there others out there who knew what he could do? For all he knew, there was someone around the corner waiting to take her place.

"Is she dead?"

"Not yet." If she was dead, her spirit would be here, hounding him still.

"Did she tell you where the second bomb was?"

"No. I don't know when or where, or even if the bomb is real."

An ambulance was already on the scene, and the paramedics rushed forward as the three of them hurried from the building. Gideon didn't know what Tabby had taken, so he couldn't be much help. He did warn the EMTs to keep her restrained, in case she did come to. Anyone in her path was likely to end up dead if she woke up.

Gideon spotted one of the private security guards he'd hired to watch The Silver Chalice and the apartment above. He made his way roughly through the crowd of cops and onlookers, and grabbed the man by the collar, slamming him against the wall. "Where the hell were you?"

The kid didn't put up a fight. "While everyone was rushing out of the store, a woman's purse got snatched. She screamed, and people were running and talking about a bomb. It was a mess, and I was distracted. I'm sorry."

"Where's the other guard?" Gideon asked. "I specifically asked for *two* people to be on duty at all times."

The kid—and he really was just a kid—paled. "Joe went to the hospital in the first ambulance. He was checking the perimeter of the building, and a woman out back stabbed him in the gut. He was hurting, but he was able to tell the officers what happened before the ambulance left. The paramedics said he'll be all right."

Gideon released the boy and shook off his anger, running agitated fingers through his hair and turning away.

Hope was talking to her mother, maybe making explanations or offering daughterly, calming words. When their eyes met, she placed a hand on her mother's arm, patted it gently and then walked away, heading for Gideon.

He wrapped his arms around her and held on as they met, not caring who was watching or what they thought.

"I love you," he whispered.

"Love you, too," she said comfortably, as if she'd already accepted everything. Their love, Emma, who and what he was, who and what she would become. Amazing, for a woman who just a few days ago had admitted without reservation that she didn't believe in anything she couldn't see or touch.

"Let's go home," she said as she smoothed a wayward strand of hair from his cheek. "We can leave word for the hospital to call us if Tabby wakes up. Or if she doesn't. I just want to go home."

There was such longing in her voice as she said the word. Home. His house. Their house. "Yeah. I just have one thing to do first."

He released Hope and turned to face what was left of Lily Clark's ghost. She was fading at last. "Thanks."

The spirit smiled at him, almost shyly. "I did help, didn't I?"

"I couldn't have done it without you."

The justice she'd demanded had been done, but Lily wasn't quite ready to go. Her smile faded. "If she dies, will she be there? Where I'm going? Will I have to face her all over again?"

Gideon didn't have to ask who *she* was. "No. Tabby's

going to another place." He didn't know where or how, and didn't want to, but he knew for sure that Lily wouldn't be seeing her killer again.

Lily glanced up as she began to fade away. "They're so proud of you," she said, her voice growing distant.

"Who?"

"Your mom and dad. They're so…" Lily Clark didn't fade. She simply disappeared with a small and distinct pop that only Gideon heard.

How odd, that this house was home. Not her mother's apartment, not the house she'd grown up in, not her Raleigh apartment where she'd lived for years. Here.

The hospital had called not five minutes after they'd walked into the house. Tabby was dead. They knew from the remains of the capsule in her mouth and the way she'd died that it was a poison of some kind that had killed her, but they hadn't yet identified the toxin. It could be days before they knew exactly what it was.

Hope planned to call the lab on Monday morning and harass them about the dust Tabby had thrown into Gideon's face. Maybe the two drugs were related somehow.

Gideon was distracted. He'd undressed her slowly and made love to her without saying a word. Tonight he didn't cheat. He didn't arouse her with caresses colored with lightning or make her come with a touch of his hand. He just pushed inside her body and stroked until she climaxed hard, and then he found his own release in her. He did still glow in the dark a little, though, her own personal flashlight.

Eventually the warm glow faded, and he pulled her body against his and held on tight. If not for his breathing and the way one hand occasionally caressed her, she would have thought he had fallen asleep. But he hadn't. He was nowhere near sleep. She felt it; she knew it because she knew *him*.

"You can tell me anything, Gideon," she whispered. "What are you thinking about right now?"

At first she thought he was going to ignore her, and then he answered, "I never saw my parents."

"What do you…?"

"After they died. I never saw their ghosts. Everywhere I turned, there were spirits, but not theirs. Never theirs. I was so mad at them for not coming back. For a while I was mad at everybody."

She stroked his face with her fingertips.

"I started to get into trouble not long after they were murdered." He lifted his hands, studying them as if they weren't his at all but those of a stranger, hands he didn't know or understand. "Think about it. No security system or lock is going to stop me from getting to what I want. No jail is going to hold me. With enough lightning I can pop any lock. I would make a fine thief, and for a while I was so furious with the world that I almost went there."

He might not know that such a thing never would have happened, but she did. Gideon was one of the good guys. Heart and soul. "What stopped you?"

"My brother. My sister. Knowing that maybe, just maybe, even though I couldn't see my parents, they could still see me."

"You made that choice a long time ago, Gideon. Why are you thinking about it now?"

"Something Lily Clark said before she moved on, about my parents being proud of me, as if…as if she'd spoken to them. Maybe she did. And you. You have me thinking about things I haven't faced yet. Emma…I don't even know where to start there."

Hope led his hand to her bare stomach, where it rested comfortably. "You're going to teach our daughter everything your parents taught you. Whatever she can do, whatever her gifts, you will always know the right way to teach her." She grinned. "And I'm going to teach her how to shoot a gun, along with a vast repertoire of self-defense maneuvers."

Gideon kissed her. In the deep silence, music drifted into the room. Honey and the brunette bimbo next door were having a party tonight, and they had their stereo cranked up high. They could hear bursts of laughter, too, as the party got more earnestly under way.

Gideon pulled his mouth from hers and sat up quickly. "Party. Tabby said she was going to a party tonight. You don't think…"

"It's Saturday night, Gideon. There are lots of parties going on." So far they hadn't had word of another explosion. Maybe there wasn't another bomb and Tabby *had* been bluffing.

Gideon slid from the bed and reached for his clothes. "I'm going to walk over there and look around, just in case. She mentioned the surf outside my window, so I have to believe she knew all along where I live. If Tabby did plant a bomb there earlier in the day, it would probably be under the house."

"I'll come with you."

"No." He leaned over and kissed her. "You stay here. I'll be right back." He exited by way of the bedroom door, stepping onto the deck and into the moonlight.

Hope fell back against the pillows and closed her eyes, but there was no way she could possibly sleep. After a few minutes she left the bed and pulled on one of Gideon's T-shirts, then stepped out onto the deck herself. Leaning against the rail, she looked across the way to the crowded deck next door, which was well lit by the fading sun and the colorful lanterns the women had strung across the deck. It was very festive, and very foreign. Hope had never been a party girl. She'd always been too serious, too concerned about what was right and proper.

Young and beautiful members of both sexes, most of them in bathing suits even though they didn't look to be going anywhere near the water, drank beer and danced and laughed on the crowded deck. Hope couldn't see Gideon from here, but then, she could only see a small portion of the house from this vantage point. She couldn't see the front of the house, or the entrance to the area under it where Gideon would check for a bomb—just in case Tabby hadn't been bluffing.

Honey had one arm wrapped around a too-thin young man with longish blond hair and a killer tan. The brunette bimbo was similarly engaged. She and her young man were dancing. They were tanned and dressed in bright colors, and they'd probably spent hours on their seemingly casual hairstyles.

The life those women led was entirely alien to Hope. Had she ever been so young? Had she ever smiled that way, without a thought beyond which CD to play next? No. Never. Most of the people on the deck were the same way. They smiled as if they didn't have a care in the world. They danced and touched and kissed and laughed.

She'd never had that before, but in an unexpected way she had it now. Maybe her party was just a party of two—or perhaps three—but Gideon Raintree made her laugh. There were moments when he made her feel absolutely giddy. He made her truly happy, for the first time in her adult life.

Hope studied the partygoers as she waited for Gideon to return. One blond woman, wearing a short, colorful dress well-suited for the beach, stood alone by the rail, much as Hope did, and turned toward Gideon's house as if she knew she was being watched. Seeing Hope, the woman lifted her hand and waved, fluttering her fingers. Hope's heart stuttered, and her knees went weak.

Tabby.

Chapter 16

If a bomb had been planted at Honey's house, it was likely either under the house—perhaps under the deck—or in the garage. Gideon walked around the house, checked out the garage, then opened the hatch that led under the house through a half door. It didn't take fifteen minutes to discern that there was nothing out of the ordinary here. Maybe Lily Clark had been right and Tabby's talk of a second bomb had been nothing but a bluff.

Gideon didn't head straight for home but walked toward the ocean. Sunset and the brief period of half light that followed was a beautiful time of day, peaceful and powerful. If not for the thirty or so people crowded onto Honey's deck, he would reenergize himself here and now. He would reach for the power that was uniquely his and drink it in. Even though many of the partygoers were already drunk, it was a chance he couldn't take. Someone might see, and that was risky.

Maybe one day he would buy himself an island and build a house for his family, a house so isolated that he could recharge whenever he felt like it, and no monsters would dare to come near him or Hope or Emma. In many ways it was a comforting idea, but could he do that? Could he literally hide away?

No, he couldn't, and neither could Hope. Somehow they were going to have to make it work in the real world, with bad guys and heartbreak and uncertainty.

He turned toward home, and Honey—dressed in a bikini top and a scarf worn like a skirt—waved at him. "Come on over!" she called.

Gideon shook his head. "I can't. Sorry."

She gave him an exaggerated pout, and someone else on the crowded deck began to wave at him. Another blonde. Tabby's ghost.

Crap, she looked solid and real. Did that mean she would stick around for a while? Did that mean she was going to be everywhere he turned? He'd been sending sad spirits on for years, but he'd never gotten himself stuck with a malevolent ghost.

The ghost stopped waving, turned and walked toward the stairs. She actually wove around the party guests, as if she was afraid she would bump into them. Did Tabby think she was still alive? Gideon stopped, his feet digging into the sand, and waited for her. Somehow he was going to have to get rid of her once and for all, but he had no idea how to send on a dark spirit who didn't want to leave.

Tabby walked toward him, smiling that sick, confident smile of hers. If Lily Clark had been able to affect this world, what could a spirit as dark as Tabby's do? He knew how to handle sad spirits and monstrous bad guys, but this was a new situation, one he didn't know how to handle.

As she moved closer, Gideon got a sick feeling in his stomach. Tabby looked too real, too solid. Her feet left impressions in the sand.

This was no ghost.

She pulled a small revolver from her pocket. The knife she preferred was locked away in evidence, but she seemed familiar enough with the gun. "Surprised to see me?"

"Yeah. I heard you were dead."

"Not really. I just appeared to be for a while. Imagine the coroner's surprise when he goes to the morgue to perform an autopsy and finds the body missing."

"Where's the bomb?"

Tabby nodded toward the deck. "Right up there with the dancers. Waiting."

He didn't think she was bluffing. She took too much pleasure from the pain of others not to take advantage of the opportunity. "Waiting for how long?"

"Not long."

Gideon had left his weapon sitting on the dresser, so he was basically a sitting duck. He didn't wear his weapon when he walked on the beach, or when he sat on the deck at the end of the day and listened to the waves, or when he met the night storms and traded energy. He didn't want to get to the point where he was always on guard, always waiting for someone like Tabby to come along.

"You could shock me again, I guess," she said. "But how will you explain that to the people who are watching? And they *are* watching, Raintree. They're curious and bored, and that one blonde, she really wants you to jump her bones. She'll settle for any other man who comes along, for the time being, but she really wants *you*. She's sad that your new partner has been hanging around so much. Sad and jealous, spiteful and envious."

"What do you want?"

Tabby cocked her head. "I want the same thing your neighbor wants, but in a very different way." She lifted her weapon and fired. Gideon saw the move coming and jumped to the side. A bullet creased his shoulder before he landed hard and rolled through the sand. His shoulder stung, but he was able to rise to his feet and run. He didn't run away from Tabby but toward her. She aimed the gun again.

He had to get close enough to shock and incapacitate her without creating a light show that would have everyone on the beach and on Honey's deck pointing at him. It was risky not to immediately take his shot, but he had to believe that his protection charm would give him an edge, as it always did. A few feet closer and he would be able to stop her without revealing his ability to those who were watching. Another step or two…

"Gideon!"

He and Tabby both turned sharply toward the sound. Hope was bounding from the boardwalk onto the sand, her long legs bare beneath one of his T-shirts. The gun was steady in her hand. "Drop it!" she ordered.

Tabby spun, took aim and fired in anger. Not at Gideon this time, but at Hope. Hope didn't fall; she fired back. Twice. It was Tabby who dropped onto the sand, one shot to the forehead, the other to the dead center of her chest. Gideon rushed forward and moved the revolver Tabby had dropped when she fell, tossing it away from the body as Hope reached them.

"Come back from that, bitch," Hope said softly. Then she looked at Gideon and said, with less venom, "You're bleeding."

Gideon turned and ran. "The bomb's on Honey's deck."

Hope was right behind him. "I'll call the bomb squad."

"No time."

Gideon ran up the deck stairs that led to the party. The music was still playing loudly, but there was no more laughter or dancing. The guests were somber; none of them had ever seen anyone shot before.

"I called the cops," one young guy said.

"Good," Gideon replied. He found Honey in the crowd. "That woman, did she leave anything up here?"

"Like what? She said she was a friend of yours, and that you'd come over later. What was she—"

"Did she leave anything here?" Gideon repeated more tersely.

Honey glanced around the deck. "She was carrying

a big purse. I guess she might've left…" She raised her hand and pointed. "That's it, over there by the beer."

Gideon rushed past the subdued partygoers, grabbed the purse and ran from the deck.

"Hey!" Honey shouted. "You're bleeding!"

Gideon ran toward the water, the heavy purse dangling from one hand. Hope was still standing near Tabby's body, watching, her eyes alternately on him and on the bag. "Get back to the house!" he shouted.

"No way, Raintree."

He looked her dead in the eye as he passed her at a run. "For Emma, not for me."

Hope reluctantly did as he asked, hurrying away from the shore as he ran into the water. While the surf crashed around his calves he gave the purse a mighty heave. It flew through the air, tumbling and sailing. He prayed the bomb was no more powerful or complicated than the one Tabby had planted at The Silver Chalice. If that was the case, then he was far enough away. Hope and the people at Honey's were more than far enough away. If not…

He couldn't allow a live bomb to float out into the ocean or perhaps wash up somewhere else into innocent hands. With his body shielding what he had to do as much as possible, Gideon let loose a stream of electricity as the bomb landed in the water. It exploded when the spark hit the bag. The force of the blast knocked Gideon back, out of the water and into the wet sand. In an instant it was over, and all that was left were bits and pieces of debris floating on the waves.

Less than a minute later, Hope was there. She didn't

help him to his feet but instead dropped to sit beside him in the sand.

"You're a good shot," he said as he placed his arm around her.

"Don't sound surprised."

"That's relief, not surprise."

Hope rested her head on his uninjured shoulder. In the distance, sirens approached. "For a second tonight, just a second, I thought I was seeing ghosts." She scooted closer. "It's not a whole helluva lotta fun."

"Nope."

"I thought my heart was going to come through my chest."

He threaded his fingers through her hair. "You didn't panic."

"No. I only panic when I find unexpected fertility charms hanging around my neck," she teased. "I called it in, grabbed my gun and walked outside just in time to see her following you onto the beach."

Night was falling quickly, but the lanterns on Honey's deck lit the beach well enough.

"You're going to make a good partner."

"I've been trying to tell you that all along."

"The chief will try to split us up once we're married. Annoying rules and all."

"Rules are made to be broken. We'll find a way." Hope stood and offered him her hand, as paramedics and two uniforms ran onto the beach. "Come on, Raintree. Let's go inside and have a look at that shoulder before you blow up the paramedics' equipment."

* * *

The police and the paramedics and Tabby's positively dead body had been taken away, and explanations had been made to the neighbors—which wasn't easy, since a couple of young men swore they'd seen lightning jump out of Gideon's fingers before the bomb exploded. Fortunately they'd been drinking heavily, and no one gave their account much credence.

Hope was still shaking a little. She'd never fired her weapon in any situation that wasn't controlled. Target practice, training and testing, that was it. But when she'd seen Tabby shoot at Gideon, she hadn't had any choice. She hadn't been thinking about Emma or marriage or special gifts—or nights on the deck, making love in the moonlight.

That psycho was shooting at her partner.

All the officials were gone, and the party at Honey's was over. Hope locked the doors and led Gideon into the bathroom, undressing him and herself as they went. She let her fingers trail over the bandage at his shoulder. It was just a scratch. Would he heal it anyway, with a tickle of lightning or a surge of electricity? Or would he leave it alone and let it heal on its own?

"A couple of those kids saw me, didn't they?" he asked, sounding unconcerned.

"Yes. I convinced them they were too drunk to see anything clearly, and I think they believed it by the time I was done."

"You're very convincing."

"Thank you."

They were mostly undressed when she leaned against Gideon's bare chest and tipped her face up to look him in the eye. "I have an appointment to interview Frank Stiles Monday afternoon."

"You're going to make him confess, is that it?"

Hope nodded. "Yeah. You did your part, now I'll do mine."

She was good at getting criminals to confess. She and Gideon hadn't been working together long enough for him to know that about her, but he would learn. Soon enough.

"What makes you so good at getting confessions?" Gideon teased as he brushed back a strand of hair that had fallen across her cheek. "You think just because you're prettier than all the other detectives, the bad guys are going to give it up for you?"

"No. I'm actually an excellent poker player, Raintree. I'm very good at bluffing my way to a confession. You give me enough information so I can bluff well, and I'll charm a confession right out of Stiles."

"Poor guy doesn't have a chance."

"Yeah, well, life's not fair."

Gideon held her, and she melted into him. It felt good to be embraced with love and passion and unexpected tenderness. She'd never known it would be so good to have a place to rest at the end of the day, a special person to rest with.

"I was so worried about you," she confessed. "When I saw Tabby point that gun at you and fire, and you fell…"

"I'm fine," Gideon said.

"I know, but…" The words caught in her throat. With the good came the bad. With the happiness, the worry.

Gideon leaned Hope back a little and kissed her throat. "Since you're feeling vulnerable, partner, maybe we should renegotiate that sex on the desk ban…."

Sunday—11:36 a.m.

"At least she didn't get up and walk away from us this time," the coroner said as he walked around Tabby's covered body.

Gideon had tried to convince Hope to stay at home this morning, but she wouldn't have it. She'd insisted on coming with him. One of these days he was going to have to quit protecting her so diligently. She didn't like it much.

But he wasn't going to quit today.

"It was the shot to the head that killed her," the coroner said without emotion. "The bullet that hit her torso missed the heart and lodged in the spine. That alone wouldn't have killed her. Would've stopped her cold, though."

Hope, who had never killed anyone before last night, paled a little. She'd been the one to pull the trigger and stop Tabby; she'd done what had to be done. Neither of them felt one iota of guilt. Tabby was one of the most evil people he'd ever met, and she didn't deserve a place on this earth.

"What was it you wanted me to see?" Gideon asked. He hated this place. He could live down here for years and never find a way to send all the ghosts to a peaceful place.

With help from an assistant, the coroner uncovered the

body on the slab and gently rolled it over. "I've never seen anything quite like this. I thought it was a tattoo at first, but it's actually a birthmark. I know some birthmarks are shaped in such a way as to resemble something else, but this crescent moon on the corpse's shoulder blade is absolutely perfect. And it's such an unusual color. I thought it might be helpful in identifying her."

Gideon stared at the blue birthmark of a crescent moon. It was, as the coroner had already observed, perfect in shape and color.

"Oh, shit," he said softly.

"What is it?" Hope asked.

Gideon ran for the door as he reached for his cell phone, and Hope followed him. "Tabby said *they*," he muttered. "And she was afraid for her own life if she missed killing me. Of course she was afraid. She wanted Echo, too. She said so at your mother's apartment."

"Raintree." Hope followed him up the stairs at a run. "What are you talking about?"

He couldn't get a signal, so he cursed at the phone as they burst from the building and stepped into the sunshine. "Her name is Tabby Ansara. We thought they were down. Defeated and powerless and…dammit. This changes everything."

While he was moving away from the corner of the building in an attempt to get a decent signal, the phone rang. Instead of giving Hope the phone, as he often had in days past, he answered himself and got an earful of static.

It was Dante. Gideon couldn't make out every word, but he very clearly heard the two he most needed to hear.

Ansara.

Home.

Gideon turned to Hope. He loved her, and even though she didn't like it much when he tried to protect her, he wouldn't put her in the middle of what was coming. Wouldn't and couldn't. "I have to go home. The Raintree homeplace."

Concern was clear on her face, startling in her brilliant blue eyes. Had he ever told her that he loved her eyes? Not yet. When he got back, he would make sure to tell her. He had so much to tell her.

"I'm going with you," she insisted.

"No."

Her eyes widened. "What do you mean, *no?*"

"There's trouble at the homeplace, or soon will be." Trouble of an unimaginable sort. Trouble she wouldn't understand even if he tried to explain it. "I want you and Emma safe."

"I have a gun," she said. "I know how to use it."

How could he explain to her that a gun blazing in each hand wouldn't be enough in the battle to come? "Stay here," he insisted. "Please."

Hope sighed and accepted his order, but she didn't accept it easily. Would she ever? "Call me when you get there."

"I will." *If I can.*

"I still don't see why I can't go with you," she grumbled. "I already know about your family, so it's not like there's anything left to hide." He saw the unspoken *Is there?* in her eyes.

He took Hope's face in his hands. "I love you. I love you so much that it terrifies me. I didn't expect to ever care about anyone the way I care about you, and it happened so fast my head is still spinning. It's important, and I want us to have a real chance. One day I will take you to the homeplace, I promise," he said. "But not today."

"I don't understand," she said softly.

"I know, and I'm sorry."

He kissed her, long, but not nearly as long as he wanted to, and then he jumped into the Mustang. "Call Charlie and have him take you home. I'll call as soon as I can."

Gideon left a confused Hope standing in the parking lot. She wasn't a woman accustomed to waiting, he knew, but she would wait for him. He didn't have a doubt in his mind.

Today was the summer solstice; that wasn't a coincidence. Tabby's attempts to kill him and Echo in the past several days, also not a coincidence. The Ansara wanted the homeplace, they wanted the sanctuary and the power it harnessed, and they always had.

They weren't going to get it.

One day his wife and his daughter would discover the beauty and power of the land the Raintrees had always called sanctuary. It was Gideon's duty to protect the Raintree sanctuary, just as it was his duty to protect Hope and Emma and any other little Raintrees that came along in years to come. It was his duty and his honor to protect what was *his,* and if that privilege came with ghosts and electrical surges and the occasion battle, then so be it.

Gideon drove as fast as the Mustang would allow once he reached the highway. The wind whipped his hair, and the homeplace grew closer with every second that passed, and when the unexpected storm approached from the south and gathered in the darkening skies over the car, there was no one for miles around to see.

* * * * *

THE ROYAL HOUSE OF NIROLI
Always passionate, always proud

The richest royal family in the world—united by blood
and passion, torn apart by deceit and desire

Nestled in the azure blue of the Mediterranean Sea, the
majestic island of Niroli has prospered for centuries. The
Fierezza men have worn the crown with passion and pride
since ancient times. But now, as the king's health declines,
and his two sons have been tragically killed, the crown is
in jeopardy.

The clock is ticking—a new heir must be found before
the king is forced to abdicate. By royal decree the interna-
tionally scattered members of the Fierezza family are
summoned to claim their destiny. But any person who
takes the throne must do so according to The Rules of the
Royal House of Niroli. Soon secrets and rivalries emerge
as the descendents of this ancient royal line vie for position
and power. Only a true Fierezza can become ruler—a
person dedicated to their country, their people…and their
eternal love!

*Each month starting in July 2007,
Harlequin Presents is delighted to bring you
an exciting installment from*
THE ROYAL HOUSE OF NIROLI,
*in which you can follow the epic search
for the true Nirolian king.
Eight heirs, eight romances, eight fantastic stories!*

Here's your chance to enjoy a sneak preview of the first
book delivered to you by royal decree….

FIVE minutes later she was standing immobile in front of the study's window, her original purpose of coming in forgotten, as she stared in shocked horror at the envelope she was holding. Waves of heat followed by icy chill surged through her body. She could hardly see the address now through her blurred vision, but the crest on its left-hand front corner stood out, its *royal* crest, followed by the address: *HRH Prince Marco of Niroli...*

She didn't hear Marco's key in the apartment door, she didn't even hear him calling out her name. Her shock was so great that nothing could penetrate it. It encased her in a kind of bubble, which only concentrated the torment of what she was suffering and branded it on her brain so that it could never be forgotten. It was only finally pierced by the sudden opening of the study door as Marco walked in.

"Welcome home, *Your Highness*. I suppose I ought to curtsy." She waited, praying that he would laugh and tell her that she had got it all wrong, that the envelope she was holding, addressing him as Prince Marco of

Niroli, was some silly mistake. But like a tiny candle flame shivering vulnerably in the dark, her hope trembled fearfully. And then the look in Marco's eyes extinguished it as cruelly as a hand placed callously over a dying person's face to stem their last breath.

"Give that to me," he demanded, taking the envelope from her.

"It's too late, Marco," Emily told him brokenly. "I know the truth now...." She dug her teeth in her lower lip to try to force back her own pain.

"You had no right to go through my desk," Marco shot back at her furiously, full of loathing at being caught off-guard and forced into a position in which he was in the wrong, making him determined to find something he could accuse Emily of. "I trusted you...."

Emily could hardly believe what she was hearing. "No, you didn't trust me, Marco, and you didn't trust me because you knew that I couldn't trust you. And you knew that because you're a liar, and liars don't trust people because they know that they themselves cannot be trusted." She not only felt sick, she also felt as though she could hardly breathe. "You are Prince Marco of Niroli.... How could you not tell me who you are and still live with me as intimately as we have lived together?" she demanded brokenly.

"Stop being so ridiculously dramatic," Marco demanded fiercely. "You are making too much of the situation."

"*Too much?*" Emily almost screamed the words at him. "When were you going to tell me, Marco? Perhaps you just planned to walk away without telling me anything? After all, what do my feelings matter to you?"

"Of course they matter." Marco stopped her sharply. "And it was in part to protect them, and you, that I decided not to inform you when my grandfather first announced that he intended to step down from the throne and hand it on to me."

"To protect me?" Emily nearly choked on her fury. "Hand on the throne? No wonder you told me when you first took me to bed that all you wanted was sex. You *knew* that was the only kind of relationship there could ever be between us! You *knew* that one day you would be Niroli's king. No doubt you are expected to marry a princess. Is she picked out for you already, your *royal* bride?"

* * * * *

Look for
THE FUTURE KING'S PREGNANT MISTRESS
by Penny Jordan in July 2007,
from Harlequin Presents,
available wherever books are sold.

Romantic

SUSPENSE

**Sparked by Danger,
Fueled by Passion.**

Mission: Impassioned

A brand-new miniseries begins with

My Spy

By *USA TODAY* bestselling author

Marie Ferrarella

She had to trust him with her life....
It was the most daring mission of Joshua Lazlo's
career: rescuing the prime minister of England's
daughter from a gang of cold-blooded kidnappers.
But nothing prepared the shadowy secret agent
for a fiery woman whose touch ignited something
far more dangerous.

My Spy

#1472

Available July 2007 wherever you buy books!

Visit Silhouette Books at www.eHarlequin.com   SRS27542

Do you know a real-life heroine?

Nominate her for the Harlequin More Than Words award.

Each year Harlequin Enterprises honors five ordinary women for their extraordinary commitment to their community.

Each recipient of the Harlequin More Than Words award receives a $10,000 donation from Harlequin to advance the work of her chosen charity. And five of Harlequin's most acclaimed authors donate their time and creative talents to writing a novella inspired by the award recipients. The More Than Words anthology is published annually in October and all proceeds benefit causes of concern to women.

HARLEQUIN

More Than Words™

For more details or to nominate a woman you know please visit

www.HarlequinMoreThanWords.com

MTW2007

REQUEST YOUR FREE BOOKS!

2 FREE NOVELS PLUS 2 FREE GIFTS!

Silhouette®

nocturne™

Dramatic and Sensual Tales of Paranormal Romance.

YES! Please send me 2 FREE Silhouette® Nocturne™ novels and my 2 FREE gifts. After receiving them, if I don't wish to receive any more books, I can return the shipping statement marked "cancel." If I don't cancel, I will receive 4 brand-new novels every other month and be billed just $4.47 per book in the U.S. or $4.99 per book in Canada, plus 25¢ shipping and handling per book plus applicable taxes, if any*. That's a savings of about 15% off the cover price! I understand that accepting the 2 free books and gifts places me under no obligation to buy anything. I can always return a shipment and cancel at any time. Even if I never buy another book from Silhouette, the two free books and gifts are mine to keep forever.

238 SDN ELS4 338 SDN ELXG

Name	(PLEASE PRINT)	
Address		Apt. #
City	State/Prov.	Zip/Postal Code

Signature (if under 18, a parent or guardian must sign)

Mail to the **Silhouette Reader Service™:**
IN U.S.A.: P.O. Box 1867, Buffalo, NY 14240-1867
IN CANADA: P.O. Box 609, Fort Erie, Ontario L2A 5X3

Not valid to current Silhouette Nocturne subscribers.

**Want to try two free books from another line?
Call 1-800-873-8635 or visit www.morefreebooks.com.**

* Terms and prices subject to change without notice.. NY residents add applicable sales tax. Canadian residents will be charged applicable provincial taxes and GST. This offer is limited to one order per household. All orders subject to approval. Credit or debit balances in a customer's account(s) may be offset by any other outstanding balance owed by or to the customer. Please allow 4 to 6 weeks for delivery.

Your Privacy: Silhouette is committed to protecting your privacy. Our Privacy Policy is available online at www.eHarlequin.com or upon request from the Reader Service. From time to time we make our lists of customers available to reputable firms who may have a product or service of interest to you. If you would prefer we not share your name and address, please check here. ☐

nocturne™

**DON'T MISS THE RIVETING CONCLUSION
TO THE RAINTREE TRILOGY**

RAINTREE: SANCTUARY

by *New York Times* bestselling author

BEVERLY BARTON

Mercy, guardian of the Raintree
homeplace, takes a stand against
the Ansara wizards to battle for
the Clan's future.

*On sale July,
wherever books are sold.*

SNRT2

nocturne™

COMING NEXT MONTH

#19 RAINTREE: SANCTUARY Beverly Barton
The Raintree Trilogy (Book 3 of 3)

The Raintree Trilogy comes to its earth-shattering conclusion as Mercy, guardian of the Raintree homeplace, takes a stand against the Ansara wizards to battle for the clan's future.

#20 DARK TRUTH Lindsay McKenna
Warriors for the Light

Born of the Light and the Dark, Ana Elena Rafeal had two paths to take. The sorcerer known as the Dark Lord has offered her a chance to rule the world—or die. And the one man she doesn't trust may be the only one who can lead her on the proper path—with the love in his heart.

SNCNM0607